ASCENSION:
Return of the Gods

by Stephen H. King

TOSK – The Other Stephen King

ISBN: 978-0-9989355-1-5

DEDICATION

This novel is dedicated to my lovely wife Heidelinde, who spent so many evenings elsewhere as I sat quietly on my computer and wrote, revised, revised, and re-revised. I couldn't do this without you, my love, and if anyone deserves to Ascend, it's you. You're my goddess, and my life.

Table of Contents

Irritation Grows

Crystal plucked a purple columbine flower from its stalk, glaring at it for several long moments before she twisted flows of fire around its spiked petals and watched them melt. She knew that using her powers to destroy one of Matt's favorite wildflowers was petty, but it was better in so many ways than trying to melt Matt. It didn't sooth her aggravated mood as much as she'd hoped, though, so she hurled the stem to the ground, stomped on it for good measure, and turned back to her steed.

Lady, Crystal's dappled mare, backed away, shaking its head in an almost-human gesture as if to say, "No, not in that mood." Crystal recognized the gesture and stopped, planted her balled fists on her hips and glared at the horse. Her frustration-fueled anger ran deep, but she knew that she could never inflict it on the gentle creature. That thought added to Crystal's frustration, her emotions building into a screaming, stomping fit that suited Crystal's daughters more than it did her.

Once the pain in her feet built up enough to cut through her anger, she stopped. Ruefully meeting Lady's gaze, she sighed in defeat. The huge mare, knowing the tantrum was at its end, approached, whinnied softly, and pressed the soft side of its face against Crystal's cheek.

Crystal threw her arms around the horse's neck and stood, nuzzling with the gentle equine for several silent minutes.

"Why is he being so difficult?" she finally asked into the horse's neck. "He promised. He promised! And now all he does is stall and come up with reasons not to teach me."

Lady nickered quietly in sympathy. Crystal pulled herself away and watched as her steed pumped its head up and down twice. Crystal knew that signal—it was the mare's indication that it was time to run. Frustration and anger dissolving at the thought, Crystal grinned and leaped up onto the horse's back, using a flow of air to springboard lightly onto the horse's saddle. At nineteen hands high, Lady was the tallest horse she'd ever ridden—ever seen, for that matter—and the leap to the saddle was exciting. Not as exciting, though, as riding Lady at a full gallop, which presented an ever-present opportunity for Crystal to lose track of her anger in the thrill of the sensations that went with hurtling rapidly on horseback across the meadow.

Hoping to lose herself once again, she pressed Lady's sides and the muscular mare shot forward. Crystal delighted in the quick, sharp thrill that splashed over her as the horse launched into a gallop. The thrill was followed, as usual, by a deep calm. From within the protected serenity of the rhythmic gallop, Crystal's mind flowed back over the past few weeks. Matt, her husband, hadn't meant to anger her. She knew that. He loved her dearly. She knew that too. And he'd promised to make her a goddess. That—well, that was the problem.

Okay, she corrected herself, he hadn't *promised* to make her a goddess. He'd said that there was a way, and that he would help her find it. Of course she understood the difference, as she'd told him already in the numerous times she'd challenged him on it. But it had been days since the battle, and he hadn't done her anything at all toward getting her on that path.

The battle—what a vivid memory. She had nearly died. Would have died, in fact, if not for Sorscha's quick action. The thrakkon had saved Crystal's life thanks to the imperviousness to magical flows that the gods had built into her race. Gods like her husband, Matt, who also used to answer to the ancient names Mars and Ares and Tyr, she had recently found out. He had been a pretty darn good but otherwise perfectly normal husband before the earth-destroying cataclysm mere weeks ago, yet now he was a creature out of ancient myth. And goddesses, too, like Aphrodite, who at one time had gone by the name Stacy and been Matt's ex-wife, as she had also recently found out.

Luckily, the calm imposed by the rhythmic power of Lady's gallop moderated Crystal's anger at the thoughts of Aphrodite and allowed her to focus on the more pleasant memories from the battle. Memories of her husband taking on the true form of the God of War and hurtling down from the heavens to save her from Aphrodite's suffocating spell. Of Sorscha, Matt's shape-shifting servant, transportation, and battle partner, careening in, exhaling a river of fire from her mouth in her dragon form as she attacked a goddess she could never have defeated in order to distract her, giving Matt time to loosen the elemental bonds of magical force that kept Crystal from moving and breathing. Of Mars, the massive, powerful warrior god fighting toe-to-toe and weapon-to-weapon against an evil goddess to save his beloved.

Hell, it was like a goddamned fairy tale. Only it wasn't a fairy tale; it was her life, and that, she realized, was the source of her frustration. There wasn't necessarily going to be a happy ending. It was her life that was ticking rapidly away one moment, one hour, one day at a time. The promise of immortality made it even more painfully clear that as it was, her time was limited. What was he waiting on?

She pressed her knees into Lady's side, pushing the mare faster as she returned to the estate from the secluded area around the little cottage. Matt had taken the family to the hidden cottage when they had first arrived, shown them their own hideaway accessible only to the loved ones of the property's master. Well, them, and Aphrodite, as the goddess had demonstrated by showing up during that visit. But Matt had been correct in his prediction that Aphrodite wouldn't come back after the grand fight. It had been remarkably quiet, and the only strife, really, was what Crystal carried inside.

Lady pounded right up to the gate of the stables before putting on the brakes, her hooves throwing dirt against the open door. A thrakkon hurried out with a stool, but Crystal beat him to it by levitating herself gently down even as Lady was sliding to a stop, a broad smirk on her face. Yes, she was proud of how far her command of the elemental flows had come in just a couple of weeks, but most of her pleasure at the moment came from being contrary.

"My lady," the stable master said, holding the stepstool and looking uncertain of his next move. "I, ah, trust your ride was pleasant?"

"It was," she said, holding onto her contrariness despite knowing that she had little reason to be angry with the thrakkon.

He nodded. "Well, then, I will be pleased to take care of Lady if my lady wishes to return to the estate."

Crystal shook her head and released her angst. "No. Thank you, Marschon, but I want to brush her down myself after our run."

The thrakkon bowed and reentered the stables, leaving Crystal on her own to walk Lady to the mare's stall.

A First Step

Over an hour later, Crystal left the stables and walked back toward the manor. She had brushed Lady for longer than was really necessary, but it felt good. It hadn't done anything for her mood, since it proved an opportunity to brood on all the things she wasn't learning, but it had at least worked the knots out of her muscles.

Crystal stalked down the curving hall leading to the round stone room known as the sorcerer's chamber. This room had been shielded by Matt in order for new mages—battle mages, he called them—to train without fear of causing significant damage to the rest of the manor, and it was where the newest groups of mages always worked until Matt felt confident enough in both their skills and their good sense to let them out. A clearing outside was another protected area that was preferred by the mages in training due to the presence of pristine sunlight that nearly always magically graced the estate, but its use required the god's approval. So far three separate groups of mages had survived the training in the sorcerer's chamber, succeeded in lifting a rock off of their own hands and then throwing a small ball of fire, and in doing so graduated to the clearing. Many, including some of her best friends, had shown promise but not made it, a fact Matt assured her was normal.

Reaching the end of the corridor she turned to the right and pressed one of the bricks, causing a secret door in the side wall to open. Crystal stepped in rapidly and closed the door. She had made this trek many times and so far had not been seen. Matt had only grudgingly given her permission to enter this hallway at will, and she knew he still wanted to keep his private battle chamber a secret.

At the other end of the hall she approached another solid oak door, but she avoided reaching out to it immediately. Instead, Crystal formed the magic that Matt had taught her, using flows that wrapped around his own, flows that both appeased and soothed the elemental locks he'd placed on it.

She was getting much better very quickly, she realized with a smile. This time the door opened on her first attempt, unlike previous trips when it had proven inaccessible through three, five, or even several dozen tries. She stepped into the room.

Crystal smiled. The offensive tapestry featuring her husband and his lovely wife Stacy at his side had been taken down, a blank stone wall left in its place. Matt had removed the tapestry before she had seen it a second time, and that fact still felt like a major, if slightly petty, victory. Aphrodite—well, the picture of her, anyway—was gone now, never to bother Crystal again.

Still angry, Crystal strode to the desk in the corner and selected a figurine of a Roman legionnaire from the many on the desktop. Matt had taught her how to tell the Roman legionnaires from the Roman cavalrymen from the Greek hoplites based on the shape of the shields and the armor they wore, but the thought of that lesson just frustrated her more because it didn't help her move toward becoming a goddess. Shrugging off that frustration, she activated the figurine with a flow of energy and watched as a legionnaire appeared, life-sized, in the chamber. The man, seeing an unarmed woman, bowed and then looked around the room with a confused expression until Crystal slapped him across his face with a flow of air, her hand moving in sync with the element. Confusion shifted to anger, and the legionnaire charged. His first sword strike came in at waist level and then rotated up toward Crystal's chest. Crystal easily blocked it with a hasty shield of air and earth, noting that the legionnaire had struck with the flat of his blade. Apparently he still didn't see her as much of a threat, so she directed a fireball at his genitals in order to change his perception.

Later, she might be willing to admit that the purpose behind the fireball wasn't just to change his perception. She was still angry. There's nothing quite as soothing, after all, as throwing a fireball at one man's crotch when you're angry at another man.

But that was something to be admitted later and enjoyed now.

If changing the way the centurion looked at her had been her main goal, she'd succeeded in spades. He leaped to his left, using his shield arm to cushion his fall and the fist wrapped around the sword's pommel to propel himself into a somersault, vaulting into a position to charge her right flank. In the blink of an eye the agile Roman avoided the fireball and charged in, attacking Crystal with the sharp edge of his sword this time.

Crystal responded by flicking her right hand up and away. At the same time, her mind reached out, seized the flows of air, and used them to propel the centurion in the direction indicated by her flicking fingertips. The attacker's body sailed against the wall, hit with a loud thud, slid down and collapsed for a split second against the floor. The warrior, though, was not going to be put down so easily. He uncoiled, rising into a defensive position and circling her warily.

Crystal smiled and drew her knife. She'd worked out her aggressions already, and was done toying with the Roman. He wasn't real, just a lifelike representation of one of the battle archetypes that had impressed Matt during the last cycle. Matt had even once described to her how they were created from his memories upon his return to the manor, fashioned from elemental magic which was then condensed and stored in a figurine shape, ready to be called upon for battle practice. They could also be put back through powerful magic, but such magic was still beyond Crystal's reach, and so her only available exit from the current situation was through the dispatch of her foe. To that end, she searched her mind for the attacks that would give her the greatest chance of being successful while killing the apparition as cleanly as possible.

Unfortunately, she didn't have time to execute the strategy. The Roman feinted to the left and then bashed at her with his shield, raising his sword for what should be a death blow. Crystal felt the scutum, which she vaguely recalled Matt explaining was Latin for 'ugly rectangular chunk of wood,' hit the flows of air and earth in which she had wrapped herself, and wielding another flow of air she stopped the man's sword arm above his head. Spinning deftly around his shield, she planted her dagger in his chest, and then removed it and spun away. With a pop, the centurion disappeared in defeat.

"Bravo!" Matt's voice sounded behind her, causing her to jump in surprise and spin around yet again. Smiling broadly, he held his arms out for her, clearly expecting his wife to collapse into his willing embrace.

Crystal glared, sheathing her dagger. "Thank you," she said curtly and then walked past toward the exit door.

Matt sighed.

The sound stopped her in her tracks. Turning, she spread her hands to her side and said more evenly, "Thank you. I have to do what I can, since you won't teach me anything."

Matt's face hardened. "I am teaching you what I can. I've told you that. I can't, though, teach you what you most want to know. You must discover the path yourself."

"A hint or two might be nice."

Matt shrugged. "Okay, a hint it is."

Crystal sidled in closer, half expecting Matt to whisper a truly valuable tidbit, and half expecting her smart-aleck husband to honk her nose or tickle her.

He surprised her by doing neither. Instead, he said, "Go see Gaia."

She frowned. "I can't just go see Gaia, can I?"

"Sure you can. At least, you can with my help. It's easy, really. I go there frequently, myself. I enjoy the mother's company."

"Your frequently, or mine?"

"I suppose every thousand years or so is my frequently, isn't it?"

Crystal hadn't needed another reminder that her husband was immortal and she wasn't, but there it was. She grimaced.

Matt sighed. "I used to be able to be a little, and sometimes a lot, sarcastic with you. Now, though, everything you do and say is dreadfully serious. Crystal, you said not long ago that you don't know the man you'd married anymore. Now I have to say the same about the lovely, talented, and brilliant woman I married."

Crystal locked stares with Matt for several moments. He was right, though she was unwilling to admit it. Her attitudes had changed since she found out that he was a god and that—well, that she wasn't. She sighed and gave Matt a wistful smile.

"I don't know, Matt. I really don't. I mean, I love you dearly, still and forever, so it's not that. But ever since you said that you'd help me on the path to becoming a goddess, that's consumed my thoughts. Look, I know it shouldn't. I'm still your wife, and the girls' mother. I know that. But I so desperately want to be able to count on spending eternity with you that, no matter what it takes, I want to get started so I can get it over with. I dread the 'whatever it takes' part, since I have no idea what that may mean, but the dread just makes me want to get on with it, which in turn makes this waiting an irritation. Do—do you understand?"

Matt nodded. "I do." Crystal was cheered by his expression, one that really did say he understood. That he wasn't holding it against her. That he accepted that her desire to become a goddess was borne out of her love for him. Her heart, for the first time in several days, lightened.

Matt continued, "But that's why you need to go spend some time with the mother. You know how much I love you, right?" She nodded, meeting his eyes, and he continued, "My love is actually a handicap in this. There are some things—a whole lot of things, truly—that you'll have to learn if you have any hope of ascending. They're hard lessons, all. If I had the heart to teach them to you, I would, but I can't. It's just not mine to teach."

Crystal sighed again. This was the first time that Matt had opened up to her on what was bothering him in her quest to become a goddess. She'd pushed, and he'd blocked, and it had felt like they were fighting for different goals entirely. All these days of frustration, the pent-up feelings of stagnation, and the silence were now broken because she had made herself vulnerable. Before the cataclysm, she had no problem being vulnerable with him. Now, though? Why was it any different now?

"So," Matt said, "are you ready to visit the mother? I won't send you before you're ready, since she can be a bit—well, a bit particular."

Crystal suddenly realized what Matt was hinting at. He actually was a higher being. So, for that matter, was Gaia, possibly even higher than Matt. She was petitioning Matt, and soon to be Gaia, to become a higher being herself, and yet she had no idea what to base her petition on. She didn't even know the ground rules. In fact, she didn't even know what question to ask, much less how to ask it.

"Matt?"

"Yes, love?"

"I don't have any clue."

"Did you doubt my words when I said it would be difficult?"

"No, of course not. I just keep hoping that at some point you'll take mercy on the poor human here and give me an idea."

Matt's voice grew somber as he replied, "Mercy, my love, would be telling you no, commanding you to remain my human wife. Becoming a goddess, if it even happens at all, will take more out of you than you've ever thought possible. But we've been over that already, no? You keep saying you want to be a goddess, and that you want to move forward. At the same time, you seem to want me to give you the next step, the next move forward. It doesn't work that way. If you're going to be a goddess, then you tell me. What's the next step?"

It dawned on Crystal in that moment what Matt had been trying to teach her for the last several days. She realized how useless her questions had been, how useless the delays had been. Her path was up to her. Unfortunately, that terrified her more than just about anything else she could imagine. How do you find and follow a path that isn't even supposed to be there? A path that your own husband is warning you will be nearly impossible?

No matter, she concluded. If it led to eternal life with her beloved, it was worth it.

"To Gaia, then."

Preparing for Gaia's Glade

The next several hours flew by. Matt had waited till she mustered her resolve to go to Gaia before pointing out that she might be there a while.

"Love, it's not like you can go to the mother goddess and ask, 'Hey, like, how do I become one of you?' and have her give you twelve simple steps. The key part of whatever she tells you is going to require you learning something, and odds are it will be something so complex that even the least hard-headed pupil will take some time to grasp it. You're not, ah—well, you're...."

"Hard-headed."

"In a wonderfully sweet and joyous sort of way that I've come to cherish with all my heart and what little soul I may have— well, yes. It's an aspect of your personality that actually gives you a chance of succeeding in this quest, but it's also a bit of a weakness."

Crystal stopped, pulled Matt in, and kissed him passionately. "Thank you."

Eyebrow quirked, Matt asked, "For what?"

"For knowing my strengths and my weaknesses. For loving me anyway."

Matt shrugged. "You put a spell on me, love. I could do nothing else."

Crystal stood with a couple of weeks worth of comfortable clothes packed in boxes. When she'd asked why she wasn't packing them into suitcases, Matt had explained that she wouldn't be carrying them. She didn't want to look like she was trying to move in. Instead, she would go with just the clothing on her back, and the mother would send for whatever she felt appropriate. It made sense, though the open question of how long she would be there still bothered Crystal.

"What are you packing for, Mom?" Heidi asked from the doorway.

"I'm going to visit Gaia," Crystal said, walking out into the sitting area followed by Matt. She sat in the middle of the couch, Heidi sitting to one side and Linda the other, both arms extended around her daughters. Matt sat in the chair opposite, hands gently rubbing the upholstered arms.

"Why?" Linda asked.

"Well," Crystal started to explain and then faltered. She hadn't let the two girls in on her desire. She hadn't known how. Deciding that a partial truth would suffice, she said, "Well, I'm hoping she can teach me something." The words had barely left her mouth when she realized how inadequate they sounded.

"Like what?" Heidi asked. Heidi had always been the curious, playful child, while Linda was the suspicious one. True to form, Linda was paying close attention to what her mother said.

Crystal's mind flashed anxiously over all the different ways to broach the subject. Her daughters weren't just children any more, and they'd know if she tried to tell them something like the Easter bunny story. Somehow, though, the truth seemed so petty in that moment—she could see her daughters wondering why she'd want to outlive them. Crystal thought that she had the most adult 13-year-olds on the planet, but she had no idea how they'd take the news that she might be gone long-term, especially when the purpose was for her to become a goddess like their dad's ex-wife.

She knew better than to bring the ex-wife into it at all. The girls were still angry toward Aphrodite thanks to the stunt in their old home, to say nothing of her later attempt to get them hurt in Matt's battle room. To tell them that she was trying to become like Aphrodite in any way would be a bad move.

All that said, though, she knew that it was best to address the issue directly with her daughters, to give them the truth, and then let them help guide the discussion.

"Like how to become like your father," Crystal blurted out, hoping it came out stronger than it had seemed to her. "Your father is a god. He's already lived a long time, and he will live forever. I want to be his equal, girls. I love him, and I want to be able to spend forever with him."

Linda's mouth worked soundlessly as she looked from her mother to her father, and then back to her mother, and then she repeated the cycle. Her sister regained the ability to speak much faster, asking, "Is that—how is that possible, Mom?"

Crystal sighed and answered, "I don't know, dear. At least one other goddess has done it, but it's apparently a very hard thing to do. I'm—we're—hoping Gaia can give me some wisdom to send me down the path."

Linda peered at Matt, asking, "Dad, weren't you born a god?"

Matt nodded. "I was. Some of my peers were too. But some weren't."

"Like Aphrodite?" Linda said, her voice making it clear that the name carried a bad taste with it.

"Right," Matt said. "Like Aphrodite. When I married Aphrodite, she was Stacy, a human woman I'd worked with in the technology era."

"Well, if Aphrodite did it, can't you just tell Mom how?"

Matt smiled. "That's a good question, Linda." Crystal caught his tell; Matt always stalled answering a question he found difficult by praising the question. Well, at least he wasn't blowing it off. "I didn't really watch Aphrodite do it, though," he explained. "She went away as a powerful human magician, and later on— much later—she was a goddess. She only told me that it was a very difficult path to walk. We split up and went our separate ways, so that's all I know."

"How long is Mom going to be gone?"

"A day, or a week. Possibly a month or even a year," Matt replied with a tender smile on his face. "We don't know, and we can't know. It's not like your mom is going away to learn to crochet, Heidi."

"How can we talk with her while she's gone, then?" Heidi's question surprised Crystal. She'd been so focused on starting the adventure that she had just assumed that she would be able to talk to her husband, the god, and her daughters regularly. The expression on Matt's face, though, told her that he had made the same assumption, and that it was incorrect. Crystal found herself suddenly missing the cell phone that had made communication so easy before the cataclysm.

"Wait right here," Matt instructed. He walked into the bedroom and returned a few seconds later holding the glass shard that Crystal had picked up on the beach during their recent visit to Atlantis. Crystal saw him push the essence of magic, that pure stream of energy that represented all four magical elements and was the sole province of the gods, into the cobalt blue glass. She saw it, but that was all she could claim—it was a very complex weave.

He handed the shard to Crystal and instructed, "Speak my name to it no matter where you are, and it will open a conduit back to me. You and I will be able to talk mentally through it, and if you need to speak with the girls I can set up an avatar here to anchor the communication. Girls, if you need to talk to Mom about something—something important only, because she'll probably be very busy—just ask me. I'll be able to reach you, Crystal, without the glass."

"Of course you will, you studly god you," Crystal said, waggling her eyebrows playfully at him. Matt's snort was his only response.

"Do you have to go this evening, Mom?" Heidi pouted.

"Well—I don't know, dear. When do you think is the best time to go, Matt?" Crystal asked her husband, not certain what she was most hoping he would say. She wanted desperately to get her quest kicked off on its way, but now that the beginning was hurtling rapidly toward her she was already missing her girls and husband. Butterflies suddenly seemed to fill her midsection.

"Well, Gaia doesn't sleep, so there isn't any time better or worse than any other for her," Matt said. "But you might wish to consider your own needs. I have no idea what she'll have you do first. Might be sit and listen, might be show her some of your skills, might even be mopping the floor for all I know. Which, by the way, will be a neat trick since her floor is grass. Anyway, you're probably better off if you get a good night's sleep and a solid breakfast tomorrow morning and then go."

"That makes sense. So girls, what are we going to do tonight?"

"Um," Linda quickly jumped in, "can we do something that includes Steve and Corey? I want to spend time with you, of course, Mom, but we shouldn't leave those poor boys to do nothing all night. Can we all do something together?"

Crystal and Matt exchanged amused looks, and then Crystal adopted a fake pout. "Aw, those poor boys would just die if they had to spend an entire night with just themselves and their mommy and daddy to be with, wouldn't they, Matt? Do you think we should spurn them, turn them out at their most tender time, or welcome them into our family group tonight?"

Matt said, "Oh, I suppose we can bear a night of their company in order to save their very souls, love."

As if on cue, a knock followed by one of the boys' voices called to the girls. Both girls shot out of their seats, but Sorscha waved them back as her lithe body glided to the door, opened it, and greeted the boys and their parents, who were standing behind. The boys' father, a broad-shouldered physicist whom they had rescued from the halls of Stanford, kept a hand clapped on each of their shoulders to prevent them from darting around the thrakkon. When they both turned to glare at him, he smiled at Sorscha, let go of the boys just long enough to bow, and asked, "May we have the pleasure of an audience with the master and lady of the house?"

The boys started to turn again, but a dangerous growl and a glare from their mother stopped them. Crystal glanced over and saw that Matt's grin was as wide as hers felt, Matt sitting at his ease facing the door while Crystal stood.

Sorscha, her well-apportioned humanoid frame rooted in the middle of the doorway, turned her body half around to look at Matt, a mix of formality and humor on her face. Matt's voice boomed, "Of course. We are pleased to receive Doctor Phillips and his family. Sorscha, please see them in and find enough chairs for our guests."

As they walked through the door, a male thrakkon followed immediately carrying two wooden chairs. With the two empty chairs already in the room, it made seating for all eight.

Natalia, the boys' mother, walked over to Crystal and whispered, "How'd he get here so fast?"

Crystal smiled and said, "Magic. The thrakkoni can speak telepathically and they can also teleport around the estate at will in their humanoid forms." She was surprised that Natalia didn't know that already after three weeks at the estate, but she knew that the librarian had been spending most of her time in the sorcerer's chamber, rapidly becoming another of a group of powerful mages in the process, and whatever time she was not down there was either with her husband or in the estate's massive library, or both at the same time. Crystal had met a great many very intelligent people, but never anyone who read as much or as quickly as both Dr. and Mrs. Phillips did. Between the two of them they had already become a source of discussion among the thrakkoni, according to Sorscha, because Natalia had already become fluent with two of the dead languages represented in Matt's library and had made use of that familiarity in translating several prior-cycle manuscripts on physics to her husband.

"Sit, sit," Matt said as he gestured to the chairs. Crystal grabbed both girls' shoulders and pulled them down beside her on the couch, preventing them from sitting anywhere else. "And please, Ben, I appreciate the formalities, but they're truly not necessary. Please, relax."

"Well, thank you," Ben said. "It's just not every day that we're invited to the suite of a god."

Matt's expression changed only slightly. "No, I suppose it isn't," he said, directing a questioning look at the couch. Crystal fielded his look, but was as perplexed as he was till she saw a quirk in Heidi's lip. Linda, the quieter and more reserved twin, had always been able to hide things well, but Heidi wore her thoughts like lipstick on her forehead.

Natalia caught and correctly interpreted Matt's expression. Turning to face her son, she said in a dark and angry voice, "Please, Steve, tell us again how the lord of the estate expressed his desire for our presence before dinner."

Ben caught on too but reacted very differently, looking at Matt with a pleading expression in his now-paler face. "Lord, it's not the boys' fault. We must have misunderstood what they were saying. We'll leave you to your business now, and you can punish me if it is your will."

As Ben vaulted out of his chair, his wife turned an incredulous look his way. The boys clung to their seats, terrified. Crystal's head swung side to side, glaring at each of her daughters in turn. Matt began laughing, a loud belly laugh that filled the room.

"*SIT DOWN*, Ben," Matt projected to everyone between his peals of laughter. "Please, sit down," he continued verbally when he caught a breath. "Natalia, your husband has obviously not told you how we met, has he?"

"No. Why?" Natalia asked, peering curiously at her husband's still-terrified face.

"Well, I was ten feet tall and waving a flaming sword in a quite godly fashion," Matt said, still chuckling. "I'm afraid I probably gave him the impression that I was a pretty mean guy. Hey, I am the God of War, after all. But it worked. The show convinced him and his crack team of ninja experimental physicists to put down their metallic clubs of doom and save their fight with me for another day."

Ben, having relaxed as Matt told the story, chuckled at Matt's description of the defensive weapons they'd brandished the day Matt rescued them from the physics laboratory. "Hey," he parried, "mine was a tungsten steel alloy rod. How many ninjas have weapons made of that?"

"Not many," Matt said. "Tungsten is difficult to work with due to its high melting point, and because of that it wasn't even discovered as a workable metal till the 18th Century, while most of the real ninja activity ended about the same timeframe. Even a few cycles ago, when engineers in Asia had an electric arc melter going at the same time as their version of ninja were going strong, it wasn't popular for a ninja weapon. It's true that a little bit of tungsten added to, say, a glaive blade, makes it unbelievably tough, but ninja swords require more finesse, more—well, more flexibility. Carbon steel works better for that, while tungsten steel would rather break than bend."

"Wow," Crystal said. "I'm constantly amazed by how much you remember from cycles long ago."

Matt shrugged and smiled. "It's weapons, my love. It's what I do. Besides, most of it is pretty repetitive. Every other two thousand years, in the magic cycle, humans find ways to kill humans using flows of elemental energy. Every two thousand years in between, in the technology cycle, humans find ways to kill humans using sticks and stones at first, and then atom bombs later."

Ben interjected, "Well, that's a bleak picture."

"Picture, hell. You should try living through each one, always hoping that someday humans will get it and quit killing each other."

"Aren't you the God of War? Should you really be hoping that humans stop warring?" Natalia asked.

"It's not like I'd lose my job, Natalia. I could just as easily be the God of Dangerously-shaped Plowshares."

"I'm not so sure about that, Matt," Crystal said with a wry smile.

Ben grunted and changed the subject. "If I may suggest, now that it's clear that you're not going to kill us for impertinence, it's probably time that we acknowledge that we were duped into coming here and find out why."

"I suspect, Ben, that your boys and our girls share equally in the blame," Matt said, giving their daughters a fake look of consternation that Crystal was sure they saw right through.

"Linda?" Matt asked, eyes locking on their quieter twin's face.

"Yes, Daddy?"

"You have something to tell us, don't you?"

Crystal tried to maintain a stern look herself despite feeling a touch of the same amusement Matt was struggling to hide. It had been a relatively innocent machination, after all. She thought back to when they'd retrieved their daughters from jail at a fairly significant cost on the Rio de Janeiro trip—now that was dangerous. Heidi had jumped to accuse the boy, a fellow American tourist about the same age as the girls, of dragging them into trouble, and Linda had smiled and nodded along with Heidi's tale. When the story was unraveled, though, it had been Linda who had thought it might be funny to watch what happened when an American boy called a Brazilian police officer a couple of rather dirty names in the man's native language. She, the studious one, had learned the words from some local children and had then convinced Heidi to talk the boy into believing that they were terms of honor and respect.

A substantial payoff or two later, the family had returned to the quiet of their hotel suite. Matt had been furious—while the girls were in the room. After he'd sent them to bed, he'd sat on the couch giggling, cycling between repeating the words softly and making a mocking version of the expression the offended policeman had worn.

"I wonder where they get their trouble genes," she had said at the time, glaring playfully at her husband before giving in to giggles herself.

"I wonder," Matt had replied, and pointed out that it was Crystal who had pried the story out of Linda by describing in just enough detail what might happen to little American girls left in a South American prison overnight. "The look on Heidi's face was priceless when you said we'd leave them there if we didn't get the whole truth."

Crystal's attention snapped back to the present as Linda lost her battle of wills and said, "It was meant to be harmless, Dad. We just wanted to get Steve and Corey's parents to meet the two of you. You and Mom spend all day away training your mages, and Natalia and Ben spend all their time in that magic chamber and in the library. We figured that this was the only way to get you to really meet each other. And look, we were right."

"That your story, too, son?" Ben asked, looking from Steve to Corey and back. Both boys nodded. The physicist looked at Matt, a half-smile on his face.

"Well." Matt stated. "I guess this might be awkward, if it weren't so damn funny." Both men erupted in laughter. Crystal and Natalia looked from one to the other, both women arching their eyebrows.

"The kids conspired to set us up, and you find it funny?" Natalia said, looking directly at Ben. Crystal realized she was thinking of asking Matt exactly the same question, but decided it didn't need to be voiced twice.

Ben stopped laughing, wrestling a serious expression onto his face. Matt followed suit as Ben said, "Well, 'Talia, they've got a point. You and I have talked about wanting to spend some time with Matt and Crystal, but it didn't look like it was ever going to happen."

Natalia glared at her sons for several more long seconds before shrugging and saying, "Well, okay. I concede that it was a good end. But Steve, Corey, don't you ever lie to me again, or I'll chop your knees off." Both boys nodded vigorously to their mother.

"You'll chop their knees off?" Ben asked, eyebrows arched.

"Oh, shut up."

"So, Matt, the boys were telling me you said you'd studied physics at Stanford?" Ben asked, his question shifting the mood. Crystal listened closely, having wanted to hear more of that part of Matt's story.

"Indeed," Matt said. "I've actually studied physics at many different locations, and in several different cycles, due to my interest in the subject. I did attend graduate studies for a few years at Stanford for the purpose of spending some time with Felix Bloch."

"But Professor Bloch died well over four decades ago," Ben argued.

Matt nodded. "Yes, he did."

"Well, I guess—it's just strange talking to an eternal being."

"Ben, I'm immortal. I've been around for hundreds of millions of years. Eternal isn't right, though, because the universe and I both have a starting point. That was a long time ago, and I don't recall much of it, but there really was a Big Bang, without the bang, of course. And, honestly, without the big, too. So—anyway, given all that, me studying physics mere decades ago shouldn't surprise anybody."

"Where did you get your undergraduate degree?"

"Nowhere. Why should I have bothered with that?"

"Well, because—how did you get into Stanford graduate school with no undergraduate degree?"

"Oh, that. On paper, I graduated with honors from—oh, where was it? Helsinki, I think, or somewhere in Denmark. It's pretty easy, really, to make up a solid academic history when you have unlimited financial resources, a few million years of experience in falsifying who you are, knowledge of several dozen languages, and a thorough understanding of how the world actually works when palms are covered in money."

"Well, no matter what that says about the admissions process, I guess you probably knew more about physics already than most of the professors," Ben admitted, though he appeared to still be bothered. "But why Professor Bloch?"

"Because of his own work, in part. The way that nuclear particles behave hasn't changed in any of the previous cycles, but the approach humans take to defining it has, and that difference fascinates me. The discovery of superconductivity—and Bloch's activities in that field—fascinated me, because that was only the second time it had been discovered. But my interest in him was also due to Bloch's own connections. How many other men in the world had studied with Pauli, Bohr, Heisenberg, and Fermi, just to name a few? The stories he told were amazing."

"I never would have thought of it that way. It must've been wonderful to spend time with him, then."

Matt grinned. "I got onto his research team and spent several years with him, in fact."

"Out of curiosity, what was the topic of your dissertation, and when was it published?"

"Oh, I never wrote a dissertation. Wasn't what I was there for. I kept appearances up by talking about it, but I think I greatly disappointed the good doctor when I said I had to leave for family issues back in Europe."

"I bet. It would've been something to have a dissertation signed off on by Professor Bloch. Say, did you ever get into studying string theory?"

"Not this cycle. I did once, but all I really do since is check into the status of the theory every so often. It's not very interesting."

"Not very…. What do you mean? Why is the study of nuclear mechanics interesting to you, but string theory isn't?"

"I know the end result. String theory relies on multiple dimensions to prove its mechanics, and on huge energy levels to prove its particles. Neither is possible for humans to observe, unfortunately."

Crystal's ears perked up, her mind finally grabbing a word she understood. "Didn't you tell me that Olympus was in a different dimension?"

"Olympus?" Ben asked.

"Yes, love, I did, and it is," Matt replied to Crystal. "You were able to go there because I took you. It's the province of the gods."

"You went to Olympus?" Ben asked, awe resonating in his voice.

"She did. You can't." Matt said.

"Oh. Well. So anyway," Ben said, "you're saying that string theory will never be resolved because mankind will never be able to experimentally measure the defining evidence."

Matt nodded. "Exactly. The god particle was an appropriate name for the Higgs boson, since it can only be observed by a god."

Ben rubbed his face. "So everything some of my colleagues were working on was a waste of time?"

"Not really. It kept them gainfully employed, and there were some useful discoveries made along the way."

"Like what?"

"Um—well, I can't really think of any right now, except for the fact that a single bird really can shut down the most expensive physics experiment ever created, and that seems a bit trivial."

"Mm hmm."

Crystal asked Natalia, "Are you as lost in the conversation as I am?" Natalia responded with a nod, a grin on her face.

Matt chortled and said, "Ben, it looks like we're being banished to the smoking room."

"You smoke?" Ben asked.

"No, of course not. But every mansion needs a smoking room. Guys toward the end of the most recent cycle took to calling it a man cave, but I like the more genteel term for it. In any event, it has everything a man needs: plush leather furniture, velvet curtains, large stuffed animal heads, and plenty of all varieties of whiskeys. You'll probably feel the need to scratch yourself in private places just from walking in. In fact, it's so manly that Sorscha doesn't even come in unless I ask her to."

"I think the smoking room sounds like an excellent place to go, then."

"Dad, can we come?" Corey asked.

Ben and Matt both stopped. Neither said anything, but both looked meaningfully between the boys and the girls sitting across the room from them.

"I, um, just wanted to see it, and then come back here," Corey objected.

"Mm hmm," Ben said.

"Sure," Matt said, chortling. "Come on."

"So what have been the alternatives to string theory over the cycles?" Ben asked as they waited for the boys.

The men walked to the wall opposite the door that led from the sitting room into the hall, the boys scurrying after them while casting apologetic smiles toward the girls. Matt opened a door that hadn't been readily apparent in the blue wall design, though now that Crystal saw it she wondered why she had missed it before. All four walked through it, the men chatting about the concept of string theory as it had changed over the eons, and the boys looking around in amazement.

"So how does it feel to be a god's wife?" Natalia asked Crystal, grabbing her attention as the door shut.

Crystal shrugged. "I'm still a human."

"Right, but not every human gets to be the lady of an estate like this," Natalia said, missing Crystal's point. Then again, Crystal wasn't sure she wanted to press the point that was on her mind. She doubted Natalia would understand.

"It is a breathtaking place to live," Crystal answered. "And having my own horse readied for me to ride whenever I want is, of course, an amazing benefit. It's like having all of my childhood dreams come true."

"If it's that good, why are you going to see Gaia tomorrow to become a goddess?" Heidi said.

"Oh?" Natalia's eyebrows shot up in surprise. "Forgive me if I'm intruding in a topic, but it doesn't seem as though becoming a goddess should be—easy."

"Apparently it isn't," Crystal said. She hadn't gotten to know the librarian very well, but she found herself instinctively liking and trusting Natalia. Crystal's instincts for people had nearly always been correct, so she decided to open up and talk freely. Come to think of it, she mused, she had been without a woman friend since the cataclysm. She had Sorscha to talk to, and speaking to the thrakkon was always interesting, but it just wasn't the same as having close female, human, friends.

She opened up to Natalia, telling her of the discovery that her husband was a god, her initial and incorrect suspicions of Sorscha, and the encounters with Aphrodite. Natalia listened closely, as did the two girls, who Crystal realized hadn't heard much of the stories she was telling either. How much had she closed herself off with her own emotional roller-coaster recently? There had always been a slight barrier between her and her girls; they weren't what she would consider friends, nor did she consider that type of relationship appropriate between mother and daughters. But she had always, up to the cataclysm, taken time to sit and talk and sometimes dream with the girls. Unfortunately she couldn't remember doing that a single time since their arrival at the estate.

As she concluded the story, she noticed that both girls had leaned in, snuggling under each of their mother's arms as they used to so long ago. She stopped, sighed, and squeezed her daughters tight. "I've missed this."

Natalia's eyes twinkled at seeing the mother-daughter bonding moment. "So it appears," she said, nodding.

After allowing several long moments to pass in silence, Natalia cleared her throat quietly and then asked, "So, do you have any idea what Gaia is going to require of you tomorrow?"

"No," Crystal said. "I wish I had some clue what was coming, but I don't. All I know is that it worked for Stacy."

"And you could be gone for a while, right?"

"Yes. That's part of what is really bothering me. Matt either won't tell me or doesn't know how long I need to prepare to be gone. I don't know when I'll get to see Heidi and Linda again."

"Well, they're always welcome at our suite," Natalia said. "The boys have taken a liking to their company, and I have to say they're pretty good girls. Is Sorscha going with you, or staying here?"

Crystal shrugged, realizing that she hadn't considered the question. She turned to Sorscha, who was waiting by the wall, and was disappointed when the thrakkon shook her head.

"I can't," Sorscha said. "My kind rarely, if ever, accompany their gods to other gods' estates. For me to go with you would not only leave the master unaccompanied, but would also send a signal to Gaia that might make her less willing to teach you anything. You need to go as a supplicant, and not as an equal."

"Well, then," Natalia said, "never fear. Sorscha will stay and keep Matt safe, and the girls can hang out with us and the boys as much as they wish while you're away. All will be fine."

Crystal had to chuckle at Natalia's pluckiness. "I hope so," she said.

"Before you go, though—how did you get so good at magic?"

"I don't know," Crystal said. "It honestly just came naturally to me. Matt refused to teach me at first, which made me very angry. I could see the elemental flows clearly, and I knew that I could touch them. Matt says I can see things that a human shouldn't be able to."

"Like this essence of magic I keep hearing and reading about?"

"Exactly."

"Mom, what's the essence of magic?" Heidi asked.

"Girls, magic is made up of four elements: earth, air, fire, and water. But above all of those, and kind of combining them all, is a supreme essence. It's how your father's most powerful spells are weaved, and it's the force behind the spell that Aphrodite cast that felt like a nuclear bomb. Humans are not even able to see it—except, somehow, for me. I can't touch it yet, but I can't help but wonder if my ability to see it is what made your father agree to give me a shot at becoming a goddess."

Natalia nodded and then added, "Girls, your mother is already legendary among us initiates. It was she who was first to be able to throw a rock, and then it was she who stood up to Aphrodite. She's beyond powerful and into amazing."

Crystal found herself blushing. Legendary? She didn't realize the other students saw her that way. She had assumed they would remember her most for the outbursts that were unusually emotional for her, but then again, messing with the elemental flows of magic seemed to bring out the unusual in people.

The door opened and the men returned, boys leading the way. Crystal started, and then realized that the window had gone dark.

"I thought you were just looking and then coming back," Crystal teased the boys.

"Um, we were," Steve answered with some hesitation. "But the talks that Dad and Matt had were awesome. You wouldn't believe what they were doing four, eight, and twelve thousand years ago. It was amazing."

Heidi shrugged. "That's okay," she said. "It gave us a chance to snuggle with Mom and hear what she's been going through. I'm glad we got the chance."

"Well, I'm glad we got the chance, too," Crystal said, heart soaring, "but everybody is probably getting hungry. Let's go downstairs and find something to eat."

Both families rose and walked down to the dining hall. Sorscha and a young kitchen's helper named Shane helped move chairs up to the facing side of the head table so that the four Phillips family members could sit across from and converse with Crystal and her family as they ate.

"So what has Rellgll got you doing in your work details, Ben?" Matt asked as they started in on their food.

"Grounds maintenance," Ben said. "Grass cutting, believe it or not. I kind of just took that because it sounded better than being in the kitchen, but I find myself really liking it. The weather here is lovely, and it's good to be outdoors doing something physical. Besides, the work really isn't all that hard. I'd like to find something to do with my mind at some point, but I don't know how that would work here."

"Actually, Ben, the time will come, probably pretty soon, when we'll need to break away a few of you who understood the work of science to start taking down information. I do this every magic cycle to record as much as possible of what you recall from the technology cycle that just ended."

"But you know more than we do. You spoke with Professor Bloch himself."

Matt nodded. "Yeah, but that doesn't mean I'm going to sit and record it all. Besides, I only dabbled in the sciences. You folks lived them."

"So I assume you'll need me to jump over to librarian duties to keep track of all this?" Natalia asked, eagerness in her voice.

"Absolutely not. You're too valuable as a battle mage. Besides, I have a perfectly good librarian already. Any of your old colleagues who aren't cutting the mustard in the magic arena will be welcome to assist, or to join other details, but I protect the battle mages' time."

"Why do you call us battle mages?" Natalia asked. "I don't think any of us in the sorcerer's chamber know where that came from, especially since you call the room by a different term."

Matt smiled and said, "I guess I could call you magicians, or magi, or sorcerers. There are plenty of terms in the English language that apply to people who can cast magic spells. But I'm the God of War, as you know. It only makes sense that I train mages for battle. Hence, battle magi. Some of you will never fight a single battle, while others will fight many. Still, the term makes me happy, so just go with it, okay?"

Natalia bowed her head. "Yes, my Lord," she said.

Matt saluted her gesture by raising his glass. "Wise answer, young battle mage."

Crystal turned her attention on the teenage conversation rolling along smoothly to her right. The boys were taking turns telling the girls of their exploits on the swim team in the season that had just been cut short. They were both, according to the story, well known stars of their school. Corey had been born with the lankier body and was slightly faster than his brother in the crawl and the backstroke, while Steve was the stouter and had gotten his father's wide shoulders. They were saying that Steve was considered by many the favorite to go to the state meet in both breast stroke and the butterfly, and their four-man medley team hadn't been beaten all season. Crystal was impressed, but wondered what swimmers could do to keep up their love for the sport at the estate.

Regardless, it was good to hear the kids conversing normally. When the boys had arrived, Heidi and Linda had reported to their mother that the girls spent nearly every moment consoling the boys on the loss of their sister. The courage they had displayed at the elementary school where they had discovered and laid her corpse to rest had been part façade, it seemed, adopted to avoid looking weak, but beneath the surface the boys had been devastated. They had spent days telling the girls about their sister and her exploits.

Matt, Crystal thought, had been considerate with their loss, as well as with the other loss of life, but he hadn't mourned. He clearly understood the mourning process and how necessary it was, but that understanding seemed academic. Crystal doubted if her husband, the god, had mourned the loss of anyone. It was a strange dichotomy; Matt could be the most caring, unselfish, feeling man she knew, but human death didn't bother him much. Logically, she knew why he wasn't bothered, but it made no emotional sense to her.

Crystal finished the meal in silence, the conversation flowing around her. In her own mind she worked over the question of whether, should she succeed, she would be more like she was now in caring for human life, or if she would ever, for some reason she didn't know as a human, adopt Matt's cavalier attitude toward human death.

"Well, my love," Matt interrupted her reverie, "in honor of your departure, the thrakkoni have another concert prepared for us. Would you like to join us?" he asked the Phillips family.

"Absolutely!" Ben answered, his and Natalia's expressions both brightening. "We've missed having music in our lives."

"This is like nothing you've ever experienced," Crystal felt moved to warn Natalia, and then realized she couldn't explain further. Luckily, she didn't need to, as Natalia smiled and nodded and followed them outside to the amphitheater.

The concert that followed was even better, Crystal thought, than the first one she had attended the night they had arrived. There wasn't as much background noise; the audience was about half the size of the previous one, which admittedly happened when most people didn't have any alternatives calling for their time. She was also prepared, this time, for the mental imagery that Matt provided to add sensory dimension to the music, and she even managed to glimpse some of the magical flows he was using to power it. She had thought it must be the essence of magic, but it was really just delicately used touches of air and water with rare glimpses of fire and earth.

Matt's lights came back up as the final number, which Crystal recognized as The Queen of the Night's Aria from The Magic Flute, trilled out its final bars. She wondered if the number had been chosen as a commentary on her quest—it was definitely possible, given Matt's love for classical music and his ability to communicate with his entire thrakkoni ensemble telepathically. Ignoring the question, though, she rose with the rest of the audience and applauded enthusiastically. Looking to her side at Natalia, she saw that the physicist and librarian looked as enraptured by the musical display as she had felt the first night.

"That was lovely!" Natalia squealed. Turning to Matt, she asked, "Did you create the music also, or just the imagery?"

Matt waved a hand grandly toward the musical ensemble of thrakkoni. "The music was all them. Not only do they craft their own instruments by hand, but they have mastered the art of playing them too. It's impressive, isn't it? My magic does create the imagery, but with the music it requires just the lightest of flows."

The party walked back inside, stopping at the junction of the hallways leading to their separate chambers.

Natalia said, "Matt, Crystal told me of her trip. I'm sure you have plenty of servants to watch after the girls, but please let us assist."

"Well, thank you. You're going to be too busy, though, practicing magic, and your husband will also be busy. I'm sure that the boys and girls can be trusted to not get too bored together, and there's not a lot of trouble to be gotten into. That said, in the evenings, I would have no problem with you having the girls over."

Natalia and Ben each shook Matt's hand, and Natalia gave Crystal a tight hug, whispering "Good luck!" into her ear. Then the Phillips family walked away toward their suite, Matt and Crystal and the girls turning toward their own.

A Rude Awakening

The girls safely in bed, Crystal relaxed next to her husband in their own chamber. The war god, she thought. And soon, perhaps, she would be the—the something goddess.

"How do you pick what you're going to be the god or goddess of?" she asked Matt.

"If you ascend, you're offered a closed shoe box that contains all the 'god of' options that are left over. You pull a slip out, or if you're really feeling persnickety, you pull out two. Nobody has yet pulled out the 'god of sewage plants' option, so I'd be wary of pulling two out if I were you."

"You're joking."

"Yeah," Matt loosed a chuckle and tickled her. He knew she wouldn't get upset at him when she was laughing, so it was unfair that he knew exactly where to tickle her.

"Seriously, though," he said, "it's kind of up to you. I've always enjoyed the martial activities, so god of war was a natural persona for me to adopt. Stacy had always fancied herself the most beautiful person on the planet, so her persona was obvious too. Others, like Helepatus, pretty much just play around a lot and come up with whatever trips their triggers for each new civilization."

"Oh, of course. So it's based on civilization, not cycle or some even longer history."

"Right. Sort of, anyway. Some of us pretty well have our roles knocked down, and taking on the same role as us biggies would be awkward. The world only needs one love goddess, for example. Only needs one Apollo too, but there are a lot of areas you can kind of overlay onto his without much trouble. For example, there can easily be a god of magic in addition to Apollo, who is the overall god of magic, arts, and healing. Does that make sense?"

"Yes, it does. I'm probably putting the cart way before the horse, anyway. It just struck me as curious."

"Love, you need to ask questions like that. Your quest is to become a goddess, right? That's pretty much a matter of discovering the undiscoverable. You'll have to ask many questions, never knowing if the answer to the question you're asking will lead you closer to the ultimate end."

Crystal sighed.

"How long did Stacy stay at it?"

"A long, long time. And I don't think that was all with Gaia. It seems as though Stacy went to visit other gods too, though who and what and for how long I don't know the story of."

"How am I going to be able to stand being away from you for so long?"

"Well, keep in mind that the other option is coming home and living out the rest of your life as my beautiful and amazingly human wife. I've told you that that would be a great option to me, but I also know that it's not what you want, and trust me, I understand why. I just don't want to see you going through the trials I know are ahead, since they will be the hardest you've ever been through. That said, I know that your options are either to remain home and live your human life with me, or stay away as long as you need to eventually come back and live an immortal life with me. Knowing that those are your options should help you keep your courage up."

Crystal hugged Matt, a long, deep, and comforting hug. He had always been the guy who let her follow the path she wanted, no matter whether he agreed, and she considered him a greater man for allowing her that freedom. Now it was even greater; he trusted her to go away and then come back a goddess, knowing that the last time it had happened the result had been horrible.

"When did you know she wasn't coming back to you?"

Matt sighed, long and deep. "I'd like to say it was right after she ascended, when she turned her back to me and announced that she would make her own estate and her own thrakkoni. But truth be told, I knew before that. I had a feeling about it even before she went off to speak with Gaia."

"I take it you don't have that same feeling with me."

"No, not even close. You're not seeking to become a goddess to immortalize your own beauty, but rather to immortalize our relationship. I'm pretty comfortable that you'll come back to me."

"Mmmm," Crystal murmured, nuzzling her head into his side. "I don't know if I'll be able to sleep tonight, but at least it will be a wonderfully comfortable night."

"Oh, you'll be able to sleep. Close your eyes and relax."

Crystal did as Matt suggested. She was surprised to see the flows Matt used without having her eyes open. She had never tried casting magic with her eyes closed before, and she supposed that she should have expected to be able to sense the elemental flows even without the help of her eyes. Regardless, she could tell that Matt was weaving a complex web over her using various elements including the essence of magic itself, using it to convince her systems to slow down, relaxing her mind and body and sending her gently toward sleep.

Her eyes snapped open suddenly. It was dark, and she was alone in the bed. She sat up, easily casting the small globe of light as Matt had taught her. "Matt?" she called out.

A laugh she recognized chilled her to the bone. She looked past the foot of the bed as both Aphrodite and Gaia came into view, one to each side of the bed, in the sphere of light cast by her globe. Both advanced on her. Neither moved particularly fast but both were already past the metal posts of the foot of the bed.

Metal posts? Crystal looked around. The light didn't reach any of the walls or the ceiling, stopped by some unseen force, but the bed was definitely the one she'd grown up in. It must have grown, she thought, since she had outgrown the bed in her early teenage years, but it was definitely the same simple metal bed frame, and—she checked—yes, the same hard mattress and rough sheets.

Looking back to the sides, she was alarmed to see both Aphrodite and Gaia standing halfway up the bed. As she focused on them she was alarmed to hear them begin chanting in an unknown language. She could feel the powers beginning to bind her, keep her from moving, shut off her air once again, just like on the day when Aphrodite had attacked her in the field.

"Matt!" she screamed. "Matt! Matt! Oh, Matt!" she screamed over and over, terrified of not being able to breathe again.

"Shhhh. Love, it's okay," Matt's voice infiltrated the scene. She felt something shake her shoulders, and then found herself able to open her eyes again. This time, she was greeted by Matt's concerned face and the now-familiar painted view of the heavens above it. Willing herself to breathe normally, she looked around tentatively. She was once again in their wood-framed poster bed.

Calming down finally, she leaned into Matt's embrace. "I—I had a bad dream."

"Yeah, that was obvious," he said. "Wanna tell me about it?"

She told him the details as she could remember them, though the images were fading fast now that she was awake again. Matt listened intently, nodding as she described key details.

"What do you think it means, Matt?"

"Well, there's a world between the worlds, a world of dreams. The paths of this world can be walked by the gods, and sometimes they use this power to attack humans or to dissuade them from following dangerous paths."

"Really?"

"No," he said, sticking his tongue out at her. "This isn't some weird Wheel of Time thing. Nobody can enter your mind, my love. You just had a bad dream caused by your stress over the coming trials."

Crystal stuck her tongue out as far as it would go. After so many years of his humor she should have known better, but he had gotten her going anyway. His approach had worked, though. The tension was broken.

"Ugh," she said. "That was horrible, regardless. How am I going to be able to get back to sleep after that?"

Matt wiggled his fingers in her face. "May-ya-jick!" he exclaimed, mimicking a performer they had both long ago forgotten about except for his silly amplified gesture and pronunciation. His expression morphed into seriousness and he stroked her face a couple of times before continuing, "Bad dreams or not, my love, you need to get your sleep. I'm sure you'll be able to handle tomorrow one way or another, but it will be much easier after a full night's rest. Please, relax, close your eyes, and let me help you drift back off."

Crystal looked in Matt's eyes for several minutes, knowing this would be the last night in a while that she would spend with him. She reached up to stroke his cheek, feeling the stubble. She knew now that he exhibited stubble on his face because he chose to, but it just made him feel even more a man. A male god, anyway. And, she finished the line of reasoning, she owed it to him to become a goddess, which meant that no matter how much she wanted to stay awake and stare into his eyes all night, she needed sleep.

Crystal nodded and then settled into her pillow. As she closed her eyes and felt the flows passing over her once again, she muttered, "Good night. I...."

Preparations

Crystal woke again, more gently than the time before. She recalled the nightmare vividly and felt a little scared to look around for fear that she was in another one. Despite her terror, she willed her eyes to open, first one and then the other, and found herself looking this time into the comfortably muted light of the morning, brightening the sky scene above her enough that she could tell the heavenly bodies portrayed there one from another. She took in a deep breath of relief and let it out in a long, resonant sigh.

"Good morning," Matt's voice called from the windows. She could see his silhouette against the curtains as he reached for the string to draw them back and let in the full morning light.

"Wait!" she called. He stopped and turned with a quizzical look on his face. "Come here," she commanded. Matt followed her order, walking slowly to the bed and sitting on its edge.

"Yes?" Matt's eyes twinkled as though he was expecting something from her, but he played coy.

Reaching up to grab his hair, Crystal used the hold to pull Matt's face down to hers and savored a burning kiss.

"You didn't think I was going to meet the day I would leave you for an unknown period of time without saying farewell the right way, did you?" she asked as she released her hold.

"Of course not. You do know that I'll miss you while you're away with Gaia, yes?"

Crystal gave him her sexiest leer in return. "My goal is to make you miss me even more," she said, and then pulled his face once again to hers and, with her other hand, tugged his body beside hers at the same time. Matt responded, hands gripping her body longingly. His kiss moved from her mouth to her ear, pausing to nibble on the earlobe before continuing their path down the side of her neck to the spot he always found, the extra-sensitive point where neck meets collarbone. She gasped, and Matt moaned his pleasure at her response.

Matt continued kissing her body up and down, covering every spot before moving to the core of her heat. Again Crystal showed her pleasure with a sharp gasp, and again Matt moaned. Soon she was swept away from the world and its worries by the passion they shared.

Once god and wife were satisfied, both collapsed onto the sheets and held each other close, not saying anything for several long minutes as Matt caressed Crystal's thigh, shoulder, and arm with his free hand.

"Nervous about today?" Matt asked, surprising Crystal out of her trance despite his tender tone.

"Shouldn't I be?"

"Sure. But have you always felt the way you should?"

"Point. Yes, I'm nervous. Terrified, in fact."

"Of what?"

"Of what might happen."

"What might happen?"

She stuck out her tongue before answering, "You know I have no idea."

"Then...."

"...why be scared of it?" she completed the sentence for him, having had this same talk with the girls many times.

Several long, quiet seconds later it was obvious Matt wasn't going to go on to a different topic, so she did the most useful thing she could think of: stuck her tongue out again.

Matt chortled. "Sticks and stones may break my bones, but that tongue will just get you in trouble."

"Didn't you say something about me needing to be well rested?"

"I said it might be a good idea if you went well rested. I have absolutely no idea how you need to go. Isn't that the exciting thing? You get to go do something today that very few humans have ever done before."

"And what if....?"

"What if what?"

"I don't know. What if she doesn't like me? Or if I ask the question wrong? Or if she just decides not to teach me?"

"Then you come back home and continue being a great mother and a magnificent wife. And we keep looking for a way for you. It's not the end of the world if she says no, my love."

"How do you know?"

Matt shrugged. "Call it intuition, I guess. Remember, this is still fairly new ground for me also."

"Well, then, I guess we better start."

"That's my girl."

She slipped lightly out of bed, just avoiding his tickling fingers. Giggling like a little girl, she danced over to her closet and selected some clothes that were of a standard cut but made of a fine fabric.

"These should work."

"Are you asking me?"

"If I'm going to be a goddess, I better be able to choose my own clothes, right?"

"Yeah, did you see how well that worked with Aphrodite?"

Crystal leered at Matt and pulled her naked frame as tall as she could, pirouetting. "Does it work better for me?"

"Immensely."

"So maybe I should go to Gaia naked?"

"No, I doubt she would be impressed as I am."

"Okay, fine," she said, and then slipped on the clothes. Matt rose, suddenly dressed in an outfit perfectly matched to the one Crystal had chosen.

"Speaking of Aphrodite," Crystal said, something Matt had said suddenly bothering her.

"Yes?"

"You said she took her closet full of clothes with her to her estate?"

"I did. And she did, right after she left me."

"I've never seen you need a closet. You wiggle your nose, and attire of your choice just appears on your body. Why did she take her clothes with her?"

"She always loved the way silks feel against her body. Her entire closet was silk, in fact, and most of it naga silk. You'll find that there are certain human things you take with you, or simply assume as I have, into godhood. My love for fried okra is that way, in fact. I don't need to eat, especially not the pod of a spiny ugly plant deep fried in corn batter, but I love the taste, and I love the feel as the crunch gives way to the pop of the little seed pods. Thus, I cherish eating them, and Aphrodite wears her silk for the same reason. When she wears clothes, anyway."

"Makes sense, I guess, in a strange way, though I have a hard time equating silk clothing to fried okra. Regardless, I wonder what I'll take with me," Crystal said.

"You'll have plenty of time for that later, but for now there is a grand feast prepared for you downstairs." Crystal joined her family as they processed solemnly to the dining hall, where a massive brunch buffet had been laid out for them. Sorscha smiled when Crystal oohed and ahhed over it and explained that she had created most of the food herself, wanting to give Crystal a grand send-off into her destiny.

****

Crystal followed Matt to the throne room, the butterflies multiplying in her stomach, rapidly filling her midsection after the pleasure of her daughter's hugs and kisses waned. The uncertainty that she was headed into was one thing—one thing that probably wouldn't have bothered her much by itself. She had felt a little bit nervous when traveling with Matt the first time into a foreign land, but had quickly found that she enjoyed the uncertainty of heading into the unknown.

No, what bothered her most was that she really had absolutely no idea how to address the issue with Gaia. As little as she knew about what she should say when meeting the mother goddess, she was certain it wasn't, "Hey, Gaia, I'm here to become a goddess, so please help me." She was as good as anyone at handing matters delicately, of course, but Gaia was—well, *the* mother. She was hundreds of millions of years old, and had probably quite literally heard it all by now.

"What should I do?" she asked, more aloud than she'd intended.

"Be yourself," Matt replied. "The Mother will have no problem figuring out why you're there, so just be open and direct with her. Of course, I doubt she's going to just come out and give you a recipe. It won't be that easy, can't be that easy, and besides, I'm sure she'll want to test you first."

"Test me?"

"Yeah, of course. She's got to find out how sincere you are. Don't sweat it, though. I'm sure you'll do fine."

"That's what you said when you talked me into bungee jumping. Little did I know at the time that *you* couldn't die."

"You did fine, didn't you?"

"I lived, and didn't break anything. Is that your definition of fine?"

"For a human? Sure."

She glared half-heartedly, appreciating the interjection of humor that seemed to kill off about half of the butterflies that were intent on beating her stomach out of her chest.

The pair walked into the throne room, Matt striding over to stand on the golden circle in the alcove. Crystal hesitated. Matt smiled warmly and held out his hand, and she found herself giving in to his confidence in spite of the butterflies.

"This is going to feel like it did when we traveled to Olympus, only not quite as wrenching because we're ending in the same dimension," Matt said. "Ready?"

Crystal smiled, not certain enough in her readiness to respond any stronger. She saw Matt reach up to the bell above them with the essence of magic and ring it once, then again, and then a third time. His gaze seemed intent on a far-off place, and suddenly he nodded and asked again, "Ready?"

She nodded, and closed her eyes as the world folded around her.

Gaia's Glade

When she opened her eyes, she gasped.

Crystal found herself outdoors in a landscape more beautiful than she could have imagined. Trees of all types stood proudly around the clearing; she saw fruit trees, pines, and several varieties of hardwoods that she would never have thought might grow near each other, in addition to some trees she didn't recognize. A lemon tree full of fruit squatted to her right, while a cherry tree was to her left. Looking behind, she thought she recognized both avocadoes and pomegranates. Between the trees, the ground was carpeted with a lush and vibrantly green grass, wildflowers spaced around as perfectly as if they'd been planted. She recognized several wildflowers, also, and once again was struck by the incongruity of cool-weather plants growing happily next to warm-weather species.

Movement caught her eye, and she focused just to their right to see a pair of deer leaping. As she calmed down from the internal jostling of the teleportation, her eyes spotted more animals. Many birds flew unafraid between the branches of the trees, and she saw several squirrels and what could only be monkeys flipping between the branches, stopping to stare every few jumps. Another, stranger animal peered over its furry snout at her from the tree line, and then wandered casually away once it had satisfied its curiosity. Butterflies—real ones this time, not the ones that terrorized her stomach—flitted about, landing on the wildflowers and posing in the sun.

Crystal, so taken in by all the beauty that she forgot her mission, giggled. Matt, who had been watching her as she absorbed her surroundings, smiled and grasped her hand.

A throat cleared from near the tree to their front—an apple tree, Crystal saw—and a silver-robed figure stepped out away from its trunk, face smiling. Gaia, as Crystal recognized her, was even more radiantly beautiful in her own garden than she had been on the day of the cataclysm. Her long brown hair was braided; for a cynical moment Crystal observed that the blossoms that were braided into Gaia's hair were clichéd, but then realized that the entire garden served one grand cliché.

"Greetings, God of War." Gaia's voice twinkled over them, reminding Crystal of a mountain waterfall. "And Mrs. Of War, I presume?"

Matt bowed. "Mother, thank you for agreeing to entertain us. This is indeed Crystal, my wife. Crystal, allow me to formally introduce the Mother, Gaia."

Crystal curtsied as deeply as she knew how. It felt rough and jerky, but Gaia didn't comment.

"I am always pleased to see you, Matthew, but you've never brought a human to my clearing. Are you here for tea and cookies, as I hope?"

Matt shook his head. "No, but that is for the two wisest ladies I know to discuss. By your leave?" Matt asked, and then immediately vanished.

Crystal's head jerked toward where Matt had just been standing, panic slamming her throat to the roof of her mouth. She felt a flash of irritation toward Matt for disappearing the way he had, but then she calmed down as she thought back to what he had said about her being tested. This was her test, not his. She knew he must have thought that he would only be in the way of her making an impression on Gaia, and she also knew that he was right. As much as it terrified her, she appreciated that Matt had gotten her to exactly where she needed to be, alone in front of the mother goddess.

"So—tea and cookies?" Gaia asked again, smiling and spreading her hands in what seemed to almost be a welcoming gesture.

Crystal summoned her courage with an enormous effort. This was the mother goddess, whom Matt had said was an approachable being. She knew that Stacy had done it, and she knew that anything Stacy had done must be doable for her as well.

That knowledge did little to diminish the fact that she was standing in front of the Earth Mother, the grand being Matt had said was number two of the deities and the only one around who outranked and out-powered him. Crystal was certain that Gaia wouldn't appreciate a waifish, timid approach, so she drew in a deep breath and pressed her diaphragm into service while forcing her lips into a broad smile. "Tea and cookies aren't what I came for, Earth mother, but I'll be happy to share them with you if you wish."

"Perhaps later, child. Matthew has always been known for speaking to the point, and I trust that his current wife has a similar penchant."

"Indeed. I've come to you, Earth mother, hoping to learn what I must to transition from human to goddess."

"I see."

Crystal allowed the pause to expand. As a teacher, she'd learned the power of silence, and she decided that now was a good situation in which to apply it.

"Why do you stand there silent, child? Don't you have a question to ask?"

Careful, Crystal's subconscious voice screamed. She'd won the silence game, but this felt like a trap.

"Earth mother, I have many questions that beg to be asked of your wisdom. Probably more, in fact, than I have the remaining heartbeats or you have the patience for. But for now, one question is central. Matthew told me that you might point me in the right direction to discover the path to becoming a goddess. Can you do that?"

Gaia snorted, but the smile that played in her eyes gave Crystal hope. "I can," she said, "but why should I?"

"So that the love Matt and I share can be eternal."

Gaia snorted again, sharper this time. "Didn't work so well for Matt and his former wife."

"I'm not like Stacy, Earth mother."

"No, you're certainly not. You don't have half her skills in magic, and you're useless in physical battle. At least Stacy could stand by Matt as an equal partner."

Crystal shrugged and carefully kept the sting of Gaia's words off of her face. "I've only studied magic for a few weeks. With training I can best any ability Stacy showed."

Gaia's smile broadened and Crystal saw she had hit a home run. Deciding to press her advantage, she added, "Abilities aside, Matt and I love each other dearly. I can't imagine life without him. He's told me the same himself. I don't know what Stacy said, and honestly I don't care, but I really am doing this for the promise of living forever with Matthew, my one true love."

Gaia nodded. "Well, then. You've argued a fine case for yourself. Whether you'll live up to your argument remains to be seen. I will help you, in any event, in finding the next step along the path you seek."

Crystal prevented herself, barely, from gasping in relief. The victory had been won much faster than she'd expected. Clamping down tightly on her emotions to maintain control, she nodded simply and said, "Thank you, Earth mother. What, then, if I may be so bold to ask, is the next step along the path?"

"So bold to ask? Your stepping foot into my garden is bold enough, mortal." Gaia's laughter pealed through the trees. "Still, you do impress me a bit. A goddess you may, in fact, make some day. Today, though, your magical skills impress no one. Go to the one you know as Apollo and beg for his teaching. Matthew can only teach you war magic, and powerful though that may seem to you and the rest of his human following, it's pitiful for one who would try to claim a spot at Olympus."

"Earth mother, thank you for your wisdom. I will go to Apollo and seek his tutelage. Should I seek Matthew's magical help to get back to his estate to travel from there, or would you assist me?"

"Are you ready to travel?" Gaia asked.

"I am."

Gaia nodded, and suddenly Crystal's world blinked again. Once her stomach untied itself, she found herself once again standing on the gold circle in Matt's throne room.

"So, how'd it go?" Matt asked from behind her.

She spun to see Matt smiling, holding his arms out to her. Crystal leapt into his arms and held him tight in silence for several minutes.

"Ow!" Matt said playfully as Crystal finally ended the embrace, leaned back, and socked him in the chest.

"You vanished and left me there to stutter."

"Surely you know why."

"Of course. But that doesn't mean a little warning would have been unappreciated."

Matt answered by pulling her into another kiss.

After several more minutes of embrace, Matt pulled away and asked, "So, it looks from your demeanor that you got the answer you were hoping for."

"Not really. She said you suck at magic and that I needed to seek out Apollo to teach me better first."

"Excellent."

"Excellent? That's—not the response I expected," she said.

"She's right," Matt said. "I do suck, comparatively speaking, at teaching magic. Why do you think I became the god of war and any other things related to smacking people in the face?"

"I guess I understand, but I've been getting used to changing the way I think of you from Matt my husband to Matt the god who can do anything. Now you're asking me to change it again, this time to Matt the god who can do almost anything?"

"Well—sort of. I'm not omnipotent. None of us are. I can't touch you on the forehead, for example, and make you into a goddess, and neither can any of my peers. So the almost any-thing is correct. But I can do as much or more of almost anything as any of my peers can. It's just that my methods are straightforward, and that's what I teach. Apollo's mages are busy still learning the basic framework of magic, and all the underly-ing theory, and won't work up to an actual casting of a fireball for a long time. He and I are peers, but his mages become well-rounded magical scholars while mine become fireball-casting warriors. That's why you need to go study under him. You'll probably have to try to forget everything you've learned so that he can build up your knowledge in a way that, to him, is correct. You've come a long way very quickly here, and you obviously have a great deal of power. Gaia just wants you to develop your power beyond the ability to melt faces, and to be honest, so do I."

"So you're saying I ought to go."

"Of course. But not right away. We've missed you terribly."

"But I was only gone for a few minutes."

"Yeah, but it seemed a lifetime to us." Matt smirked.

Crystal stuck her tongue out at Matt, and then asked, "So how did you know to wait for me here?"

"I didn't. Gaia is always one to follow protocol, so she rang the bell before transporting you back."

"Oh."

Crystal related the entirety of her meeting with Gaia to the girls, who hungrily pressed her for details as they oohed and ahhed over the beauty of Gaia's special glade. Later, Crystal found herself repeating the entire story again to Natalia and her family over dinner. She didn't mind; she enjoyed storytelling, and this one was special. How many people could describe Gaia's meadow?

That night, as they lay in bed following another powerful session of lovemaking, Crystal said, "I'm probably going to be gone a long time to Apollo's, if he's going to teach me magic."

"Yeah, probably months. I doubt if he'll let you come home during that time, either, as I'm sure that his teaching methods require a fair amount of immersion."

She peered at what she could see of his face, searching for a telltale hint of sardonic humor, hoping that the last had been a joke. Not seeing it, though, she felt her chest tighten.

"Months?" she asked. "I'm really hoping you're not serious."

"I am."

"I'm not sure I can do that."

"You must, if you wish to continue in your quest."

"I know that. I just don't know how I'm going to manage being away from you and the girls for that long."

Matt rolled onto his side and looked directly into her eye. "Oh, come on," he said. "You've done much more difficult things. You carried twin babies inside of you for months, remember? You have a far greater pool of strength than you give yourself credit for sometimes."

Crystal smiled, thinking of the girls. Relaxing, she found an uneasy sleep.

Learning Magic

The next morning found the couple once again in the throne room facing the circle on the floor. Crystal looked at Matt, uncertainty fueling the butterflies in her gut once again. Matt just shrugged.

"Remember, my love," he said, "Apollo is very, very strong in the arcane, probably the strongest in that aspect of all my peers. He's also a cool, calculating jerk who won't respond at all to any degree of sucking up to him."

Crystal started to protest, but Matt waved her comments down. "Dear," he said, "it wasn't an insult. Quite the opposite, actually. You're going to use every weapon in your arsenal to wring the teaching out of him as fast as you can; I know that. But I also know how he's going to respond to any attempt to win him over, so please let me warn you away from them."

When Crystal nodded, Matt said, "Well, then, I think we're ready to go. You'll probably need to stay for a while, but we won't transport your bags till he suggests it. Unlike Gaia, the twit won't be impressed by your personal supplication, so I'll make the request for you."

"You keep giving me snide remarks about him. How about some actual information?" Crystal let her irritation show, knowing that she needed every possible advantage to get where she wanted to go.

"Sorry. I'm really not certain what will help you, though. By all means, ask anything you want."

"Well, let's start with—did we see Apollo on our trip to Olympus?" She took a shot in the dark.

Matt snorted. "Apollo? At Olympus? Only time he ever shows up there is for official meetings."

"The gods have official meetings?"

"Running the universe does take some actual meeting activity, yes. But back to the matter at hand, Apollo doesn't deign to be associated with his lesser peers, a group that happens to include all of us, any more than he has to. His arrogance is unparalleled."

"Why didn't you tell me this earlier?"

"What difference does his arrogance toward his peers make in your approach to him? Besides, if I fill you with my own notions before you meet all my peers, it might prejudice you against learning anything from them—and especially from that nasty little twerp."

"Nasty little twerp?" Crystal stepped back, eyebrows raised. "I don't think I've ever heard you call anybody that."

Matt grimaced. "I reserve that term only for the one who truly deserves it. Look, Apollo is rightfully known as the master of the arcane arts. Neither I nor any other of my peers is his equal, nor can we train our mages to be equals to his. But he is quite aware of his superiority, and lets you know it every chance he gets. He treats his thrakkoni more as beautifully-decorated slaves than as capable servants, mostly because nearly every task around his estate is performed by magic, it is said, rather than through allowing the humans and thrakkoni to dirty their hands with work. He is, in short, as opposite to me in manner, taste, and style, as you can get. Now, does knowing all that make you feel more prepared to meet His Twerpitude?"

"No, I guess not," Crystal admitted. Regardless of what Matt told her about Apollo, she was still going to approach the god with obeisance, trying to learn as much as she could from him, and that there was no love lost between him and Matt made no difference in her mission or in her approach to it.

"A couple more questions, though, mostly because I'm curious. Was Apollo born a god, or did he rise from being human also?"

"He was one of the originals, along with his twin Artemis, and the gods the Greeks knew as Hermes, Zeus, Hera, Poseidon, Athena, and me. And, of course, Gaia and Yahweh and a couple more."

"Oh," Crystal said, filing the information away for later. "So, does Apollo have a real name, like your name is Matt?"

"None of us really has what you would consider a real name. He usually changes his name during the magic cycles, but it's always some variant of Apollo. I never see him during the technology cycles, so I have no idea what he goes by then. He was once called Michael, but don't call him that now."

"Why not?"

"He won't react kindly to it. Long story, and hardly worth telling now."

Crystal nodded.

"Oh, one more thing. Don't try to communicate with me telepathically in his presence. I'm sure he has wards to sense it, if not to prevent it entirely. Be careful what you say, but anything that must be said, say out loud. So, ready?"

Crystal nodded again and then followed Matt to the gold circle. She heard what she now recognized as his standard rings, followed immediately by the lurching sensation of a teleport. Either Apollo had been very quick to reply, she thought, or Matt just hadn't waited. In either case, she found herself in an overly white throne room, standing on pearlescent floor tiles, facing a huge gold throne on which a handsome robed man sat. A large raven perched on the high back of the throne seemed to be leering down at Crystal.

A thrakkon stood behind and to Apollo's right, and Crystal realized what Matt had meant. This servant of Apollo was beautifully decorated, to the point that Crystal wondered how she could move. Sorscha was beautiful even in the simple tunics and breeches that she always wore. The thrakkon behind Apollo, in comparison, was enrobed in an ensemble that was so beautifully artistic that the thrakkon herself was practically invisible in it.

"Matthew, how nice to see you," Apollo said, his soft voice carrying an overtone that made it clear that it really wasn't nice to see Matt in the slightest. "I trust your pet humans made it through the cataclysm relatively unscathed?"

"Of course," Matt replied jovially. Crystal glanced sideways at Matt to see if he was reacting to the sarcasm, and was surprised to see that her husband had switched to Greek god form for the meeting. It shouldn't have surprised her considering the long rivalry between the two gods, she thought. The tension between the two was so thick she could feel it, could even taste an electric charge building in the air.

"That one looks uncomfortable," Apollo sneered. "Did you bring her for healing? I'm pretty good at that, you know."

"I am aware of your prowess in the arcane, Apollo. This is my wife, Crystal. And no, I am bringing her to you in the hopes that you will teach her to wield the elemental powers as only you can."

Apollo's eyebrows shot up in surprise, and it took the god a couple of seconds to respond. "That's one I didn't expect, Matt. What, is your beloved already tired of poofing around with fireballs and airballs?"

"She was attacked by Stacy, as you are already aware. I'd like her to be able to defend herself a bit more competently next time."

"Well, well, well. This isn't really your idea, is it? Not that you've ever been accused of sprouting an idea that could be considered unique or interesting, but this is well beyond your realm."

"Gaia—suggested it."

Apollo sat forward, his interest stoked by Matt's revelation. He rose and stalked to Crystal, walking around to assess her as though she were a prized sculpture at auction. Matt's jaw, Crystal saw from the corner of her eye, clenched, but otherwise the God of War stood passively.

"Cast something for me," Apollo whispered into Crystal's ear. She obeyed, holding out her hand and lighting a globe over it.

"Hmm," Apollo purred as he walked closely around the globe, assessing her work. "Clumsy, but strong. You have some latent ability, don't you—um, what did you say your name was, dear?"

"My name is Crystal." The light floated unblinking. She noticed Matt's lip corner turn up slightly, confirming her belief that in keeping her focus, or perhaps in not calling Apollo on his apparent mistake, or even both, she had passed a test.

"Good. You can let the light go now, child." Apollo turned from her and walked directly back to his throne, taking his seat imperiously.

Crystal let the globe wink out as Apollo continued, "Who am I, when the Mother asks, to say no? I cherish my relationship with her, as do we all, don't we, Matthew? Certainly I will take your beloved into my home and provide her the opportunity for the best magical training available anywhere in the universe. Should she fail, well, at least we will have tried."

Matt nodded once. "Of course. I'll have her extra clothes sent, as I am sure she will be here for a while."

"No need, mate," Apollo said, his voice jaunty in its air of superiority touched with an edge of sarcasm. "My mages in training all wear the same simple garments. I trust your pretty wife doesn't expect any special treatment, does she?"

Crystal stepped forward and said, "No, his pretty wife does not."

"Oh, oh oh oh, she has spirit," Apollo scoffed. "Excellent. It should make her training most interesting. But no, my dear old friend Matthew, she won't need any of her grand effects from your estate while she's here. And I'm afraid, dear Crystal, that I'll need to ask you to surrender that little communications bauble also."

Crystal panicked and looked at Matt, whose clenched jaw was his only sign of distress. "Matt?" she left the question unspoken.

Matt turned to face her, a fake smile plastered across his face. "Love," he said in a grand voice, "it is acceptable. I am sure that Michael has a good reason related to your training for requiring you to be stripped of the ability to contact me directly, and I am equally certain that he will arrange for that communication should the need arise. Am I correct?"

"Of course, Matthew. The first part of my training requires— oh, bah, why am I explaining it to you? Go back and teach your battle mages to poof their little fireballs, and I'll make sure that your beloved here can actually do something useful should she face Stacy again."

Matt held out his hand and accepted the blue glass shard from Crystal before turning back to Apollo. Drawing his flaming sword, the god of war flicked it up and at an angle in front of his face in an apparent salute. Apollo lifted his chin in return and Matt sheathed his sword, rotated to face Crystal and bowed deeply, and then vanished.

"Well, well, this is an interesting development," Apollo said, folding his arms over his chest and leering at Crystal.

Crystal bowed deeply and said, "Master, I thank you for your offer of tutelage, and I..."

"Oh, shut up," Apollo cut her off. "I'm sure your husband enjoys your babbling, but I do not. You're here to learn magic, and learn magic you shall. That, or get sent home in disgrace. Do you understand me?"

Crystal nodded and said, "Yes, I do."

"I told you to shut up. There's a reason I made you surrender your communication bauble. Mages in my training must first learn to conquer their inner voices. You know what your inner voice is, don't you?"

Crystal started to open her mouth to reply, but squelched the impulse just in time and merely nodded instead.

"Good. I'm impressed; most humans are too slow-witted not to say something there. In any event, the buffoon you call your husband is good at teaching people to throw rocks and energy around, but that's all his mages are ever good for. If you follow my training correctly and fully, you will eclipse all of them. The elemental flows are there for all uses, but in my house you will learn to wield them to heal as well as to harm."

"By the way," he said, "and I command you to speak out loud in response to this. Does your husband like me?"

Crystal watched as Apollo directed an intricate flow of ka, the essence of magic, over her head. A truth spell of some sort, perhaps?

"He said that you and he are opposites in taste, manner, and style, but he didn't say that he dislikes you."

"You saw my flows, didn't you?"

"May I speak in response?"

Apollo laughed, a smirk spreading across his face. "My, my, my, you are a treasure. Yes, you may speak until I tell you otherwise."

"Yes, I did see them."

Apollo nodded once from his throne and looked at her for several silent seconds, his expression unreadable. Finally he rose. "Okay, Crystal," he said, "you may end up being one of the most powerful mages I've ever trained. You may also end up going back to your husband in disgrace. The choice is yours, honestly. It won't be easy, no matter which way you go. But I do feel moved to offer you an out now. Right now, you can go back to your husband, head held high, saying whatever you wish about me and my methods. Consider the option well, as after you accept, any early departure will be a failure on your part. And—I really do mean it when I say that the path won't be easy."

Crystal considered her options briefly, as Apollo had asked her to. As frightened as she was of failure, she knew that her only way forward toward being a goddess lay in earning the blessing of Apollo's training.

"I will do whatever you require to learn to be a mage," she said, keeping her voice as neutral as possible.

Apollo nodded, and then sat on his throne. A thrakkon moved out from an unseen side passage and touched Crystal on the arm. "Fine, then," Apollo said. "Follow the thrakkon to your room. You may not speak from the time you depart this chamber until I release you from the restriction. You may not leave your room. You will find three books in your room. Once you have absorbed the three books, seek audience with me by speaking my name, once and only once. Do you have any questions?"

Crystal's experience as a teacher worrying over precise phrasings of test questions came back to her as she asked, "What, exactly, do you mean by absorbing the books?"

"I mean that you must be able to discuss their passages with me, showing that you have understood the subjects discussed within."

"Do I need to have them memorized?"

Apollo chuckled pleasantly. "The human brain can't memorize the contents of the books, so no. You need to be conversant."

"Then to what standard is passing measured? And what are the outcomes if I fail?"

"Passing is measured by your ability to intelligently converse on every page of each book, and as much as I would like to see you succeed, should you fail, you'll be sent back to Ares in disgrace. I mentioned the disgrace part before, didn't I?"

Crystal nodded. "Yes, you did. No more questions, then."

Apollo looked to Crystal's left, and the thrakkon tugged at Crystal's sleeve. "In that case," Apollo said, "you are now one of my apprentices, and as such you are forbidden to speak with any save me, and that only when I permit it. Go study the background information provided, and once you have mastered it I will provide you with further knowledge."

Crystal allowed herself to be led quietly out of the throne room through a side passage, and from there down a series of halls to a nondescript door. The thrakkon opened the door, smiled and bowed. Inside the room was a single bed, a candlestick on an end table, a porcelain construct that was shaped like a primitive privy, a simple pine wardrobe, and a small desk with three books on it. Crystal walked in and the door shut behind her, sealing her away from the outside world.

Well then, Crystal thought, *this can't be too difficult, can it?* She had been quiet for periods before, and all she had to do was to go through the books on the desk and she would be done with this test. It couldn't be that hard.

Crystal moved over to the desk and looked at the books, picking them up and thumbing through a few pages of each. The book titled Origins of Magic didn't look too hard. Neither, for that matter, did A Matter of Color. But Classical Mechanics, on the other hand, looked more like a book Matt might enjoy than she. Flipping its pages, she was dismayed at the level of complexity—and the number of equations. She had no idea how she could absorb it.

She was unsurprised when she opened the wardrobe to see it filled with identical simple white gowns. Accepting her fate, she stripped out of her sturdy travel clothes and put one on. It was itchy, of course. She let loose a quick, voiceless chuckle and thought back to one of her college classes on the history of the educational process in which she had learned how quite a few different teaching systems over the years introduced physical discomfort to train the mind to focus on the academic matter at hand. Pain or discomfort could also, she remembered, be used to condition the mind into recalling lessons when a similar pain or discomfort was applied. It could also, she thought wryly, be used to train a dog not to bark, but she wasn't a dog, nor did she have a barking problem.

So. Crystal knew what Apollo was doing. While that didn't mean she wanted it done to her, Matt had said Apollo's methods were very effective, and Gaia had said that Crystal needed to go through this to find the path to becoming a goddess. She could endure it, she knew, and she was going to do just that.

The door opened suddenly and a pretty young man entered balancing a tray with one hand. With the other hand, he held a finger up to silence her, and she realized that she had been opening her mouth to greet him. *Shame on me*, Crystal thought—not an hour into her training and she had already nearly failed out.

The boy noticed Crystal's chagrin and chuckled softly. "I nearly did the same thing," he said. "My name's Patrick. I'm studying fire now, as you can tell," and sure enough, now that he pointed it out, the connection between his red robe and his task of studying fire made sense.

He set the tray down on the desk beside the books. "The food for newbies is a little rustic, but it'll get better once you've mastered the books. By then, you'll be able to speak again, and you'll join the rest of us in doing the chores. Till then, you won't ever leave this room. One of us will bring you food a couple of times a day. Newbies always get plenty of food in the morning and the afternoon, but none at night, so keep that in mind if you're used to eating several meals a day."

Crystal nodded, and her new friend left. As the door clicked shut behind him, Crystal considered the task ahead of her. Stay in the room, be silent, wear scratchy robes, and memorize three books. Somehow she had expected it to be harder, really. She examined her lunch—sausage, bread, and water. Patrick's description of it as rustic was overly kind, but the food wasn't bad, and would certainly keep her alive for the few days it would take her to absorb her assigned readings.

Idly, Crystal wondered if Stacy had done the same. She had to have become an expert in magic somehow. Had Apollo been her teacher, too? If so, had Apollo used the same methods back then? Crystal cut off a hunk of the sausage and ate it with a piece of bread, imagining herself with her new powers after completing the training.

She needed to focus, though, she realized. Her mind was already going around on useless tangents in the quiet of the moment. She had only one task ahead of her, and though it seemed gargantuan, she should approach it as she had coached her students to take on projects. *How do you eat an elephant?* she remembered asking, and her classes responded in unison, *one bite at a time!*

Crystal shook herself out of her reverie. Memories of her classroom time weren't getting her any closer to switching to colored gowns. She wondered which element Apollo would have her learn first. Matt had taught air because it was the least damaging for the pupils. Would Apollo go straight to fire, instead? Absently she scratched her neck line where the hem of the robe was causing her skin to itch.

Focus.

With an effort, she wrenched her thoughts out of both past and future and looked at the books to be read. She caught herself starting to dwell on the question of whether Apollo had placed a ward on the rooms to cause distraction, and diverted her attention back to the books. Focus, focus, focus. Which book to begin with?

Origins of Magic, she decided, since it seemed the most normal. Her approach would be to read quickly through each in turn, surveying the topics covered in them. She would use the skim-read-skim method she had taught her reading classes. Then, once she had properly surveyed each of the books, she would go back through with further and deeper reading.

She was on it! She would be done and back to Matt and the girls in no time. She smiled, imagining the girls' faces already, glowing with pride at their mother for buckling down and doing it, for dealing with the guy her husband called a nasty little twerp, for becoming a great mage. Speaking of the nasty little twerp, she realized that she would likely have an opportunity to get to know him better over time. There had to be an interest of his that she could relate one of her own interests to, thus building a bridge between them and hopefully getting whatever special training he must reserve for his best students.

Mentally she kicked herself again. She was never going to get there if she couldn't focus now. She spent several moments with eyes closed, repeating the words in her mind over and over till they became a mantra: *Focus, Crystal! Focus! Focus!*

Crystal opened her eyes and gazed down at the book in front of her. She sighed and, with some effort, opened the cover of Origins of Magic to read the table of contents. She forced her brain to adopt the disciplined approach she had taught her reading students. The book's organization looked straightforward: a chapter on the nature of elemental magic followed by a chapter on each of the seven elements—wait, seven? She had thought there were four. The seven elemental chapters were followed by a chapter on the essence of magic. Each chapter except the last was between twenty and thirty pages, the last being about twice that. Fewer than three hundred pages, then, and considering her normal pace for alternatively skimming and reading, she should be done pretty quickly. She set to the reading at hand.

Sometime later she looked up from the last page of the book. There were no time pieces, she realized, with which to gauge her time line. Ah, well—one book down, regardless. Now she could give her brain a break, let it wander a bit before setting back in for the discipline of surveying the second book. The lack of a clock, she realized, would be a significant problem when she set into phase two, the intense study phase. She had always vigorously enforced on her students the need to maintain strenuous study activity for no more than forty-five to fifty minutes, followed by a well-deserved ten or fifteen-minute mental break. It was the way the human brain worked, she had explained, and she could show them the psychological studies that proved it, assuming they ever asked. None ever did, though. It seemed that no matter how hard she tried, the students never really got into the topic enough to absorb it, to ask the questions that needed asking. Such, indeed, was the curse of....

Focus.

Coming back from her memories, she realized that she'd have to find a way to time the study periods.

Rising from the desk chair, she performed the physical exercises she had taught her students while explaining that it was important to keep the body moving while studying. Too often pupils engaged in long study sessions would find their body fatigued, not from movement, but rather from the lack of it. Thus, study breaks not only gave the brain a chance to untwist itself, but they also gave the student a chance to untwist her body. The fatigue, Crystal knew, was....

Focus.

Crystal sighed, tired of having to remind herself of the task at hand. The silence combined with the dichotomy of the directness of the task and the complexity of learning the three books was getting to her.

Feeling invigorated and hopeful from her exercises, Crystal sat back down and turned her mind to the issue of timing. She had to find a way to regulate her study. There weren't any windows to let in the sun's rays to use in tracking its movements. She didn't even know if the sun existed in Apollo's little section of the world, and even if it did, the technique wouldn't work in the evening. She rose again and looked in the wardrobe—nothing useful. She opened the single drawer in the desk, and found candles and matches.

Holding the candles up to see that they were all the same length, she realized she held her solution. Candles usually burned at a standard rate. She set one up in the provided candle stand and held a piece of paper up beside it, creasing the paper in order to track the top of the candle.

One of her normal exercises in the reading class had been to have the students time their reading pace, in order to contrast that with their skimming pace as well as to track the improvement in their reading speed over the course of the term. She had done it herself several times, and as a result she knew that she consistently read standard prose at the speed of about sixty-five paperback-sized pages per hour, a pace that worked out to about two hundred seventy words per minute. None of the books in front of her were standard trade paperback size, of course, so Crystal picked up A Matter of Color and counted the number of lines per page and used a few lines to estimate the number of words per line, and then multiplied—three hundred fifty words per page, give or take a few. The math wasn't easy to do in her head, but it proved a useful exercise in focus to work through it completely. Besides, she didn't have to be exactly exact, she thought—this exercise was just aimed at measuring time using frigging candles. In any event, the speed of two hundred seventy words per minute times fifty minutes was half of two hundred seventy with two zeroes at the end—one thousand three hundred fifty—no, not enough zeroes. Thirteen thousand five hundred, then.

Crystal hadn't been a math major for a reason, but she had learned a few tricks over time in tutoring math to some of her study hall attendees. Thirteen thousand five hundred, the average number of words Crystal could read in one fifty-minute time block, was tough to divide by three hundred fifty, or the number of words per page, in her head, but she could go the other way. Twice three hundred fifty was seven hundred, and twice that was fourteen hundred. Ten times that was really close to what she was after, and she reminded herself that it was all just a stupidly rough approximation for measuring candle length, anyway. So, twice and twice again and then times ten was an overall multiplication by forty. Fourteen thousand was five hundred more than thirteen thousand five hundred, which was about a multiple and a half of the original page length of three hundred fifty words, so she backed her estimate down by a page and a half.

So, forty pages was close. Back it down by a page and a half, and that's closer. Forty minus one and one-half is thirty-eight and one-half.

There. She was done. Math wasn't her favorite or best subject, but by god—she'd have to, someday, investigate how she felt about that phrase, she thought briefly before continuing—she had come up with something useful. By her estimate, she should be able to read just about thirty-eight and a half pages of A Matter of Color in fifty minutes. Now she needed—deserved, even—another break, she thought to herself and chuckled.

"Something funny?" Apollo's smooth voice sounded from behind her. She spun around to see the god standing, fists on his hips, watching her. Remembering the stricture against speaking, she just shook her head.

"Good. I see you've received your food, and you found the correct attire, and you're into the books already. Good girl. Is there anything else your heart desires?"

Yeah, she thought to herself. *A nice steak for dinner, to start with, in addition to the presence of my family. And while we're at it, how about a nice silk blouse instead of this scratchy one?*

As much as she wanted to voice her opinion, though, Crystal just shook her head and worked at maintaining a pleasant smile.

"Ah, good. Well, I won't disturb you for long. Feel free to go low tech with the candles that I see you found, or to use your light globe, whichever. When you are ready to be tested, speak my name out loud—but not till you're ready, right? You won't like the cost of failure."

The god blinked out of her room.

Crystal found herself unsure what to think of the interruption. On one hand, it was nice that Apollo had checked in on her. On the other hand, though, it would have been nicer if he'd knocked first.

Turning her focus back to the task at hand, Crystal counted out the first thirty-eight pages in A Matter of Color and creased a line halfway down the next page. Stopping point marked, she lit the candle she had measured and started reading from the beginning. She knew that if she deviated from her normal reading pace she would throw off the measure, but she had done the paced reading exercise enough that she was confident in her ability to regulate it.

Thirty-eight and a half pages later, Crystal put the book down and blew out the candle. She was going to have trouble, she knew, absorbing the book. It was mostly repetitive nonsense. It seemed like someone had started out to create clever repetitive poetry extolling the greatness of each color in turn, and failed. In his failure, then, the author had turned the bad poetry into worse prose. Crystal had no idea, nearly thirty-nine pages into it, what the book was about, and that realization didn't lend much hope to her ability to learn it.

The book contents would be a problem for later, though. Crystal took the sheet of paper and measured the candle's height again. Once again she creased the paper. Two inches. Ish, anyway. The actual length between the two marks didn't matter; what was important was that she could now go through and mark that distance several times down each candle. She had her timer; all she had to do was to burn from one mark to the next mark, and that would be fifty minutes of reading. Ish, anyway, she found herself repeating. Crystal reminded herself that nothing had to be an exact science and then started marking candles. Each candle turned out to be long enough to last two full cycles, giving her forty study sessions, and Crystal was sure that if it came down to it she could make the remainder of each candle work also. Still, she hoped to be done before then.

Candles marked, Crystal got back to the business of surveying her books. It took her another hour (ish) to survey the book on colors, though she realized after she finished that she still didn't really know what the book was supposed to be about. It was—the term gibberish poetry seemed too nice for whatever it was.

After a short break, she launched into Classical Mechanics, wondering how what seemed to be an intermediate-level knowledge of theoretical physics would possibly improve her ability to wield the flows of elemental magic. It didn't matter. She would likely never have to work a problem using the equations contained in the book, she knew; Apollo had specifically said she only needed to be conversant on it. Crystal had studied science education a little back in college, and so she was already vaguely familiar with Newton's laws, which was where the book started its discourse. Apparently Newton's laws, or Newtonian mechanics, as the book preferred to call them, couldn't adequately be used to write the equations covering many physical situations, and so the purpose of the book she was reading was to build other tools. That much, anyway, Crystal understood immediately, and she was confident that with some effort she could grasp enough to satisfy Apollo's questioning.

Finishing her survey of the third book, she leaned back in her chair to consider the breadth of the test laid out before her. She had to read and understand three very different works: one that was both interesting and quite useful to her goal; one that was totally uninteresting, quite strange, and didn't seem useful at all; and a third that sailed well beyond her ability to grasp in its entirety. Each presented a different challenge, and she idly wondered how many previous apprentices of Apollo over the years had failed because they took the ostensibly easy one of the three less seriously than they should, or because they gave up on the gibberish or the physics.

Crystal yawned, the physical action alerting her to the fact that she was very, very tired. She'd been presented with a great deal of mental exercise. An itchy sensation grabbed at her collarbone, and as she scratched it lightly she realized that she hadn't felt the itchiness of the gown the entire time she had been focused on the books.

Despite her desire to move on quickly, she was having a difficult time keeping her head up and her eyes open. Since she had relaxed for the moment, her exhaustion was now taking over. Cupping her chin in her hand and supporting that arm's elbow on the desk, she fantasized briefly that she could actually hear the bed calling her name. Crystal looked at the wall for a few moments wondering whether Apollo would call her smart or lazy for dozing off, and then realized that she didn't really care. She did some of her best effort late at night, and so it made sense to rest for a while and then get back at it after she was refreshed. She laid down, unwilling to undress due to Apollo's demonstrated lack of consideration for her privacy, and closed her eyes, letting the light globe wink out of existence. She drifted off to sleep nearly immediately.

Crystal came to sometime later, throwing her light globe up and blinking the sleepy feeling out of her eyes. She felt like she had been asleep for a lot longer than she had intended, but without a clock or a window or any other time reference she had no idea. She knew she had to relieve herself, though. The white porcelain privy looked too exposed, but she was happy to find that its flushing was magically enabled.

Moments after she rose, dropped her gown back down, and stepped toward the desk, she heard a quick rap on the door and it opened. Surprised, she turned and barely remembered the prohibition against speaking. A young girl in brown entered carrying a tray. "Breakfast time, luv," the yellow-garbed girl said as she placed the tray down on the desk, turned, and left quickly without meeting Crystal's eyes.

Well, at least Crystal now knew how long she had slept. She was mildly irritated that she had wasted so much time sleeping, but she also realized how tired she must have been to have slept so solidly overnight in an uncomfortable, unfamiliar bed wearing a scratchy gown.

Crystal examined the tray, suddenly feeling very hungry. It held plenty of food, though the fare still qualified as "rustic." She pulled off a hunk of the baguette and chewed it, then pulled a couple chunks of an unknown type of melon from the bowl of fruit. Well. If she continued to get all the fruit, sausage, and bread she could eat, and plenty of water to drink, the experience might not be too bad after all—save the scratchy clothes, the imposition of silence, the separation from her family, and the really difficult task. That, and she was craving a cup of coffee. Otherwise, all was good.

Smiling to herself, she pulled the bowl within arm's reach of her seat and returned to the task of studying. Crystal lit a candle and dove into Classical Mechanics, trying to tackle the toughest one first.

Five candle burns later, the door opened again and another tray was brought in, this time by a boy in a blue robe. He said nothing as he set down the tray, collected the other dishes left from the previous two meals, and then departed. Crystal hadn't noticed how hungry she was becoming till she looked at the sausage and felt her stomach roll excitedly.

Another five candle cycles later, Crystal sat back and thought about the book she had just completed. She wasn't comfortable, and probably never would be, with the mathematics involved, but the book was written clearly enough that she had been able to slowly unwind the story in it. She was pretty certain she could quote Newton's three laws of motion as well as Hooke's law of spring dynamics—those were the initial, easy part. She remembered thinking that Newton's Laws were overly simple for all the grandeur associated with them when they'd been presented in her science teaching classes. A body in motion remains in motion, check. Force on a body of mass m is directly related to the acceleration caused by that force through Newton's equation, F equals m times a, check. Principle of equal and opposite forces, check. Three laws, all pretty simple. And Hooke's Law, that the force a spring uses to push or pull is proportional to how much it's already compressed or expanded, made perfect sense as well.

Crystal had also learned about and felt confident in her ability to converse on the principle of conservation of energy, though the idea that energy wasn't always conserved was new. It had taken her some time to wrap her head around the idea that the "system" being studied was whatever it was determined to be, that the person doing the problem could select the boundaries of the system being studied, and in doing so could draw those boundaries so that no energy was added or removed through them. Once she got it, though, she recognized that this re-drawing of system boundaries allowed the problem-solver to assume that energy was conserved. This then led to the advanced calculations in the Lagrangian and the Hamiltonian formulations that made Crystal's head spin. The working in of initial conditions had been tough to follow at first, but after a few times re-reading the same passage she at least understood the purpose if not the equations.

Crystal thought the spring mechanics were particularly interesting. Most people, she thought, neither knew nor cared what went into describing oscillatory motion, but the periodic nature of it fascinated her once she read about it. If she had more time, she would probably try to work some of the problems, but—she needed to finish the text to get on to others.

Tomorrow, she decided, after finding herself nearly too exhausted to reach over for the book on colors. With one book per day, and a little time the last day to review all three, she should be done soon enough. Letting her light globe wink out once she was safely lying on the bed, Crystal drifted off to a deep sleep once again.

The Test

A dozen candles and a couple of nights, or what she assumed was nights, of sleep later, Crystal woke up confident in her ability to discuss the material in the three books. Through her studies she had seen the connection intertwining the topics, but she didn't feel certain without discussing her theories with someone first. Unfortunately, the only discussion she could have was the test. Still, the combination no longer seemed outrageously silly, and that bolstered her confidence significantly.

Crystal took a few minutes after enjoying the breakfast that, once again, a young person brought right after she had finished with the privy. As she ate, she considered that either her internal clock was taking over and running her schedule perfectly, or the room had some enchantment that warned the kitchen when its occupant was rousing herself from a night's sleep. She suspected the latter, since her internal clock had never been all that perfect before.

Best to be safe, she reasoned, and review all three books briefly before calling in Apollo. She would only get one shot. Apollo himself had said it was impossible, and thus not expected, for her to memorize all three books, but she had no idea where he would pull questions from. She knew, based on her own experiences both giving and taking oral examinations, that the more the test-taker knew in general, the more likely she would be able to at least say something from the books about a topic in the event that she got stumped.

After about an hour and a half of review—she hadn't bothered using the candle timing trick this time—she put the three books down in a pile and stood up. It was time.

"Apollo," she stated aloud, and was answered immediately by the appearance of the god, a bemused expression on his face.

"Already? If you succeed you'll be only one, ever, to do so after a mere four days. Remember what happens if you fail. Are you certain you're ready?"

"I'm ready," Crystal stated simply.

"Fine. Please sit, though. I hold the examination as more of a discussion. No need to make you feel as though you are on stage."

As Crystal pulled the wood chair around from the desk, Apollo summoned a comfortable chair for himself and sat, looking appraisingly over his steepled hands at Crystal. He eyed her silently for several minutes before saying, "Let's start with one of my favorite subjects, shall we? Describe for me a Lagrangian, and tell me its purpose."

Crystal was relieved. Apollo had selected as his lead-off question the topic that had been, and still was, the most difficult for her to grasp, but he asked the question in a way that made it straightforward to answer.

"The Lagrangian of a physical system is defined as the system's kinetic energy minus its potential energy." That much she had understood easily. She remembered from science tutorings that energy had two parts: potential, which described its ability to start moving, and kinetic, which described the fact that it was moving. The two parts were easily transferred one to another, she recalled, as they were in a pendulum that swung back and forth. At the top of its swing it stopped completely, losing all kinetic energy but brimming with the ability to start falling back down, which meant, mathematically, that its potential energy was maximized. At the bottom of its swing it was moving the fastest, which meant it had maximum kinetic energy, but had no way of speeding up any more. Most important, what she remembered was that at every point in its swing, the combination of its potential energy and its kinetic energy was the same, because they fed into each other.

She continued, "Its purpose was to give another method for deriving the equations of motion for a system. Prior to the work of Lagrange, they only had Newton's Laws to describe motion based on forces, and often the many forces in a system are too complicated to be useful in enunciating the system's motion mathematically." She felt proud of herself, in part for working enunciating into the talk, but also for distilling into fairly simple terms the most significant reason, as she understood it, behind the development of the system they were discussing. Newton's laws could make the math really complicated, she remembered from trying her hand at solving a few of the problems.

"Why is the Lagrangian easier, then?"

"In many situations, it is possible to choose the boundaries of the system so that energy within those boundaries is conserved, which means that the total change of energy over time for that system will be zero. That then yields a simple differential equation."

"Simple?"

Crystal shrugged, trying to downplay the fact that she had been caught using the wrong term. "Simpler than the equations that would have resulted from Newtonian force-based mechanics."

"Indeed. Tell me, then, Crystal. Speaking of forces, how many elemental forces are there?"

"That depends on how you define your terms. There are three primary elemental forces, which surprised me at first since I had originally believed there to be four. Earth, though, which I had at first considered a primary, is really just a secondary material flow caught up in a combination of two of the primaries, and the three other secondary forces also result from various combinations of the primaries. These all can be counted as the seven elemental forces."

"And what of ka, then? The essence of magic? Is it not also an elemental force?"

"No. Ka is a force, yes, but it's different from the elemental forces. It's the force that all the others split out of. It's very much like sunlight can be split into the seven colors of the visible spectrum—three primary colors, and four composites, but all seven are separate colors, and all seven when combined create white, or ka."

"And so you mention colors. Tell me, Crystal, the difference between blue and yellow."

Crystal's chest relaxed as she realized that she had been right in her guess to how the three books were related. Subjugating her urge to cheer in order to continue focusing on the success-or-dismal-failure discussion at hand, she quoted as near verbatim from the book on colors as she could.

"Blue is our color for the water true, while yellow is for air so mellow."

Each chapter had been full of what seemed to be gibberish lines of horribly weak attempt at poetic verse regarding a color in the rainbow. When taken in conjunction with the knowledge that the colors in the rainbow corresponded with elemental forces to be wielded, though, the gibberish began to make sense not only as a discussion of the forces but also as a sort of instruction manual for their use.

Apollo nodded. "Tell me what you know of oscillations," he said.

Crystal's excitement grew. Here was a topic she understood, but it also bridged all of the works, and it finally fell into place that she could explain how it did. "An oscillation is when something moves back and forth past a particular position, and each time it passes it is pulled back toward the position it just flew through. Hooke's Law describes one of the simplest examples of oscillation, an object at the end of a spring." Crystal's understanding of the chapter on Hooke's Law had been greatest, in part because of the fairly simple math. Equations describing springs that were written from force laws were devilishly complicated, while those written from energy laws were very simple. "It says that the force the object feels pulling it back to the center is directly related to how far away it is from the center. It's also a case where Lagrangian mechanics are usually far easier to use than Newtonian mechanics. In terms of magical forces, however," Crystal used her pause after the word to emphasize the importance of the shift in topic, "oscillations are the key to creating a magical effect with a degree of permanence. The light globes I've been creating have required a constantly-maintained flow of forces on my part, for example, but I have now figured out how to use oscillations to make one stay until I put it out."

Apollo unsteepled his hands, crossing his arms over his chest as he stared at Crystal with heated intensity for several minutes. Finally he sat forward slightly and said, "That was—impressive. I don't see any way for your husband to have helped you prepare for the test, but I also don't see how you could possibly have done as well as you have without significant help. Please help me understand. You've passed, certainly, and I won't take that away from you, but I must know how you made such short work of the most difficult challenge I could put a novice through."

Crystal thought briefly that Apollo's suggestion that she had cheated should be an insult, but she was too elated to bother. Instead, she smiled broadly and said, "No help. The book on physics was nearly the death of me, to be honest, but it was well-written and luckily took off where my college science education class ended. Meanwhile, I've taught classes on how to most effectively read and absorb information, and that knowledge gave me the foundation I needed to work on the complex puzzle you had set out for me. I came in prepared, but the preparation was from my life experience rather than any secret crib session."

Apollo bowed his head. "That explanation I can accept. Now, you're probably wondering what comes next."

"In truth, I can't help wondering whether I did better than Stacy."

Apollo's face darkened. "The comparison is futile. My methods have changed over the years."

"I see. Well, then, the most immediate thing I'm wondering is when I can get out of this scratchy robe and get some real food, honestly."

Apollo threw back his head and laughed. When the laughter stopped, he said, "As soon as I explain the next part of your training, I'll leave and you can put on your silk clothing again. Call out after, and a thrakkon will escort you to your next room. In the room you'll find robes of seven colors in addition to other texts that are yours to read at your leisure. Put on the robe of your choice—and yes, they're better made than the one you have on now—and tomorrow morning a thrakkon will guide you to that force's training area. Between then and now, the mess hall is available to your desires. You may, of course, speak at will from now on. You will also be expected to do your share of chores and so on, but the senior adepts will instruct you in all that is required."

Apollo rose, and his chair blinked out of the room. "Now," he said, "do you have any further questions?"

Crystal shook her head.

"Fine," Apollo said. "Good luck, and I shall see you tomorrow." He disappeared, leaving Crystal by herself again in the room.

As she quickly stripped out of her robe and promised to burn it at the first opportunity, she also considered her feelings at being able to speak again. After four days of a speech restriction, it felt far more liberating than she would have thought to have the restriction lifted. She had never thought about how important her ability to speak was to her, and now its return nearly made her giddy.

She called out as she finished putting on her silk tunic and pants, and her call was immediately answered by a knock. "Enter," Crystal called, and then giggled softly at how good it felt to be able to say that.

The door was opened by another well-decorated thrakkon who said, "Please, come with me."

Crystal followed the thrakkon down the hall to a large rotunda into which led six hallways, including the one she had come down, on each floor. The ground floor held a sculpted marble courtyard in the center. In the courtyard's benches sat several humans in each of the different colors, most reading quietly but some chatting amiably. Crystal saw others walking, apparently coming and going freely about their desired business. Looking up, she saw that the rotunda terminated two additional floors of hallways above her, and the glass dome on top let a vigorous stream of sunlight in.

"This is the central point in all your normal activities, Lady Crystal," the thrakkon said. "I would be pleased to give you a tour sometime, but for now the master believes that you would be happier to get to your room to relax after your testing. The main dining hall is there," the thrakkon pointed across the courtyard to a set of marble double doors with a golden lyre inscribed on each. "The hall operates all day and night, so stop in there at any time if you are hungry. And now, please let's continue."

The thrakkon led Crystal up two flights of circular stairs to the third floor of the rotunda, and then down one of the passages to its end. "Please, press on the door," he said, pointing to the door on the right. "Adepts' doors open only to their own touch or voice."

Crystal touched the door and jumped slightly as the door slid quickly and soundlessly back into a slot in the wall, revealing her chambers. She and the thrakkon walked in and the door slid shut behind them. "Wow," she said, impressed by the size of her new abode.

"Indeed, Lady Crystal. The master has created an impressive training and housing facility for his adepts."

"Why do you call me Lady?"

"You're the wife of the God of War, Lady."

"I guess. Hey, I hate to sound like a five year old with why, why, why, but—why is everything all white? Is it possible to get some color for the room? Maybe a picture or two?" They had entered a sitting room that was entirely white: walls, floor, furniture, and ceiling. Through a slightly open door, she could see into what must be her bedroom, and what she could see of it boasted no color either. At least in the testing room the wood desk had been wood color, and the simple metal bed frame had been the silver-grey she expected of metal. The total whiteness unsettled her.

"Rooms, Lady Crystal. The master assigned you a suite in honor of your position. You will, I hope, be pleased to find a well-appointed study for your use behind that door there, and your own privy in a door opening from the study. As to colors, your chamber is meant to be an empty palette, ready to be decorated to your own tastes. You have but to touch an item and name its color."

"Hmm, okay. Magenta," Crystal said, touching an end table. She hated the color, but it was the first that came to mind, and the table dutifully obeyed by coloring itself a bright shade of reddish-purple.

"Oh, that's bad. Grey." Again the table changed color, this time to a more soothing light grey. "Grey," Crystal said again, this time thinking of a darker shade, and the table re-colored itself once again. "Amazing," Crystal said, turning back to the thrakkon.

A hint of a smile played on the thrakkon's lips. Bowing, he excused himself to other duties and left. Crystal looked around, mind playing with color schemes. She wanted to see what she could do with the suite, though, so she poked her head through the door and surveyed the bedroom. The bed and its coverings were simple, as was the wardrobe, but at least the privy was somewhere else. Nodding her approval, she walked over and opened the door to the study.

Crystal froze, all thought of color schemes vanishing from her mind as she saw a blue shard of glass waiting for her in the middle of the white desk. "Matthew," she murmured, and rushed to the desk to cradle her communications link. Had it been so long she had actually forgotten about it?

"Took ya long enough," her husband's voice filled the room.

"Didn't want it to seem too easy," Crystal replied, trying to match Matt's playful tone.

"Heh. I bet. Knowing Apollo, he gave you a nearly impossible puzzle to solve, and knowing you, you did it in half the time he thought you might."

"Something like that. He was awfully surprised that I took his test just a few days after he gave me the material."

"I'm sure he was. I'm not. You're the smartest woman I know. Probably the smartest I've ever known, in fact. Was it about magic and its properties, I presume, or something completely out of left field?"

"It was about magic, mostly. Hey, speaking of that, did you know there are really seven elemental flows?"

"Sure," Matt said.

"Well, how come you taught us there were four?"

"The three primaries and one secondary that I teach are the only flows you can really see and touch and wield in a useful sort of way, love. It's kind of like—well, you remember that science education class you took back in college, where I helped tutor you and several other students on Newton's laws?"

"Yes, and the memories of the payment you exacted from me for your tutoring service still make me all warm and tingly."

"Heh. Well, um, yeah. Anyway, do you remember anybody later on complaining about teaching Newton's Laws first, despite them being inexact, when you were learning about relativity?"

"What I remember about relativity is a bunch of education majors smiling and nodding and pretending we understood what was being said, when we were all still stuck on that question about shining a flashlight in a spaceship."

Matt's chuckle sounded through the connection and he said, "Well, that's kind of my point. You start with what people can easily understand, even if it's not the 100% correct model."

"Wait—Newton's Laws weren't 100% correct?"

Matt sighed. "No, relativity gives them a slight twist at higher speeds."

"I guess—okay, that makes sense. Oh, by the way, part of the test involved Newtonian mechanics, so I really am glad we took the time to make sure I understood."

"Newtonian mechanics? How was that part of a test on magical theory?"

"It had to be covered, I guess, to build up to conservation of energy and working with Lagrangian mechanics."

"Lagrangian...? How the hell did you learn partial differential equations in four days?"

"You know, I saw that phrase several times and meant to ask you about it. What are partial differential equations?"

"What? Oh. You didn't—ohhhhhh. You studied oscillations and energy conservation, didn't you? So that's how he does that."

"Does what? Oh, never mind. It's probably too complicated to be explained across this link, isn't it? Anyway, I don't want to talk about magic and tests any more, Matt. I'm just very pleased to be done with the first test, because it means I get to talk to you."

"Same here, love. Hey, the girls heard me talking, so they are here and want to say hi."

"Hi, Mom!" Crystal heard.

"Hi, Heidi!" Crystal said. It was funny to her how many people claimed to not be able to tell the twins apart across a voice link. To her, they sounded completely different. "Is your sister there?"

"Hi Mom!" Crystal heard Linda yell. "Heidi insisted she had to talk to you first."

"No, I didn't!"

Matt's growl broke up the coming fight before it began in earnest.

"Sorry, Mom. We've missed you a bunch!" Heidi said, and her sister voiced agreement.

"I can tell," Crystal said with a touch more sarcasm than she actually felt. "So what have you two been up to?"

Crystal spent the next several minutes listening to the girls' exploits. They didn't admit to having gotten into any real trouble, she was happy to note, but then again she'd only been gone for a few days. Most of the stories they told were pretty mundane, and all of them included two teenage boys. Crystal, completely unsurprised, listened intently as her daughters rattled off their schedules and made sure to ooh and ahh at the right breaks in their delivery.

"Mom, when are you coming home?" Linda asked at the end of the teenage recitation.

"I don't know, dear," Crystal said. "I passed the first test and am now called an adept, but I still have so much left to learn. Tomorrow I get to select a magical flow to begin my intensive study."

"What are you gonna pick?" Heidi asked.

"There are seven really good choices, but I've always been curious, even when we dabbled in Wicca, about healing magic. I'll probably choose that."

"Oh, cool, Mom!" Heidi said. "Will you teach us any of it when you get home?"

Crystal chuckled. "Probably, dear. How else will I get healed if I need it if you two don't know the magic? It's not like your father knows how to heal. All he knows is that war stuff."

"Hey!" Crystal heard Matt protest, and blew him a noisy raspberry across the link in return.

Matt laughed out loud, and then said, "Well, love, the girls need to go down to dinner, and you probably do as well." Crystal realized she was very hungry, and said so. "Well, now that you have the glass piece back," Matt continued, "you and I can speak anytime you want or need to. Go eat and enjoy your lessons. As much as I hate to admit it, you really are in the best place anywhere to master the arcane."

"Okay," Crystal said. "Goodbye for now, and if we don't speak later on, good night."

"Goodbye, love," Matt said, and the girls echoed his words. Crystal saw something change about the flow of the essence of magic about the glass piece, and was pretty certain it meant the connection was severed. Would Apollo even be willing to teach her about the essence of magic, she wondered?

Musing on the question, Crystal walked back into the bedroom and opened the wardrobe. In it were several robes of each of the colors of the rainbow: red, orange, yellow, green, blue, indigo, and violet. There was no white, she saw. That disappointed her.

She was hungry, she reminded herself. She slipped out of her silk clothes again and into a purple robe. This time, the cloth fell smoothly against her skin and actually draped her comfortably. Crystal imagined that the raw spot on her collarbone where she had scratched at the irritation of the testing robe was thanking her for her choices, and giggled at the mental image that generated.

A knock sounded at her door. She opened it to see Patrick's grinning face and skinny body still clad in a crimson robe. Patrick looked down at her color choice. "Healing, I see?"

Crystal nodded and smiled. There was something charming about this boy, despite the fact that he couldn't be much older than Steve and Corey were. "I've always been drawn to healing arts," she said.

"Well, that's good, but I'm dying to find out how you passed Master Apollo's test so quickly. I've also been assigned to orient you to the dining hall and work charts. May I have the pleasure of your company this evening?"

"You do realize I'm twice your age, yes?"

"Oh, ma'am, I hope I didn't offend you. I've heard—well, I've heard that your husband is a pretty powerful man. I didn't mean to flirt too much."

Crystal smiled, chuckled pleasantly, and winked at the youth. "It's okay, kiddo. We women need flirting with as much as the girls do, and I won't tell my husband about it if you don't, all right?" Having set the tone, Crystal reached out and placed his arm in hers. "Am I still young at heart enough for an adept of your stature to escort to dinner?"

"Of course," Patrick said, and took off with Crystal. He proved an excellent host for the evening, explaining the unstated rules against talking in the courtyard ("to foster quiet study and contemplation," he said) and showing her how to read the work schedule in order to know when it was her turn to help with the cooking crew, the cleaning crew, or the serving crew for a meal. "Everyone takes a turn," he explained, and that seemed similar enough to Matt's requirement. Granted, Matt had excluded those studying magic from the chores, but everyone here in Apollo's estate was studying magic, as Patrick confirmed when she asked.

Crystal heartily enjoyed her first true meal in several days, downing a full plate of roast beef and vegetables. The berry pie and ice cream were a divine finish to a truly challenging day, she thought pleasantly as she sat and enjoyed the sensation of fullness in her belly combined with imagined replays of her taste buds' celebrations.

"It's getting into evening, and therefore study time," Patrick said, interrupting her reverie. "I should escort you back to your room so you can get some study as well as some sleep in for your first lessons tomorrow."

"I think that would be good, Patrick," Crystal said, realizing that she had been so intent on getting to the dining hall earlier that she hadn't learned what she wanted to.

The boy nodded and took off across the hall toward the main doors, and Crystal stayed by his side. Once they were out of the noisy hall, she asked, "So how long do adepts usually spend studying each area of magic?"

Patrick shrugged. "Dunno. As long as we need to, I suppose. A year, maybe two, or perhaps a decade. Some adepts master specific magic flows in just a matter of months, I hear, but I'm not one of those. I enjoy the learning process along the way, and so it doesn't matter to me, really, if I never move from red to purple."

"Oh," Crystal said, feeling horrified by Patrick's timeline yet refusing to show it. It couldn't take her years, or decades even, to master each flow. She had days—a week, at most—to do that. "Your patience is commendable," she said.

"Thank you, Crystal," Patrick said, and stopped walking. They had reached the door to Crystal's suites. She looked at the youth, who clearly was uncertain what to do next and very uncomfortable in his uncertainty. Inwardly she grinned. She was so tired, though, and this was the first human being who had shown her any warmth here, so she decided against any further abuse of the poor boy. It made her happy that he found her attractive, though. She grabbed Patrick's hands, and the poor boy jumped at her touch.

"Patrick, it's been a lovely evening. Thank you for showing me around. I'm afraid my old age has me exhausted, though, so I need to go talk to my husband and then get some sleep. I will, though, tell Apollo what a wonderful guide you have been." Crystal gave him a chaste kiss on the cheek and, without waiting, walked into her room and closed the door.

Crystal realized when she walked in that her suite was still shockingly white; she had been about to color it earlier when she was swept up in the reunion with her husband. She was in a mood for purple, she decided, so she set out changing the walls and furniture to various shades of the color. Acting on a hunch, she touched a wall she had just turned a peaceful lilac and said "Clock." She smiled; the large wrought-iron wall clock that appeared was exactly what she had envisioned.

Crystal went around putting color, artwork, and clocks on every wall in her suite. When she was done, she stepped back into the sitting room and examined her work. She had to admit that she really liked what she saw. Her chambers were beautiful, and she was pleased to have done it all herself. The clocks on every wall seemed a little overboard, but something about having the time available to her whenever she wished to look up comforted her.

The efforts of the day finally caught up, and Crystal allowed her shoulders to sag in her exhaustion. She picked up the blue glass shard and carried it to the bedroom. In the wardrobe she found a selection of her nightgowns; apparently Apollo and Matt had arranged for their transport while she was at dinner. She pulled off her purple dress and let a pastel nightgown flow down her body, sighing at the sensation of silk sliding over her skin.

Just last night, she thought, she had slept in a hard bed clad in a scratchy white sack of a dress, but tonight she would sleep comfortably and well.

Climbing into bed, Crystal cradled the blue glass to her bosom and called her husband. Matt's voice answered immediately, and the two spent several minutes relating the details of the dinner. Matt laughed as Crystal told the story of Patrick's infatuation. He told her that the girls were safely ensconced in their own beds for the night, and then the couple lapsed off into pleasant chatter that relaxed Crystal completely. She closed her eyes as Matt talked, imagining him laying there beside her, and she drifted off to sleep in mid-sentence. Matt severed the link with a light, soft chuckle.

Colorful Lessons

The next morning the alarm clock that Crystal had called into existence on her nightstand chirped a pleasant tune. Crystal rolled over and mashed the buttons on its top, finally finding the one that led to silence.

"Somebody tell me again why I thought an alarm clock would be a good idea," she said aloud, not expecting an answer.

She rose in the dark room and walked to the wall across from the foot of the bed. *Well, if artwork can be created here, I wonder... she* thought to herself, and then touched the wall and said "window." "Yes!" Crystal exclaimed as a view over a rolling, green hillside sprang into being.

"Oh, yeah. Curtains," she said, and black curtains sprang into existence. She pulled them closed, not certain if the landscape was an actual place or merely the product of her imagination, but not wanting to run the risk anyway. She washed and then changed back into her purple dress.

A rap at the door called her attention. When she opened it, she was surprised to see Apollo himself, who in turn grinned at her expression.

"And who were you expecting this fine morning?" he asked.

"I—I didn't figure you would come for me yourself," she said.

"It's really no trouble, child. You see, I can do this little thing called teleporting."

"A simple California girl like me wouldn't know such things existed without smart men around to guide me," she responded in kind.

Apollo snorted. "I'm not your husband, child. You really should try to toss in an honorific occasionally. You know, something like Master, or Sir, or Oh Greatest God in the Universe—something simple like those will do. Not that I need it, of course, but, well, there are appearances to maintain."

He was right, on a certain level. There was nothing to be gained from generating jealousy among her peers. "Yes, Master," she said, her smile still intact. "So do I get the pleasure of learning from you directly today, Sir?"

"I promised to teach you, and teach you I shall." Apollo turned to walk down the hall, and then stopped and looked back at her. "Purple is an interesting choice, you know. It's one of my favorites, certainly, but it's ironic that the wife of the god of war would choose the healing arts to begin with."

Crystal followed Apollo down the hall, around the rotunda, and then down another hallway that was white as it broke away from the rotunda and shifted hues slowly, gradually becoming vibrant purple as they walked its length toward a pair of golden doors that were embossed with the same lyre she had seen on the mess hall doors. As they walked, Apollo discussed her upcoming training. "Healing is challenging to teach, in part because to prove its effectiveness you must have injury to heal. Your husband just lops a human's finger, or entire arm, off, I'm sure, and if the poor students fail the test then the subject dies. We're not that barbaric here. You will find my most important rule here is that there shall be no practicing without the presence of one of the senior adepts who are skilled at healing and hand-selected by me. Got it?"

"Yes, Sir," she said, choosing not to respond to Apollo's insulting jab at her husband. There was nothing good to be gained from stepping into the middle of an eons-old enmity between gods, she knew, and she was also beginning to wonder whether the enmity was entirely sincere.

"So," Apollo continued, "For your first day, of course, I will be your safety net—not that you will need one at this point. But the child over there with the gold sash over her robe is Hillary, the senior adept on duty now. In all colors of training, look for the adept in the gold sash if you need immediate help."

Through the next several hours, Crystal found the training both exhausting and fairly straightforward. The book on colors had described violet magic well, and she found that knowing what to look for when bending the flows to your will was the hard part. Matt had been correct in a way, she knew after a few hours of practicing. The flows of air, fire, and water had been exactly that—flows that could be pulled, gathered, directed, and pushed. Healing, though, was more of a latent energy inherent in living things. Instead of wrapping her mind around elemental energy as she had when casting fireballs, healing involved reaching into the body, into the cells themselves, and tweaking the native energy into forging its own repairs. Crystal felt like she was showing a natural affinity to the magic, and Apollo's praise seemed to affirm that.

"Lunch is almost over. You should probably go eat to sustain your energy," Apollo said, surprising her. She still thought it was just mid-morning.

Crystal shrugged. "I'm more interested in learning than eating right now, Master." The honorific had come more naturally to her in the magical training area.

Apollo shook his head. "You must never skip a meal when you have one available, Adept. Food fuels your brain, which is in turn what fuels your magic. A hungry mage makes mistakes. Go."

Crystal nodded and left wordlessly, feet finding their own way to the mess hall as her brain absorbed itself in reviewing the lessons of the morning. She sat by herself and ate quickly, not bothering to taste the food she was devouring.

"You'd be Crystal, right?" a voice interrupted her feeding frenzy. She looked up at the adept standing in front of her table.

An orange robe marked her as a student of prophecy, and the gold sash marked her as a senior adept.

"I am, yes," Crystal replied, unsure how best to respond.

"I'm Maureen, loov. I'm in charge of the mess hall schedulin' this month. I wanted to mek sure you knew to check the list, as I've added ya in to the shift work for next week."

"Thank you. I will, and I'll make sure to be there when I'm scheduled." Crystal had heard Maureen's harsh British accent before but was having a hard time placing it.

"That's good. I've heard ye're a bit of a VIP, but an adept's an adept, as far as I'm concerned."

Crystal smiled and nodded vigorously. "Of course. I'm pleased to jump in." Recognition of the accent dawned, and she asked, "Are you from Liverpool, if I may ask?"

Maureen smiled. "Aye, loov. Ya been there?"

"Once, on a vacation. It's interesting that many of the adepts I've met have had either mild or more pronounced British or Irish accents, but yours is different."

Maureen laughed. "Indeed. I was visiting Dublin when the cataclysm hit, and the professor brought me with the rest of his students here. Who could've known that the man I'd gone to interview on his knowledge of occult practice was the great Apollo himself?"

"Nobody, I guess. Thank you, Maureen."

Maureen nodded and walked out of the mess hall. Crystal finished her meal quickly and headed back to the purple magic training area. So Apollo holed himself up in Ireland, eh? An interesting, though not necessarily useful, bit of information.

Crystal worked through the remainder of the day, breaking only when Apollo insisted on her need to eat dinner, and then returning to practice by herself before heading to bed. Her conversation with Matt and the girls through the glass shard was quick, but she tried to make it clear that she was working really hard, exhausting herself, in order to finish her training sooner to return to them. Matt understood; the girls not so much but they were still positive. They soon signed out, leaving Matt and Crystal to speak warm words of love until Crystal dozed off again.

The next day was a repeat of the previous, except that Apollo felt strongly enough about her progress to have her work on actual injuries. They teleported cases in from the health clinic where possible, but some adepts had to volunteer to have injuries inflicted on them in order for their fellows to heal them. Apollo was merciful in a way Crystal couldn't imagine Matt being, using his own powers to anesthetize the injuries while they were imposed. Crystal realized while participating that the sashed adept's job was to perform the anesthetization and to inflict the injury during Apollo's absence, which was a burden she couldn't imagine bearing.

That evening, exhausted, she looked at Apollo and breathed in deeply. Crystal had healed over a dozen different maladies that day by her count, and despite her pride in that accomplishment felt that something was missing. "Master, how does energy oscillation play into what we are doing?"

Apollo looked her in the eye for several seconds, and then shook his head. "You know the answer to that, Crystal. Why do you ask me?"

"I was hoping for some specific directions," Crystal said.

"I can't give you specific directions. Every body is unique."

"Yet every case involves setting up a harmonic oscillation that will keep the magical energy going, right?"

"Of course. Very, very few mages ever master the art, since it takes a delicate touch, but somehow I suspect you'll do just fine."

"So what length do I set the harmonic oscillation to?"

Apollo grimaced. "You're asking stupid questions, child."

The master's reproach stung Crystal. He was right, though. Her newfound knowledge of spring dynamics lent itself directly to the question, but the book on colors had held a more direct reply hidden within its silliness.

Nodding, Crystal replied, "Yes, Master. I guess I am. I think I am ready to change colors tomorrow morning."

A harrumph from Apollo confirmed her theory. "I certainly hope so," the god stated, then vanished.

That night, Crystal's relation of the day's activities was even more succinct than the previous evening's talk had been. She virtually kissed the girls good night, and then she enjoyed a few minutes of adult conversation with her husband before begging off for sleep. Matt sounded bemused, and she asked him about it.

"You know that Apollo and I have never gotten along," Matt replied. "Yet he seems to be teasing more magical knowledge out of you in a couple of days than I could have in an entire lifetime. He's no better a teacher than I, but you're rising to a tough occasion, and I'm proud of you for it."

"Thank you, Matt," Crystal replied, too tired to go into a discussion of teaching styles versus teaching ability and how Apollo's style was resonating with what she needed. "Thank you, and good night."

Over the next several days, Crystal chose to work on the elements she had already thought she'd mastered according to Matt's teachings. Apollo's approach was, of course, very different, but she adapted to his framework quickly. Early on, she quit asking Apollo the questions that frequently popped up in her mind based on what she had done before, as his response was always to sneer and refer to Matt as any one of several derogatory terms that included barbarian, imbecile, and worse.

Crystal could understand the dichotomy between the two styles, but that didn't keep her from wishing that Matt had taught the theories that she knew, from their conversations across the blue glass, that he was familiar with. Matt's approach to fire, for example, was useful if you wanted to light something on fire or throw a fireball. Apollo's approach covered those needs but also opened the mage up to many other options, including such useful activities as regulating the temperature in a room.

Setting up the required oscillations for self-maintaining elemental energies proved tricky. Each element seemed a little different, but all required an extremely delicate touch. The directly-touchable flows she found the easiest, because the greatest challenge with them was mostly in setting up the right length of flow. Once the correct length was established, the harmonic vibration could be kicked off with a gentle flick at one end. Depending on how close she got to the right length, the oscillations lasted for minutes or hours, and she squealed in excitement when she was certain she had nailed the correct length of a flow of air, thus creating an oscillation that could possibly have gone on forever had she not stopped it an hour later.

Healing energy oscillations were more challenging, since there wasn't a flow to measure. The colors book had suggested creating a zone of energy; the zone surrounding the energy was actually more important—and difficult—as she had to remove all the energy there. Once she managed that task, though, the oscillation fell into place with just a nudge. Apollo had been correct, she thought, when he had said she was a natural healer. Granted, Crystal disagreed with the rest of his assertion, that she as a natural healer shouldn't be married to a natural thug, but she was content in taking the silver lining out of the cloudy comment.

Apollo smiled broadly when she opened the door the next morning wearing a green robe. "Ah, emotions today. This is a fun one," he said.

As they walked down the green hallway, Crystal asked, "Master, is it more properly called emotions, or feelings? The book on colors wasn't very clear, switching between the two terms as it did."

"Interesting question, but before I answer, tell me this. What is the difference, to you, between the two terms?"

"I remember learning in one of my education classes back in college that feelings were things that humans can't change—things like hunger, pain, et cetera. Emotions are our reaction to feelings, though, and can be changed. It was one of those how to deal with misbehaving students topics, but the theory has stuck with me."

"Right. So you're choosing to define feelings as what some of this last cycle's psychologists called primordial or homeostatic emotions. Emotion, on the other hand, refers to the complex, or what some call classical or secondary, emotion. Am I correct?"

"Yes, Sir. I just didn't realize there were so many possible terms for it."

"Well, given that framework, I guess what we are about to work on is more correctly called the magic of feelings. As an adept, you can manipulate the primordial emotions, like pain and lust, that a person feels, but the higher level emotions such as anger and love aren't yours or mine to command. To do so would violate the free choice policy."

"What free choice policy?"

"The gods make it a point—a policy to us, which in turn creates a law of nature to humans—to allow humans to make their own choices about life, for the most part. I mean, you have no choice in your experiences. Take, for example, the cataclysm that the planet went through recently. Nobody had a choice in whether or not to go through it. It caused many people hunger, pain, and other primary emotions. What humans did in reaction to those feelings, though, was left entirely to them. Some got angry, some became depressed, and some shaped their emotional being into a determination to survive. We can affect the primary emotions, but not the secondary, on purpose, because if we specified people's reactions to their environment, what would be the point? You'd all be robots, not humans."

They reached the lyre-inscribed door leading to the green training room as Apollo finished speaking. Crystal opened the door before objecting, "But, Sir, if all we can do is affect the primary emotions, what good is it? Emotional pain is strong, but so is physical pain."

Apollo turned to face Crystal and smiled warmly, one corner of his lip turned upward oddly. She flashed back to the time in the sorcerer's chamber when Matt had borne the same expression toward his trainees just before he had thrown a fireball at them, but now she had nowhere to duck to.

Longing. Crystal's heart hurt—suddenly Apollo was the most beautiful man she had ever seen. She wanted him—no, she *needed* him. Every ounce of her body cried for her to reach out to him, grab him, hold him, become one with him. She loved Matt, she forced herself to consider, but even that dimmed against her overwhelming desire for Apollo. Matt was—not here. Apollo was, and every inch of his body glowed his radiant and quite edible sexuality.

There. Crystal found the spot in her head where Apollo was managing the energies, and flicked the fingers of her mind's power to disperse them.

Once again, Crystal found herself looking at the god through her normal eyes, but now she was looking up to him. Somehow in her longing she had dropped to her knees, hands gripped tightly in front of her. Tears wet her cheeks. None of that mattered, though, compared to the shocked expression on Apollo's face.

"That was impressive, Crystal. I've never met a human who could have so quickly disarmed my attack. How did you know where to find it?"

"Well, the book helped," Crystal said, "but I also recall being attacked emotionally by Stacy, though I had no idea what it was at the time. I'm susceptible to an attack once, I guess, but don't try to fool me twice."

"Well, this set of lessons will be short, then," Apollo said, his expression clouding briefly at the mention of Stacy's name. "I think we need to start with making sure you are aware of how many primal emotions there are. Most people have felt them all but have no idea, cognitively, what they are. You've already felt lust, so let me run through the other ones, a bit more gently now because I believe you've learned your lesson." Apollo sneered briefly, and then said, "There are twenty-four feelings remaining, and I shall name them as I apply them to you so that you know what they are as you watch me tweak them."

Apollo went through the twenty-four at a fairly steady pace, holding each as Crystal felt the sensation and at the same time located its epicenter in the brain's energy, naming it aloud so she had a label to associate with the feeling and the location/energy combination. "Attraction. Longing. Amusement. Zeal. Pleasure. Pride. Hope. Rapture. Relief. Shock. Agitation. Frustration. Ferocity. Revulsion. Envy. Torment. Agony. Depression. Disappointment. Regret. Loneliness. Pity. Terror. Anxiety."

Crystal sat weakly on the closest bench once Apollo was finished. "That was rough," she said.

"You wanted to learn. There's only one way to do so, child."

Crystal set her jaw and stood back up. "Unfortunately, I need to see them all again, but in smaller chunks. Could I trouble you for that, Master?"

Apollo crossed his arms across his chest. "You're resilient, too. Ares normally chooses buxom blondes as his spouses. I'm actually impressed with his choice this time."

Crystal decided to challenge Apollo while he was apparently impressed. "He told me he doesn't normally choose a spouse, actually."

Apollo shrugged. "When he chooses a spouse, it's usually a buxom blonde. Better?"

Crystal nodded, accepting the minor victory she had won. "Yes, Master."

"Well, there are six categories, as you know if you read the book, so tell me when you're ready to repeat the first."

"Ready," Crystal said, and held on mentally to feel the love category: attraction, lust, and longing. She watched each with the detached sense of observation she had grown used to while working in academics. Quickly she noticed that each of the primal emotions in that category touched the same part of the brain and wondered if all categories operated similarly. "Ready," she repeated, and she observed, categorized, and labeled each emotion as it was presented to her.

Once Crystal had suffered each emotion a second time, she started feeling around inside herself for the same spots she had watched Apollo attack. It wasn't easy.

Apollo observed Crystal's efforts for several minutes. Satisfied with her progress, he brought over an adept in a gold sash and introduced her to Crystal. "You will wish to practice on each other," he said, and then left.

Crystal and the adept, Maryse, practiced all day, alternating triggering the emotional hot spots on each other. Maryse, several times, commented on her disbelief that Crystal was new to the color. Crystal had been practicing for less than a day and was already better than Maryse, who had put every moment of study since the cataclysm into green magic.

That night, over dinner, Patrick sat at her table again. It had become a habit for him to sit with her and talk through the meal, but Crystal was relieved that he seemed to have lost his infatuation with her. She wickedly considered using some of her lessons from green flows on him and mentally chided herself for doing so.

The next morning she pulled on an orange robe to meet with Apollo. As they walked to the training room, he explained the challenges orange held. "Prophecy magic is a tough one to learn, child. If you tweak the flow of the element of fire, for example, it always gets hot. Prophecy isn't a flow, though, for one thing—it's an ethereal energy that the prophet must gather around her. Sometimes the energy isn't there. Sometimes it is there, but the prophet receives nothing from it of importance beyond the suggestion that she will have to poop later on."

"And sometimes it's wrong, Master?" Crystal interjected.

"No, child. Prophecy is always right. When it seems to be wrong, that means that the prophet misinterpreted. It's easy to do, really. The resultant prophecy will show up in your mind as fleeting images, sounds, and smells. Sometimes the best you can hope for is a guessing game."

"Unless the prophet is a god?"

"Even if the prophet is a god. Sometimes especially if the prophet is a god, because we tend to value our own opinions so highly that we never question them. The ability to truly see into the future would be extremely dangerous for any of us to own, and so none of us do. Thus we are limited to prophecy magic, which is significantly, and sometimes humorously, limited. Are you ready to try?"

Apollo opened the orange lyre-decorated door as Crystal nodded. There were only a couple of adepts in this room, far fewer than there had been in any other chamber. "Not a popular magic to practice, is it, Master?" she said.

Apollo shrugged. "It's a hard magic to work with, as I said. Who wants to put so much effort into bending prophecy energy into a vision that you may or may not understand when you can work at tossing a pretty fireball, yes? Now, watch."

Crystal turned and watched as Apollo concentrated. She couldn't see what he was doing with his mind, but she could see the energies sparkling in front of him as he nimbly massaged them, finding and folding the sparse prophecy energy into a glob.

Finally, Apollo stopped gathering energy. He stood, staring into the gathered cloud for several seconds, and then nodded and let the energy disperse. "Hmmph," was all he said.

"Am I going to poop later on today, then, Master?" Crystal teased.

"Probably. We—and by we, I mean me and the rest of the gods—are going to be summoned to Olympus in the relatively near future, though I didn't see why."

"Are you summoned often?"

"Not very. Once, maybe twice a cycle. It's only done for a significant crisis or matter of concern."

"That scares me a little."

"It shouldn't. The meeting may also be for something as simple as the discussion of a policy. I didn't see why we were summoned, only that we were all gathered in the chamber. See the difficulty with prophecy?"

"Yes, Sir, I do. My turn, now?"

Crystal set her mind to gathering the same energy that she had watched Apollo mold. Soon she had her own glowing mass of prophecy energy in front of her, and then she stopped and stared into it.

Her worry that she might fail at the magic and see nothing dissipated immediately as she was greeted by a startling image. Crystal was looking directly at Aphrodite, who in turn was glaring at Crystal and standing in what could only be an arena, wielding two swords as she had in her battle with Matt. Crystal stiffened as she saw her arm in front of her also bearing a sword. Unlike the typical sword, though, Crystal's was notably dull—the grey of pewter rather than the shine of polished steel. Aphrodite sprang at her, and Crystal gasped and let go of the cloud.

"I guess you saw something dramatic," Apollo said drily.

Crystal realized she had been holding her breath, and struggled to regulate her breathing back to normal before answering. "Uh huh. Aphrodite and I were fighting in some sort of arena."

Apollo's eyebrows shot up in surprise, and an expression of amusement lit his face. "A fight? How exciting that must have been."

"I don't—I don't want to fight her, though," Crystal panted, still having trouble normalizing her breathing. "I just wish she would leave us alone."

"Ah. Well, your human sentiments aside, let's discuss this prophecy. It's good that you got a solid one to talk about your first time. Most adepts only see a tree blowing in the wind, or ripples in an ocean, for the first several days. Hence the relative desertion of this room. But yours is interesting, a fact that is entirely unsurprising to me, of course. So tell me. How do you know it was Aphrodite you were fighting?"

"I saw her."

"You recognized her? You're sure?"

"I saw her face, and I've seen enough of it that it was easy to recognize."

"OK, then we have solid recognition. How do you know the other combatant was you?"

"I was looking out my own eyes."

"You can recognize your own eyes from the inside? How remarkable," Apollo said with a sarcastic lift in his voice.

"Well, I wouldn't be..." Crystal started to protest, but realized that she already knew the answer from the book. In a prophecy, you never knew whose eyes you were looking through. "Oh, I get it. I saw the fighter's arm, though, and it looked like mine."

"Which arm? Does it have any identifiable features?"

"This arm, and—well, no."

"So how do you know it was your arm?"

"It felt like my arm."

Apollo sighed and said, "Oh, Crystal, I know you're smarter than that."

"Master, I know what you're saying, and I will question the identity of whoever's eyes I look through in any future prophecy. But this one, I feel very strongly, was me. It's only intuition, granted, and so I know it's fallible, but I know to my core that I'm right."

"Okay," Apollo shrugged. "Remember what I said about why gods often get prophecies wrong? It's yours to take however you wish, of course, but unless you suddenly got smarter than the gods, I highly recommend you be careful in your assumptions, intuitions, and assertions."

"Point taken, Master."

Apollo nodded curtly. "What other questions do you have regarding prophecy magic, child?"

"What happens to the prophecy energy if we apply harmonic oscillations?"

"Don't do that. Don't even consider it," Apollo said in a quick, clipped voice. He continued more gently, "Prophecy energy comes vaguely and wisplike from the underlying timeframe. To hold it in place and cause it to resonate would destroy time if we allowed it. I know that sounds cliché, but in this case it's a real threat."

"Has anyone ever tried it?"

"Yes. A few cycles ago a human mage decided he was going to try to create a real crystal ball. He succeeded until several of us gods realized what he was doing and destroyed it for him."

"How did you know he was messing with it?"

"If by 'it' you mean large amounts of magical energy, each of us gods, and some powerful human mages as well, can sense large movements of energy. One of us—usually the closest—will always go investigate. In this case, it was large enough that it alarmed several of us, so Ares, Hermes, Hera, Athena, Artemis, and I, as well as quite a few of the lesser deities, popped into existence in his chamber at the same time. He wasn't hard to convince at that point to abandon his efforts."

"I guess not. Another question, Master. Are the prophecies only applicable to the adept who is seeing them?"

"Absolutely not. Only the adept can gather the energy, but any poor fool can peer into it and see visions. One would hope the adept would be better than the fool at interpreting the visions, but visions have been given to regular men before, though usually by a god who manages to stay out of sight."

"Oh. So—um, was the Book of Revelation the writings of a poor fool, or an adept?"

"Child, the Book of Revelation to which you refer was written after the end of the last magic cycle. There were no adepts at that time. Plenty of poor fools, of course, but that's irrelevant to your question."

"So who wrote it, if there were no adepts and poor fools were irrelevant?"

"You'll have to ask Yahweh for an answer to that."

"He's gone, though, isn't he?"

"For now, yes he is, it would seem. It appears that your line of questioning has reached a terminus."

"Oh. Well, thank you anyway, Master," Crystal said. She felt a little disappointed.

"Now, child, your practice today must of necessity be quite solitary. The adept in the gold sash is really only there to keep you from hurting yourself, since prophecy is an individual activity. Your task for the day involves practicing gathering the energy and interpreting it, but there is no rubric I can provide for your use. Enjoy your day, then, and I shall see you tomorrow morning."

With that, Apollo vanished and left Crystal to her own efforts. Dutifully, she molded another cloud of prophecy energy, and saw herself in the restroom. This time the viewing angle was outside the eyes, so she was clear that it was her, in the restroom, relieving herself. She sighed.

Crystal tried again and was greeted by an image of waves lapping against the shore. Another time, and she saw Sorscha smiling at her and nodding. Crystal tried, and tried, and tried, each time hoping that the vision she called would explain further the prophecy regarding Aphrodite, but nothing related came.

Her hunger overpowering her, she growled in frustration as the hours flipped into evening. Finally she gave up and headed down to dinner. Patrick had apparently already come and gone, but Maureen stood over her with a stern expression.

"You were absent for yer shift, Crystal."

"Sorry, Maureen. I lost track of time in my training area."

"That's no excuse. You need to let the gold sash in yer area know you have a shift to do in the kitchen."

"Sorry. I will tomorrow, I promise."

"See that ye do, Crystal."

With a loud harrumph, the matron of the kitchen stormed away, and Crystal meekly finished her dinner.

Back in her room, she used her blue shard again to contact her husband and daughters for the night. She cherished the utility held within the bit of glass, but Crystal was beginning to long for actual hugs from her girls as they prepared for bed for the night, and even more for the touch of her husband as they slid into bed together. Matt had always been good about touching Crystal every night, regardless of whether the physical contact that meant so much to her led to actual lovemaking. Now that his status as a god had been revealed she had changed her expectations in some areas, but in intimacy Matt had always seemed a god, and Crystal missed it greatly.

When the conversations were over, Crystal drifted off to sleep.

The next morning, Crystal considered her options. She had already been through all of the seven colors. To repeat one at this point seemed boring and a waste of time. She had done well with the four flows she had learned from Matt, but she had mastered the finesse involved in each of them while in Apollo's magical chambers. She had learned and practiced the other three till she was sick of casting spells in those categories. She really didn't think anything was to be gained by further practice in any of the specific colors.

She found a white nightgown. It was a little too revealing, but she fixed that with some minor flows. Defiantly wearing white, she stepped out into the hallway when Apollo knocked the next morning.

"White isn't an option, child," Apollo said, looking down his nose at her in distaste.

"It has to be, Master," Crystal said. "If I am to defeat Aphrodite, I must learn to wield ka."

Apollo shook his head and held up his hand. Crystal saw and felt, at the same time, the force of air push her back into her sitting room, and Apollo followed in and closed the door with the same column of elemental air.

"First of all, child," Apollo said, "Your prophecy indicating that someone would fight Aphrodite is just that. Someone will have to face her, at some point in the future. It could be anybody with an arm that you thought you saw clearly. You should be hoping that it is not you, as she is quite gifted not only in magic but also in the physical martial arts. Second, child, I won't teach you to wield the essence of magic."

"Why," Apollo asked as Crystal's expression changed, "are you smiling?"

"My husband said he couldn't teach me to wield the essence of magic. You say you won't. That's an improvement," Crystal said.

Apollo shrugged. "Can't. Won't. Not much of a difference between them."

"There's a lot of difference, actually. The book on colors made it clear how to proceed; I just wanted your confirmation that it was worth proceeding on. Thanks to you, Master, I'm pretty certain I know where to direct my efforts."

Apollo nodded. "I see," he said. "Well, you have truly been an exemplary pupil. It's no wonder that Matthew latched onto you. Do you have any final questions I can answer?"

Crystal's mind went into alarm mode. She still had so much to learn, so many questions to ask! She wasn't ready to leave, so she decided to ask questions as they came to her anyway.

"What are the differences and similarities between me and Stacy?"

"Other than basic attitude? Not much. You're both very talented in the arcane."

"What is it about a human that makes some of us so talented in the arcane when others aren't?"

"If I knew that, I wouldn't have to have a test to ascend to the title of adept. With every cataclysm, I take several that I think will make great adepts who do not, and I take others who end up being powerful magi. I've given up on predicting. Did you ever watch the Summer Olympics before the cataclysm?"

"Yes, Master, I did."

"Drop the Master, please. You are quite beyond that now. Anyway, in the Summer Olympics just past, someone ran a mile in just under three and three-quarter minutes, and won the gold medal and set a world record as a result. Do you think his coach knew from the moment of meeting that the runner would someday win the Olympics?"

"Of course not. It takes long hours of determination to win."

"So if you were to put in the same number of hours of determination, would you run the same speed?"

"No."

"Why not?"

"I'm not built like a runner."

"Precisely. Your tremendous skill with magic is in part based on a natural ability that you have in great quantity. Some humans are born with it, and of course most are not. But you also have a background in learning how the mind works, which helps, and you have been willing to suffer through many days of training to bring your background as well as your innate abilities to bear. In addition, you were wise enough to seek out the greatest teacher available."

Crystal started to grin at Apollo's self-aggrandizement, but quickly shifted her expression back to neutral when she realized that he actually seemed to believe it.

Apollo broke the uncomfortable silence. "Well, Crystal, I think your training here has reached its natural conclusion."

Crystal nodded, swept away in her emotion. She had made immense leaps in her knowledge and abilities, and she had, she felt, beaten incredible odds in succeeding. She had become accustomed, though, to the steady hand of Apollo teaching her, and she knew that further lessons would be on her own. She missed Matt and her children so much that her heart throbbed when she thought of them, but seeing them meant an end to a fantastic tutelage. As much as she wanted to find out what was the next step on her path, she feared to leave the one with which she had become comfortable.

"Am I ready?"

Apollo sighed. "As ready as I can help you become. Fare thee well, Crystal."

The world flickered again, and she found herself on the gold circle in Matt's throne room, clutched tightly to her husband's body. "I missed you so much, my love," Matt breathed in her ear.

"Am I really back? Is this really you?" Crystal asked, needing confirmation.

"Yes, and I know the perfect way to celebrate your return," he said with a lusty smile.

"It's only mid-morning, though," she said, smiling and relaxing against him.

"So?" With that dismissal, Matt carried Crystal down the circular stairs leading to their suite, laid her carefully down in the bed, and made love to her as she had been dreaming he would for days.

To Touch Ka

They finally rose at dinnertime. As they dressed, Crystal said, "I had an interesting prophecy when I studied that magic."

"Many people do," Matt said in a dismissive tone.

"I was fighting Aphrodite in an arena of some sort."

"Oh, that does sound interesting," Matt said in a voice that didn't match his words. "What point of view did you have?"

"I was looking at Aphrodite through my own eyes."

"How do you know it was your eyes?"

"That's the same thing Apollo asked."

"If both I and the twit ask it, it must be a good question, right?"

Crystal sighed and crossed her arms over the tunic she had just slipped over her head. "I know it was me. I just—know it."

"Yeah, that's the problem with prophecy. Just when you know something beyond a shadow of a doubt, you're proven to have misinterpreted. How do you know it wasn't a battle Stacy had before she ascended?"

"Doesn't prophecy only work for the future?"

"Unfortunately, no. The timeline goes both directions, and energy can flow along it both directions too. I think it flows more often back to the prophet, but that would be a good question to ask the twit."

"You two are like the worst kind of brothers."

"How do you know we're not brothers?" Matt leered at her.

"Your mother would've killed you early on, that's how." Crystal stuck her tongue out at him.

"Heh. Fine. But back to prophecy magic, there's a reason I'd rather shake a magic eight ball than use the energy. At least when an eight ball is vague, it's obviously vague."

"Alright, I concede. And I'm hungry."

"Let's go down to dinner, then," Matt said, and then he winked and threw open the door from the bedroom. When the couple stepped out into the sitting room, Crystal's eyes took in the beauty of its décor. She had missed it greatly, she realized. She had gone from the drabness of the testing room to the wonkiness of her purple chambers. She had been proud enough of her chambers as Apollo's adept that she had described them in detail to Matt, because she had formed them out of her own creative mind. It was like being back in the college dorms again, if dorms came in suites. Matt's chambers—the chambers of Ares, as Apollo had called him—had an air of imposing grandeur about them, though. He was the sovereign ruler here, and she was his First Lady.

Her thoughts were interrupted by two squeals as teenage girls buried her in a three-way hug. "Mom! When did you get home?" Heidi asked.

"A little bit ago. I've told your dad about some of my stay, but I saved the best stories for you two. Let's go eat dinner and I'll tell you all about it."

The family was joined at the high table in a chance meeting by RJ and Krista, Phoenix, and Birch and his wife. "Slow day in training?" Crystal asked.

"We decided we should all enjoy a dinner together," Birch said. "We were going to just sit at one of the round tables when we saw you walk in, and wanted to have a chance to chat with you also. We spend so many wordless hours tossing magical energies around that, well, we figured a social time would be good."

"Where've you been?" Phoenix asked as bluntly as she always did. "We haven't seen you on the practice field for weeks, Crystal."

"I've been away doing stuff," Crystal said, not sure how to proceed.

"The god you knew as Apollo is an old friend of mine," Matt interjected. "Crystal went to his estate to learn a little different approach to some of the elemental flows. She finished and came back just today."

Crystal reflected on Matt's cover story. Apparently gods were under no pressure to tell the truth. Old friend?

Birch, the mythology expert, came to the same conclusion for a different reason. "Old friend? Ares and Apollo were said to have hated each other."

Matt looked down the table, smiled, and shrugged. "Hatred is a bit strong. There's always been a healthy rivalry between us, to be sure."

Crystal nodded, glad that the fears she had of jealousy from the group had been diverted. "I can tell you now from being there. Ares and Apollo are like two brothers bickering. You know they love each other underneath all the gruff stuff, right, hon?" Crystal turned to Matt and pinched his cheek for emphasis.

"Well, love might be a bit strong too. Let's just say that we mostly get along fairly well in public, okay?"

Crystal chortled. "Mostly. Right."

Phoenix proved, once again, her incapacity for jovial chatter, jutting into the conversation with, "So what was Apollo's estate like, Crystal?"

Matt squelched the reply that he had started to make as Crystal answered, "It's white. Very, very white. And there isn't much outside. Matt's estate pretty much requires you to go outside to do anything but go from your room to the dining hall. Apollo's, on the other hand, I never saw the outside of. The walls are white, the sculptures are white, and columns are white, and all of his adepts are white from lack of sun."

Krista snorted. "You'd expect a god to have a better interior decorator, wouldn't you?"

Matt smiled and said, "We tend to be our own interior decorators, since contractors can't handle the pressure. Apollo's world is truly white, as Crystal says, so his estate reflects that."

"So, enough about my trip. Tell me what you have been learning!" Crystal said excitedly, hoping to finally divert the conversation away from her trip. It worked, as all three senior battle magi jumped to tell her all about their latest efforts. The tales took them through the main course, and Crystal was overjoyed to see Sorscha take over serving her and her family. The thrakkon had been absent so far that day, and the absence bothered Crystal.

"Sorscha!" Crystal turned and looked at the thrakkon. "I've missed you. Where have you been all day, dear?"

Sorscha smiled back at Crystal and said, "Taking care of your bags, Mistress Crystal." She bowed and took their dirty plates away.

She called me Mistress, she said to Matt.

Matt kept his chat with RJ about the laying of stone along a path as he replied to Crystal, *Yes, she did. So?*

She's never called me Mistress before, Crystal objected.

You came back from Apollo's nearly as strong, magically, as a goddess. It's proper for her to switch honorifics accordingly.

Wow, Crystal said, and then realized that Birch was asking her a question about something he had learned about fire magic. She replied with as non-committal an answer as she could and continued the conversation through the evening, mind only half engaged on the talk at hand, and the other half considering the implication of her rise in status.

Dinner over, the family bid farewell to the other diners and headed back to the room. As they entered, Heidi rounded on

Crystal, accusing, "You didn't tell us a single story about your trip."

Crystal took both her daughters by the arm and led them to the couch. "No, I didn't. I'm sorry, girls. I didn't expect the other mages to join us, and when they did I didn't want to make them jealous. But we're here now, so what can I tell you about?"

Both girls had questions, and they started peppering her with them at the same time. Holding her hands up, Crystal laughed and said, "Okay, okay. How about if I just tell you what all happened?"

Crystal told the stories she knew how to make humorous. The rest, she figured, were probably not worth telling. She went over the test she had taken, and the move, and she made both girls and Matt laugh over her exploits teasing poor Patrick. She told of the various colors and what they represented, and the lessons she had learned. Nearly done, she realized that both girls were yawning.

"Tired?" she asked, a twinkle in her eyes.

"No, Mom," Linda said, but she was stopped in the second word with a yawn.

Crystal laughed. "Go to bed, girls. We'll all still be here tomorrow."

They did, and Matt picked Crystal up off the couch and carried her into the bedroom. He laid her down gently on the bed and went around. As her eyes followed him, she noticed the blue glass shard on the pillow between them. "How'd that get there?" she asked.

"The twit transported your stuff back, along with a snide comment about your love for purple, while we were away at dinner, and Sorscha unpacked your stuff," Matt said.

"Well, that was nice of 'the twit,'" Crystal said, poking gentle fun at Matt's tone.

Chortling, Matt reached out and touched the side of her face. He ran his hand down her neck, around the curve of her breast, and then farther down. His lips connected with hers as his touch once again inflamed her body in passion. Many long minutes of lovemaking later, Crystal murmured good night wishes to her husband as she drifted peacefully off to sleep.

The next morning Crystal's peaceful sleep was interrupted by a bright flash of light. Gathering a flow of elemental fire for use as a weapon, Crystal sprang up into a seated position, searching for the source of danger. It turned out to be Sorscha, who was chortling in the peculiar thrakkoni huffing manner and walking toward Crystal from the curtains that she had just thrown open.

"Good morning, Mistress," Sorscha greeted Crystal brightly.

"Can we go back to Crystal, please?"

"If you prefer, Crystal. Your achievement was significant, though, and I honor you for that."

"Thank you. Tell me, since nobody else will. Did I return faster or slower than Stacy?"

"Stacy didn't return, Crystal."

"What do you mean she didn't return? She obviously mastered Apollo's lessons."

Sorscha stared at Crystal for several seconds, an astonished look on the thrakkon's face. Finally she drew in a long breath and said, "You didn't know, did you? Stacy left the master to live with Apollo."

"What!?" Crystal sat up straighter in bed, eyes widening in shock. "I didn't—Oh, my god, I never realized. So that's why Matt and Apollo are so acerbic toward each other."

"Well, yes, Misst—Crystal. I'm sorry, I somehow thought you knew. Stacy left here to become a pupil of Apollo, and ended up becoming his girlfriend. The master and Apollo didn't speak to each other for thousands of years after, even though Aphrodite reportedly turned around and left Apollo once she was done learning from him."

Crystal shook off the last of her shock and rose. Sorscha had laid out some clothes for her already, just one of the little services Crystal had come to miss in her absence. Crystal dressed in silence, still absorbing the news. Finally she understood Matt's reluctance to send her down her path of learning to wield the elemental powers. Finally she understood the acid relationship between Matt and Apollo. Finally—she understood.

"Matt is up in his chamber, already at his governance duties?" Crystal asked, breaking the silence.

Sorscha nodded her reply. "Yes, he's been at it for a while. Will you join him?"

"No, I won't disturb him. I think I'm going to go practice some magic while he finishes. Please let him know I'm in the war room when he's done."

Sorscha nodded and left the bedroom up the spiral staircase. Crystal left through the sitting room. She checked briefly on her daughters, who were still sleeping soundly in their beds as they had nearly every morning since the cataclysm. Crystal wondered briefly about what they were to do in the fall for continuing the girls' education, but she assumed that between Matt, herself, and an assembly of physicists and librarians now at the estate, they could figure something out when the time came. In the meantime, though, it was summer, and she saw nothing wrong in letting the girls enjoy a summer break.

Lost in her thought, she bumped into Natalia as both turned the corner into the downward-sloping hall into the downstairs magic practice areas. Crystal forced herself to smile and chat amicably, hiding her annoyance at the timing. She had hoped to go right into the hidden war chamber to practice, but none of the other battle magi could know about the room or its hidden entrance yet by Matt's orders, which meant that Crystal would need to make up some reason for going into the sorcerer's chamber with Natalia first.

Crystal entered the sorcerer's chamber and realized it was her first visit in weeks. The room wasn't attractive, but it had been the site of her first introduction to the arcane. Crystal smiled around the room and greeted the eleven practicing magi. Two had moved up to making flame, and excitedly called for Crystal to come watch. The others were still working at moving the rocks in columns of air above their hands. Crystal thought briefly that the magic-users who came to the estate initially had progressed much faster than this crew, but then she realized that there were far fewer of the first group who had stuck it through the initial failures. If more of them had stuck with it, the two groups would be about the same.

Crystal made a show of watching the tricks done by everyone who asked; she knew how it felt to be able, for the first time in your life, to do something even as simple as lifting a rock with magic, and so the students' eagerness found her sympathetic despite her own zeal to get started. Finally she worked her way over to the desk, reached into the drawer, and pulled out a rock. Without explanation, she held the rock in her palm, stared at it, flipped it over with magic, set up a column of air with resonance to keep the rock floating for hours, and walked directly out of the room.

Crystal closed the door to the sorcerer's chamber, checked quickly to make sure no one else was in the hall, and opened the secret door to the war room. She ducked into the passage and closed the door behind her, waiting till it sealed shut to let out the chuckle she had been holding. She chortled more as she walked down the hall, wondering what the newbies were deciphering out of her cryptic moves.

Once inside the war room, she dropped all pretense of humor. She had sensed ka, the essence of magic, many times before.

Thanks to the book on colors and its chapter on white, she felt like she knew how to get at it. Granted, the book had been somewhat cryptic, but she thought she knew what it had meant. If she was correct, of course, it was exactly opposite of the other magical efforts. To work most magic, the mage focused, concentrating on gathering energy or directing the flows depending on the color. The book implied, however, that to reach the essence of magic, the mage had to un-focus.

It sounded to Crystal somewhat like some old puzzles she had worked, optical challenges from her youth that presented the viewer a series of geometric shapes without any real pattern. However, by relaxing and un-focusing the eyes in a certain way, a picture could be resolved by the viewer. She still wondered how those pictures had been made, but she had been able to figure it out and "see" what was actually there as the pattern emerged from the shapes. Now, she hoped to do the same with magic.

Crystal stood and breathed deeply in the quiet of the war room. She swung her hands and arms around several times, shaking them, making sure that when she did relax them they would be truly relaxed. She relaxed her body, letting her arms hang limp, letting her shoulders rest naturally, and tried to shift her gaze to be looking at nothing.

She saw—nothing. Not only was she purposely not seeing any physical objects in the room, but she also wasn't seeing any of the energy or elemental flows. Growling, she shook herself and opened her mind to the energy as she had in the past. Suddenly the energy around her came into full view as it usually did when she was trying to mold it to her bidding. Crystal peered into the surrounding flows, trying but failing to see the pure essence.

She stood like that for many minutes, alternatively tensing her body and mind and then relaxing them fully and deliberately. When Crystal relaxed too much, the energy always disappeared to her, and she had to yank her concentration back to bring it back into view. She got frustrated.

On what must have been nearly the hundredth cycle of tensing and relaxing, suddenly the elemental energies surrounding her coalesced into pure white. Her heart raced in excitement, the blood in her ears nearly making her miss Matt's whispered, "Hello, love," from behind her. She did hear it, though, and started to spin around to express her frustration over his interference with her practice.

She found she couldn't turn, though; Matt had blocked her head in place. His voice came in a whisper from right behind her, "No. Don't move. You're almost there, love. Relax and let me show you again."

Crystal relaxed and obeyed and felt his strong hands grip her upper arms gently, smelling his aroma as his body folded itself behind hers. The energies dissipated once again, and Crystal groaned at the loss of the lovely white essence.

"Shhhh," Matt said softly. "Relax your eyes and your body. Reach out with your mind to the elements, like you were."

She did as he said. This time she found her earlier frustrations gone; it was much easier to relax when she was doing so into Matt's loving arms. She saw elemental forces sparkling in the air around her.

"Good," Matt's whisper continued. "Don't focus on the elements. Imagine them in their colors, and don't name them by type. Just let them be, and let them be according to color. Do you see the rainbow in front of you yet?"

Crystal let the energies flow freely for a little more, finally getting to where she could see all the colors. She nodded a silent assent.

"Now, pretend like they're the most delicate modeling clay in the world, and gently caress them together all at once. You can't do two or three at a time; you have to grab all of the colors at once and gently smush them."

Crystal imagined the colors all coming together and gently tried to make it happen. It didn't work; the energies just fell out of her vision. She groaned again, her frustration returning.

"That was close. Try it again," Matt whispered.

Crystal tried again, failed again, and groaned again.

"Relax," Matt urged her, still whispering. "Again."

Crystal sighed deeply. She hated failing, but this didn't make sense. The book had made it seem like it was just a matter of relaxing and mixing, but it was proving slippery. She couldn't get the energies to mix at all.

Matt read her frustration. He cooed in her ear, "My dear, you can do this. You were close both the last two times. Relax, and, believe it or not, don't try so hard."

Crystal breathed in a deep and slow breath, calming her nerves as she did so. Matt was right. She could do this. She thought back to how many times she had attempted to see the pattern in the optical puzzles. She had spent hours, as she recalled, and then suddenly she had seen it when she had least expected to, and she'd laughed at herself for all the failures before.

It was all in the relaxing, she knew.

Relax, she told herself. Crystal settled into a comfortable pose, still supporting herself but allowing Matt's presence behind her to lend balance and stability. She let her eyes un-focus around her, reaching out instead with her mind to "see" without seeing all seven of the colors of the elements. She had won the optical puzzle fight when she had stopped trying to see the image, and so she stopped thinking about bringing the colors together. Instead, she just—did it.

The colors blended together into a white stream of radiant energy, and Crystal gasped at her own success. Jubilantly, she toyed with the flow, folding it, bending it, stretching it. She formed a ball with it and sent it around the room. Finally she let it dissipate and turned to Matt, her face glowing in the joy of her success.

"Matt, I did it!" she squealed.

Matt's smile lit his whole face up. She had missed this pure expression of happiness that he had occasionally worn before the cataclysm. Crystal held Matt's hands and danced around him.

After several spins, she started getting dizzy and stopped her dance. Matt's smile remained, but he said, "Now, do it again before you forget how."

Crystal turned, relaxed, saw the colors, and put them together again. This time she paid more attention to her sensations and was amazed over the ferocity of the force that swirled through her being. The essence was indeed powerful; it felt as though she might even be able to control life itself.

She savored the power for several more minutes, and then let it dissipate. For good measure, she grabbed it once more, finding that this time it was even easier.

"Each time it will feel more natural, love. Be careful, though, that you do not wield it carelessly. With the essence you actually could destroy the entire estate, despite my wards."

Crystal nodded, suddenly and inexplicably tired. "Why hasn't anybody done it, then?" She yawned.

"Partly because it's not what gods do. Remember, gods don't fight each other directly. Partly because of what you're feeling now, also. The white force is really the magic of creation, of life itself."

Crystal nodded, remembering the gibberish about that in the book on color. "'The beginning of life, the beginning of strife, the end of life, the end of strife' the book said. That makes more sense now."

"Um, okay. Not sure where the verse came from, but it's largely correct. And when you use it, it actually takes a little of your life force to do so. Call it the cost of the magic, if you will. For a god, it's just a little tiring, but it's nearly put you into a coma. Can I help get you back to bed to rest it off?"

Crystal nodded and admitted that she did feel very tired. Matt held her up as he walked out of the war chamber, and then teleported back to their bedroom. She sat on the edge of the bed and let him undress her, and then collapsed into the bed as he pulled the sheet over her. Crystal heard Sorscha's voice ask, "Did she do it?" as her eyes closed, and Matt's happily positive murmur was the last she heard before she dozed off into a deep sleep.

The Next Step

Crystal jumped awake, gasping at the sensation. She had been in a sleep that deep only a few times in her life. Lighting a globe over her hand, she looked around at the room she was in, confirming that she was still safely tucked into her bedroom. As her eyes ran the circuit of the room, the door opened and Sorscha entered.

"Good morning, sleepyhead," Sorscha joked. She threw open the curtains, causing Crystal to yelp at the jolt of energy the light brought her.

"Morning?" Crystal asked, surprised. It had been morning when she'd gone to bed, near as she could tell. "How long—how long was I asleep?" Crystal asked, not certain she wanted the answer, but fearing that it would be measured in days. That was, at least, how she felt.

"Not long, really. It was just after noon yesterday when you were brought back to bed, and it's now early morning. So— eighteen hours, maybe?"

"Not long? I can't remember the last time I slept that long," Crystal said. She spent several minutes as Sorscha poured a bath for her and laid out her clothes thinking back, trying to recall taking such a long sleep and failing. "Sorscha, you were there when Matt and Hermes sundered the world in their fight. How often did they rely on the essence of magic to do so?"

"I don't know, Crystal. Please remember that I'm immune to magic flows, which means I can't see them either. I wouldn't know elemental fire from magic essence if I had to. It's not what I'm here for, anyway."

The door flew open and Matt walked in, a tray in his hands. He set it over her lap gently and then kissed her hand, and then her lips. "Good morning, my love. I brought you breakfast in bed this morning."

Fruit and a vegetable omelet were her favorite breakfast foods, and Matt had brought lots. She smiled up at him. "Thank you, Matt," she said, popping a small strawberry into her mouth. "What's the occasion?" she asked after chewing and swallowing the very sweet fruit.

"Nothing major," Matt said, a playful grin on his face. "You did, however, successfully manipulate ka yesterday. That's cause for celebration in anyone's book, I'd say."

"Mmm," Crystal moaned in pleasure as she bit into a sweet bite of pineapple, and then nodded. "Yes, that was amazing. But I'm so hungry now, and I can't believe how long I slept. Is it really worth it?"

"It is, on rare occasions," Matt answered. "As you grow in power, you'll find it affects you a bit less, but it will always be powerful work needing some powerful fuel."

Crystal nodded, and inhaled several bites of the omelet. Washing it down with the cup of coffee Matt had also provided on the tray, she asked, "So is today a good day to go get the next step from Gaia?"

"Already?" Matt said, his face clouding over. "I'd hoped we would have some time together first."

Crystal stopped her ravenous pillage of the plate and reached up to caress Matt's face. "We can," she said. "We shall. I just thought it best to get through and done with the lessons I have to learn, and then we can luxuriously take the rest of our long lives together."

"I expect that Mother will be surprised to see you back, successful, so quickly. That's probably a good thing. I worry, though, that you may be trying to take the learning too fast."

"Learning can't be taken too fast, remember?" Crystal said, recalling the lessons she had attended on the adult learning process. The pace of an adult's learning cycle truly was irrelevant, so long as the minute disciplines of learning were adhered to. For example, it really was possible for an adult to learn a foreign language in just a few days, providing lessons were provided over a few long days' time but in short bursts. That process was why immersion language instruction worked so well, she knew. It had also served her well in passing Apollo's tests.

"I do," Matt said. He should; Crystal recalled a paper on the topic that she had written, and received a great score on, that he had helped proofread for her. Besides, he knew well how stubborn she could be.

"Okay, fine. We'll go see Gaia today."

Crystal thought that she should be overjoyed, but instead she was both terrified and weary. She had passed the first test, but it had been hard. What would the second test require? Would Gaia, instead of being impressed by her rapid completion of Apollo's training, decide to raise the bar even higher?

She shared her concern with Matt and was waved off. "No, Gaia isn't vindictive, my love. She is the perfect example of the good kind of teacher. She'll test you, to be certain, but she'll celebrate with you at your success."

Crystal looked at the now-empty plate, amazed that she had eaten all that Matt had brought. "Thank you for the food, dear," she said, self-consciously wiping her mouth with a napkin.

Matt grinned wickedly. "No problem. Anytime you want to eat half a cow instead, let Sorscha know."

Crystal smiled passively, eyes down on her tray. Suddenly she balled her napkin up and threw it at his face. If it had connected, she would've been surprised, but it got the duck and chuckle she was looking for, and she stuck her tongue out at Matt for good measure.

Still chuckling, Matt said, "Okay, Love, I'll leave you and Sorscha to get you all gussied up, and then I can teleport you back to Gaia for your next mission."

Crystal's dressing was interrupted after Matt left by her girls running in and leaping on the bed. "Mom," Heidi said, "we were worried about you. Dad said you were just really tired, but you slept so long. Are you okay?"

"I am," Crystal assured her daughters. "I really was just overly tired after practicing magic too much yesterday, and I really appreciate how you both let me sleep in till today."

"Can we go horseback riding with you today, then, Mom?" Heidi asked. The question caught Crystal unprepared— horseback riding? It took her aback. She loved horseback riding, especially with her daughters, and let her mind wonder for the moment whether the quest to become a goddess was worth missing out on the moments she cherished.

"Not today, dear," Crystal said, deciding quickly. She had to keep going down the path. "I'm sorry, but I have to go see Gaia again today. I'll have time after I return, though."

"Okay, Mom," Heidi said, and smiled the expression Crystal had come to know meant that it wasn't really okay. Crystal wondered if this was what Matt had referred to with his too fast comment. Was she about to miss out on a crucial part of the twins' growing up? She didn't know what was next, though, and she had to assume that it would be like the last challenge, with her being given some time to travel to it.

"I'll be back this afternoon, probably. Can we ride horses then?"

Both girls' faces brightened. "Sure, Mom," both said.

Crystal wondered if she had just made a promise she wouldn't be able to keep as she shooed the girls out and finished dressing. Sorscha had chosen well, once again; it was a flattering green silk tunic over linen pants.

Matt returned when Crystal called. "Beautiful, my love," he said in appreciation of her outfit and hair, and kissed her. "Let's go see Gaia."

A few minutes later Crystal found herself again standing in the perfect woodlands glade, surrounded by its variety of trees, plants, and animals. Matt had come with her and now stood by her side.

"Either you're a very fast study or a failure who's too stupid to be embarrassed," the earth mother said. "I sense that the former is the truth. Excellent job, child."

Crystal beamed from the compliment. "Thank you, Mother," she said. "I've come to seek your guidance in what I should do next."

"Besides learning to think for yourself?"

The words stung, yet they rang true. Crystal realized, too late, that she had automatically sought Gaia's help as though this were a step-by-step project for which only the goddess held the directions. She had taken the easy out instead of spending time pondering it herself.

Gaia allowed Crystal's internal chastising to go on only for a few seconds before interrupting in a soft voice. "Perhaps I can assist you in that. You've learned to wield the flows of magic quite impressively, or you would not be standing here now. What else might a goddess need to know?"

Crystal thought back to the prophecy she had seen. She doggedly refused to believe that the unseen combatant had been anybody but herself. "It seems too simple of an answer, Mother, but—how to fight? I mean, there are a lot of things I'm sure a goddess would need to know, but I'm already versed on topics such as governance. It seems my most glaring lack of knowledge is in the martial arts."

"The art of governance is something a goddess might wish to know, but there's really no need for it, child. A goddess can make a thrakkon who can deal with the administrative duties, and as far as leadership—well, you only need the humans who follow you to be happy with you if it is your desire. But the martial arts? Yes, I'd say that is a large gap in your abilities, indeed. Funny, isn't it, that the term martial in your language comes from one of your husband's names?"

"He's not going to be able to teach me, though, is he? He loves me too much to be hard enough on me."

"What say you, Matthew?" Crystal turned to her husband, curious how he would answer Gaia's question.

"I can teach anybody anything related to fighting," Matt said directly to Crystal. "Yes, I love you, but I can be as hard on you as you need to learn something you need to learn. That said, Thor might be better suited to teaching you."

Crystal thought back to the time she had met Thor, the giant wrapped in skin and scale armor in the bar that was called Olympus. He had seemed jovial enough, and didn't have a dislike for Matt. She shrugged. "Okay, so my next stop is with Thor. That makes sense."

"No, it doesn't," Gaia objected. The earth mother walked over to Crystal, eyeing her from head to toe. Crystal was confused; she had thought they had found the right answer.

Gaia reached out and felt Crystal's upper arm once she was within reach. Crystal kept herself from shying away despite that being her first reaction. She forced herself to breathe normally. The earth mother continued, running her hand up and down the arm, and then held the arm up and shook it a couple of times.

Gaia turned to Matt. "Your princess is better suited to tea and cookies with me than to a turn in Valhalla, Matthew. You know that. Look at her. She would break within minutes."

Crystal turned a questioning look toward Matt, who responded by nodding. "She's right. Thor can be a little rough on his students."

Crystal smiled, refusing to be beaten. "Well, then, can't you teach me a workout regimen that will get me in shape to handle Thor's teaching?"

Gaia snorted. "Oh, I can see that now, child. I'm sure that Matthew would humor you. He'd build you a little track with a dumbbell station every so often, and you'll go out there once a day in your workout tights and colored headband, work out for half an hour, and then have your tea and cookies. The only question would be who, really, is the dumbbell."

Flushing slightly over the ridicule, Crystal asked both deities at once, "OK, so if a track with dumbbells isn't the way, how does one prepare for training at Valhalla?"

Gaia smiled and moved in front of her, looking Crystal in the face as the goddess spoke. "Well, you're weak and lazy, and I'd dismiss you now if you hadn't bested Apollo's tests as quickly as you did. You're smart. And, clearly, you're persistent as well. Fine. Go to Hephaestus and be his servant for a while. Service in the smithy of the gods cannot fail to forge some strength in you as well." Gaia turned, pronouncement clearly over, and walked back toward the central tree.

"Ready, love." There was no question in Matt's voice, merely a warning, as the couple teleported back to the estate's throne room.

Matt gave Crystal a few seconds to put her tummy back where it belonged after the teleport. It would take several more trips to see Gaia, Crystal thought as she stood there, for her to become accustomed to it, and she really hoped she didn't have that opportunity. The earth mother had seemed such a pleasant goddess during the flight in the cataclysm, but Crystal could see that she had a hard side as well.

As Matt led her back down the spiral stairs, Crystal asked, "Matt, who is Hephaestus? I vaguely remember his name—I think it was from reading the Odyssey. But I don't remember much of anything about him."

"Hephaestus, or Vulcan, as the Romans knew him, never was the flashy one. He is an incredible smith, but he's not really ever wanted to be the god of anything. He makes some really cool things, though. He made Hermes's hat, and he's also responsible for most of the magical armor that was worn by humans in the last magical cycle."

"What does he do in the technology cycles?"

"I—um, I don't know. I've never really been curious enough to go looking for him. I suspect he continues work in his forge. You'll have to ask him."

On a hunch, Crystal asked, "Was he born a god or raised?"

"He was raised, which probably is why he's so intent on being a master craftsman. I suspect that in his human life he was a well-known smith of some sort."

"Oh. So I can ask him about the path he took to becoming a god."

"You can."

"You don't sound like that's a good idea."

"Oh, it's not a bad idea. You're just quite unlikely to get a response from him. He's not known for opening up to—well, to anybody, really."

"Has he ever been married?"

"Now how would I know?" Matt suddenly got agitated. Irritation seeped through his words as he opened the door leading from the bedroom to the sitting area and said, "I need to go check on the mages. I'll see you in a little while, okay?"

"Wait!" Crystal called, and Matt stopped and closed the door in front of him but didn't turn back around. "What did I say, Matt?"

Matt turned, a rueful smile on his face. He shrugged and said, "I suppose I shouldn't get upset over it any more. It was a long time ago."

Realization dawned for Crystal. "He was with Stacy, too, wasn't he?"

"Yeah. Homer even wrote that he was married to her. Funny thing is that according to Greek legend, she cheated on Hephaestus with me."

"So the Greeks had it exactly backward."

"Well, sort of, except that by that point Stacy and I were done and so there wasn't anything to define as cheating. Can we talk about something else?"

"Oh, of course. Sorry, I was just curious. But now that you mention it, I do remember some of the old mythology. Wasn't Hephaestus crippled, or something like that?"

"Crippled is exactly what the legends say. That, or lame. He is as crippled as Tyr was one-handed, of course. He does love building stuff, though, and often when he appears he's riding one of his contraptions. One of his favorites is an insect-like mount with six legs for stability, in the body of which he sits and is carried along. People see gods showing up in horse-drawn chariots, and then one god sitting in his contraption, and they make assumptions. Hephaestus is just contrarian enough, then, to play on those assumptions."

"This is going to be an interesting trip, isn't it?" Crystal asked.

"Definitely. He'll be happy to put you to work, I'm sure."

"Is there anything else I need to know about him first?"

"He's grumpy, he's a brilliant smith, and he's grumpy. Not sure if there are any other facts that are relevant."

"Thanks, dear," Crystal said, a smirk on her face. "Does he have a normal name, or has he always gone by Hephaestus?"

"To the Greeks, Hephaestus was a normal name."

"You know what I mean," she said.

"You should call him whatever he introduces himself to you as. Like I said, he's grumpy. His human name once upon a long time ago, if I recall, was much harder to say than Hephaestus."

"Gotcha," Crystal said and smiled.

Matt winked. "So, wanna stick around tonight and leave tomorrow with as much fanfare as you had last time, or just get going now?"

Crystal was still feeling full from breakfast and well-rested from her long sleep yesterday. She weighed her options briefly and then said, "I'll go today. There's really no point holding off till tomorrow when today is as good as any. I would like to spend some time with the girls, though, first."

"Of course. You did promise to go horseback riding with them," Matt said as he opened the door to the sitting room.

The family went out to the stables together, Matt saddling his warhorse Phobos while the thrakkoni keepers brought Crystal and the girls their favorite horses. Crystal looked longingly into Lady's eyes. Her mare was magnificent.

"New saddle?" she asked the thrakkon holding Lady's lead. It had been several days since she had ridden Lady, so she wasn't certain, but she recalled the old saddle having simple western-style scrollwork tooled into it. This one, though, had different scrollwork—Celtic, maybe?—around its edges, and it also sported purple gemstones set around the horn.

The thrakkon nodded, smiling. "Thank you for noticing. I make saddles in my spare time, and I thought you might like this design."

"I do, I do. Thank you, Marschon. It is stunning, indeed."

The stablemaster led Lady outside, then bowed and turned back inside to whatever work he had for the day. Crystal recognized the subtle whistling sound as what served as his sigh of happiness.

Once both girls were solidly on their steeds, and Matt joined them on the feisty Phobos, who Crystal noticed was still leering at Lady in a very ungentlemanly manner, if such a term could be used for a horse, even one that was immortal and likely contained at least a small part demon. The four leaped into a gallop, sparking squeals of joy from the girls. They crossed several acres at a fast pace, led by the tremendous strides of the black stallion. Matt clearly enjoyed riding his steed, whooping war cries and laughing aloud. It lightened her heart to see him play as he was. He always took his job and his life and its inherent burdens so seriously, and even now that he had reclaimed his place as a god he kept a rigid schedule of governance. Seeing her beloved play was such a relief after the last several weeks that Crystal's heart felt even lighter as a result.

The family played outside for several hours, their path never taking them anywhere in particular. Once they found themselves by the stream that ran down the middle of the estate, and Lady and the twins' horses stopped to drink. And drink. And drink. Crystal was getting a little impatient when Phobos and Matt solved the problem by running up from behind, vaulting several yards through the air, and splashing down in the middle of the stream near the drinking horses. The trio of mortal horses, led by Lady, turned disgusted expressions at the warhorse, who in turn seemed to be laughing. Chortling, Crystal pushed Lady away from the stream.

When the family had had as much horseback riding as they could take in a day, they turned back to the stables. The sun had crested and was on its way down as they released their steeds back to the gentle care of Marschon and the other thrakkon and headed back toward inside and the mess hall where lunch would be available.

As they ate, Crystal told the girls of her plans to learn blacksmithing. They surprised her by accepting it quickly. "Mom, the last trip showed us that you won't be gone forever," Linda said, and Heidi nodded her agreement.

After lunch was eaten and the plates cleared, Crystal followed Matt up the staircase to the throne room. She stood next to the golden circle and reconsidered for a moment. "This is going to be a tough trip, isn't it?" she asked Matt.

Matt nodded. "Probably. Hephaestus is tough. He'll expect you to be his typical apprentice. You'll do fine, though. All you have to do is work and keep your mouth closed. Oh, and don't cast magic at all. Okay? He has a love for things crafted by hand, so casting magic in his realm is kind of an insult."

Crystal nodded, then said, "Any other insults I should know about?"

"Nah. Well, maybe. If he appears as a cripple, don't look at his deformity. Never offer to help him, no matter how crippled he appears. Pretend like whatever infirmity he displays doesn't exist. And did I mention doing whatever he asks—within reason, of course—and keeping your mouth closed?"

"You did," she said, wishing that just once her husband would be above a joke at her expense. What he was telling her was undoubtedly absolutely true, but he still seemed to be enjoying her discomfort an awful lot more than she was.

"Alright," Matt said. "Ready?"

She nodded. The world crunched around her, and once her stomach was back to normal she looked around.

The Forge of Hephaestus

She was in a forge. She had seen forges before, on tours of the older parts of several settlements both in Europe and on the East Coast of the United States. They were all, as she recalled, dark and noisy and hot. This one fit that description completely. It was gloomy; the only light source was a glowing—whatever it was called, where they heated up the metal—to the side. Five anvils stood in the room, four of which were occupied by shadowy figures pounding metal against them. The pounding constituted the noisy part, though it lessened considerably after a few seconds as the largest figure, standing closest to the oven-thing, stopped pounding and walked toward them. As he came closer, Crystal could see that his massive torso was completely covered in sweat; it had to be well over a hundred degrees in the forge.

The huge man stopped briefly in front of Matt and Crystal and grabbed a rag from a nearby hook on the wall. He used the cloth to wipe the sweat off of his hands and face as he nodded to Matt and then looked Crystal up and down. She watched his movements, wondering if they were going to have to try talking over the bone-jarring noise in the forge. She didn't have to wonder long. The man threw the cloth back over the hook and jerked his head toward the doorway. The pair followed him out of the forge through a leather curtain hung in the doorway and were greeted by the beautiful wooded outdoors. Crystal gasped at the sudden change from dark, loud, and hot to sunny, quiet, and moderate.

The giant smiled grandly and said, "Welcome, Matthew, to me estate 'ere in th'woods. What kin I do fer ye?" Crystal was enchanted; the giant's gentle Scottish lilt charmed her ears as the wind whispering through the ancient trees surrounding them delighted her skin and hair with its hint of springtime chill.

"What's oop with th'accent?" Matt replied, mimicking the giant's brogue.

Hephaestus guffawed, his peals of laughter ringing in Crystal's ears. "I spent some time on the isles toward the end of the last cycle, Matthew, and it was a really grand time," he said with a more natural, neutral accent. "Not only is it beautiful there, but I also met a lot of people on the isles who still enjoy an honest day's work."

Something the god said—it's beautiful there—caught Crystal's attention. She had noticed a strange glimmer around them. It was beautiful and sunny, and the wind gently moved the hair on her head, but something just out of her sight was also—was it jiggling? No, she was seeing energy oscillations, she realized. Unfocusing as Matt had taught her, she looked around and saw herself surrounded by energy constructs of magical essence.

"It's beautiful there, and it's also beautiful here," Crystal said. "But here is just an illusion of there, isn't it?"

The giant eyed her silently and then turned to Matt. "She's good. Who is she?"

Matt smiled. "Crystal, meet Hephaestus, the god of the forge. Hephaestus, this is my wife, Crystal."

Hephaestus held out his hand. Crystal joined it with her own hand, and the giant pumped her arm with three solid whacks. Still holding her hand, he looked critically at the arm he had just whacked. "You know, a little manual labor would tighten that right up," he said, and then smiled brightly at Crystal.

Crystal grimaced and said, "I'm sure it will."

Matt cleared his throat. When Hephaestus returned his attention to Matt with a question on his face, the god of war said, "Actually, that's why we're here. Gaia said that Crystal needs to learn a little of your trade."

"Well, if the earth mother says it, it must need doing, right?" Hephaestus was more cheerful at the tasking, Crystal thought, than Apollo had been. She noted that Hephaestus didn't even question why. "I'll be happy to put your lady to work, so long as you don't mind me expecting her to work as hard as anybody else."

Matt shrugged and looked pointedly toward Crystal, signaling that this was her issue to address.

"Of course I'll work as hard as anybody else, Hephaestus," Crystal said.

A cloud crossed over the god of the forge's expression. He said, "Mm hmm, we'll see. In any event, you'll need to address me as Master while you're here. I'm sure the humans and other beings at the estate where you live look up to you, but you're on my turf now. If you want my teaching, you'll need to earn it."

"Shall I send her clothes, or do you have suitable for her to wear?" Matt interrupted, and Crystal silently thanked him for the change of subject.

"What I have here is fine," Hephaestus said.

"Excellent. Also, she has a trinket she uses to communicate with our children. When she's not working, of course. Do you have a problem with that?"

"Of course not, as long as it doesn't interfere with her work. She'll be busy, but as long as she accomplishes what I give her, it's good that she speaks with her kids."

Matt smiled and pressed the blue glass shard into Crystal's hand. He kissed her, and said, "Good luck!" Then he disappeared, leaving Hephaestus and Crystal together.

Hephaestus cocked his head to the side and surveyed Crystal for several minutes. Finally he said, "You can't work in those clothes. I'll have Angus lead you to your chambers, where you can change into work clothes. When you're changed, come back here and I'll give you your first assignment." The smith spun on his heels and re-entered the forge, yelling something Crystal couldn't make out as he did.

A black-haired muscular man took the smith's place quickly, still wiping sweat off of his own arms, hands, and face with a rag. Holding out a mostly-clean hand to Crystal, he smiled and said, "Hi, I'm Angus. The Master asked me to show ye around a bit. Follow me."

Angus's gentle accent charmed Crystal as well, and this time it felt genuine. She followed him away from the forge down a path through the trees. Children's voices came to her, quietly at first and then louder as they walked.

"Where are you from, Angus?" Crystal asked, assuming the response would be somewhere on the northern end of the largest British isle. She had always been captivated by Scottish history; her own ancestry had been said to have its roots somewhere in the highlands of Scotland, and now she silently upbraided herself for never getting around to checking further into the matter. She felt an immediate bond with Angus as a result.

"I'm Scottish, from Aberdeen," Angus said. "My family was in the shipbuilding business there for centuries till it died down. Always needed strong smiths to make the hardware that held the ships together, they did."

"Oh, yes, Aberdeen," Crystal said, her mind racing back to the tour she and Matt had taken of Scotland, trying to recall as much as she could of the coastal city. "Aberdeen is just a lowland town, right?"

"Yep. And where might you be from?"

Crystal felt a twinge of annoyance at the diversion, and answered absently, "California. The Bay area." The pair reached a village, where children were darting around playing.

"Oh, yes, California. That's *just* a western state, right?"

"It's—oh," Crystal said, breaking out of her enchantment and realizing what she had said. "I deserved that, didn't I? I'm sorry. I didn't mean..."

"Think nothin' of it," Angus interrupted her. "For Americans, Aberdeen was usually nothin' more than an airport they passed through on their way to their Highland tours. Never mind it was the most prosperous city on the isle—Americans just wanted to see the wall and taste the whiskeys. It's all now a bit of a moot point, anyway, isn't it?"

Crystal wondered if she had ever seemed so silly on the tours she and Matt had taken. They had always taken the time to chat with locals and try to get the local flavor, so she knew they weren't the worst type of tourist, but who knew how many times a simple slip of her tongue had turned off a local?

"Well, now," Angus said, breaking into her reverie, "here is our village. Hopefully ye'll forgive us for not having our kilts on, but kilts and forge work don't go well together, what with slag flyin' and all."

"It's beautiful," Crystal said, hoping that the sincere compliment would help make up for her stupid comment earlier. It was beautiful, she thought, in a rustic way. Around a central green were arrayed economical living quarters. There were fifteen or twenty of them, as Crystal counted, depending on whether the larger building at the opposite side of the green had rooms on its back. The slant of the roof suggested that it should. Most quarters were pressed together into triplexes or quads, but one in the center on the right stood larger than the rest and had a long hall attached to its side. The children whom Crystal had heard, about a dozen, were darting about the green in the middle of the homes.

Angus led her around the green to the right. Passing the larger edifice, he paused and said, "The Master's home is here, though he spends nearly all of his time in the forge. That's the dinin' hall, attached. The kitchen is just behind, in a separate building. Ye're expected to jump in and help out when ye're not workin' in the forge, but the Master said ye'll be spendin' most of yer time workin' metal. Strange—ye seem a bit frail for our kind of work, though I don't mean that t'be an insult. But who am I to judge, eh?"

Continuing, Angus pointed to a couple of buildings out behind the hall. "The water closets are marked with men and women sigils to keep them separate. Each has a bath and a loo. My wife says the women's facilities are splendid."

They continued walking, and Crystal asked, "Do you have any children, Angus?"

"Aye. The red-haired lad in the green shirt in that group playin' is mine." Angus pointed to the group, his face beaming with pride.

"Good looking kid. How many families live here?"

"Thanks, and a dozen, not includin' you. There's four of us master smiths workin' directly with the Master, plus a few apprentices. The rest do the work of the village, runnin' the gardens and the kitchens and the cleanin'."

An absence caught Crystal's attention, and she asked, "Where are the thrakkoni?"

"What's a thrakkoni?" Angus asked.

"It's a humanoid-shaped dragon, a servant to the gods. Haven't you seen any?"

Angus crossed his arms, suspicion sliding across his face as he accused, "Ye're pullin' m'leg."

"No, no leg-pulling here," Crystal said. "My husband has a slew of them as servants. It seemed natural to assume that all the gods had them."

"Who is yer husband, then?"

"Oh," Crystal said, surprised that she hadn't thought that Hephaestus might leave Angus in the dark. "My husband is Matthew, the god of war. Now, at least. When we married, he was actually just Matthew, a really good-looking college dean. But things have changed a bit since the cataclysm, haven't they?"

"Indeed they have, lass. Indeed they have. The god of war, eh? Well, here we are at yer room." Angus had led her around the side of the large building at the far end of the green, and now held open the door to the unit on the end. "Everything ye should need is already here, though it was set up for a male smith's apprentice, so it may be missing a few of yer, um, delicate items. My wife Donna can help ye get those if ye find us over dinner. Any other questions?" Angus barely waited for her shake of her head before he retreated from her room, explaining that his work at the forge was calling him.

Crystal closed the door behind the smith. No thrakkoni, and no magical completion of chores? Hephaestus really put an emphasis on manual labor, for a god. Well, Crystal had spent most of her life without servants, so she was sure she could live up to the smith god's expectations now. She looked around the room. Inside a simple bureau were several sets of shapeless, genderless, one-size-fits-all work clothes. She stripped down to her underwear and then tried the sets on for size. Once she got the drawstrings adjusted right, she was surprised at how comfortable the clothes really were. It made sense, she thought; no point making the workman—or woman—feel worse than she needed to. She thought back to the itchy robe she had been forced to wear by Apollo and cringed. Yes, this was much better.

She tied on the leather boots and stood up. They weren't as protective as the modern steel-toed footwear, but they were sturdy, with a thick leather sole and a tough leather upper front. The back folded up and came around the calf, and then a strap laced them securely on. There wasn't a mirror, but she was sure that if she'd had one she would have seen a hard-working woman in it.

Newly clad in her working armor, Crystal set out for the forge, stopping briefly by the restroom to splash water on her face. She knew it would be hotter than she'd ever been for longer than she'd ever been that hot inside working with the metal, and she was sure she would learn to relish the feel of water against her skin.

She strode directly in to the forge, walking over to Hephaestus to be heard over the din. "Master, I am ready," she yelled, looking over at the unused anvil in the farthest corner away from him.

Hephaestus followed her gaze and then laughed, shaking his head. She followed him out of the building, wondering what he found so funny. The clang and clatter of hot metal being worked died down as the flap closed over the door, and Hephaestus motioned Crystal off to the side down another path. As they walked, he explained, "Are you crazy? I'm not letting you touch a hammer and anvil yet, as green as you are. Mother's orders were to teach you the craft, and the craft I shall teach you. We're going to start at the beginning and work our way up."

Crystal nodded, not certain yet what he meant. They rounded a bend in the path and came to another clearing, this one holding a huge pile of logs that were cut into rounds at one side and a ten foot tall mound covered in mud on the other.

Hephaestus stopped and held his hand out grandly toward the logs. "First, we teach you to make one of the most important ingredients: charcoal."

"What's the charcoal used for?" she asked.

"Are you daft?" Hephaestus asked, his expression making it clear that he meant it. "We burn the charcoal to smelt the ore and to fire the forge."

"Why don't you just use magic?"

"*Just* use magic? Oh, *just*? Girl, have you ever made anything with your hands?"

"Yeah, I used to do cross stitch and...." Crystal realized that she shouldn't be saying it moments after she began, but by that point her defensiveness was taking over.

"*CROSS STITCH?*" Hephaestus roared. "I'm not talking about needlepoint, damn you. I'm talking about something useful. That's what we smiths do, make stuff that's useful. In fact, a good smith can make everything he needs to use himself except for the anvil, and maybe, just maybe, by the time I'm done with you, you'll be one of those good smiths." He held up the hammer he had been using in the forge that he'd slipped into a loop on his belt before leaving. "I made this by hand. It's made of a metal stronger than any you'll ever work, in a fire hotter than any you'll ever be able to use. I made it myself, as a product of my own sweat and work, and no magical crafting will ever come close to the feeling I got from stepping back and seeing what my hard efforts had wrought. No," Hephaestus brandished the hammer under Crystal's nose for emphasis as he paused, "I don't use magic to smith, and you can't either. If I catch you at it, I'll send you straightaway back to your happy little estate. Understood?"

Crystal nodded, eyes fixed on the hammer's grey-blue head, and he continued, "Come to think of it, I don't want you using magic here at all, except that little blue trinket your husband gave you, and then only to speak to your loved ones. Everybody here accomplishes things with sweat on their brow, and you aren't special enough to justify an exception. Nobody is."

Crystal nodded again, and then a question occurred to her. "Master, why don't you have any thrakkoni here?"

"Who says I don't have any thrakkoni here?"

"I asked Angus where they were, and he had never heard of them. Thought I'd been reading too many fairy tales, I guess."

"The humans here don't need to know about them. I only keep a few around, and those are really only here to tend the place during the technology eras. Besides, I've got green fingers, and there's a huge hydroponic growing system out behind the apartment building you're in now that I keep going with thrakkoni when humans aren't available."

"Green fingers?"

Hephaestus read the confused expression on Crystal's face and said, "Oh, right. You Yanks, I think, said green thumb."

"Oh. Right. I haven't met too many smiths, but to my limited scope of knowledge, gardening seems kind of the opposite of smithing. I did notice a couple of awfully fine rose bushes outside the building Angus pointed out as yours. Were those your handiwork?"

Hephaestus smiled for the first time Crystal had seen. "Indeed," he said.

Crystal thought back on the hydroponics she had seen at her alma mater. Hephaestus must really enjoy crafting, it seemed, if he went to the trouble to grow plants in containers when he had such beautiful land. But it was mostly illusory, she remembered, according to their first chat, and so she wondered, "Master, where are we?"

"At my forge, of course," Hephaestus said with a coy smile.

"No, I mean, where is your forge located? It looks like you have good ground for gardening, but you said you use containers. I can see that most of what surrounds us is illusion. It seems a strange combination."

"You continue to prove your perceptiveness, Crystal. As much as I love the look of the British forests, we're actually deep inside a volcano. Specifically, the one your civilization knew as Etna. It's the only way to get heat of sufficient intensity to smelt and forge some of the metals I work with. I keep it nicely climate controlled in here for your sake, of course, but we're actually in a large pocket in the rock that juts off the main lava chute, and the temperature outside my protective wards is normally around a thousand degrees. It's a bit higher, of course, when the lava is flowing by."

Crystal looked around at the lush greenery with a newfound level of appreciation. "Wow, that's impressive. But, so where does all this wood come from? Surely it's not grown here."

"Supply of firewood is a task the thrakkoni handle for me. They usually teleport out and teleport back in with the logs."

"Usually?"

Hephaestus laughed. "I've got a couple of daredevils in my group who like to play chicken with the lava. At our depth beneath the cone, sometimes there's lava filling the chute, and sometimes there isn't. When there isn't, it's a straight shot up the cone to the surface, and the thrakkoni like to fly that. The danger comes in when there isn't lava out there, and then a minute later there is."

"It does sound like a dangerous sport. Have you lost any?"

"One, a long time ago. He didn't take it seriously, and so we think he hit the chute at the wrong time and didn't accelerate fast enough, and for some reason didn't think to teleport out in time. Since then, they've all been more careful." Hephaestus shifted his weight and turned his gaze back to the wood. "Now, are we going to chat all day or get some work done?"

"I'm ready to work, Master," Crystal said.

"Well, then, that's good. Did you bring gloves?"

Crystal pulled the work gloves out of her pocket and held them up; she was glad that she had noticed them on the table on her way out of her room.

"Okay, see that mound over there? You're going to build another one. First you'll split the wood. Have you ever split logs before?"

Crystal hadn't, and she admitted it.

"I'm going to have to teach you everything, aren't I?" Hephaestus said with an exasperated look. He led her over to a large round log laid on the ground.

"That's one of the widest axes I've ever seen," Crystal said.

The god glared at her. "It's a maul, not an axe. Pick it up." Crystal did and found it extraordinarily heavy. She had wielded hatchets and axes before, at least a couple of times, on camping trips. She only ever managed to dent the logs until Matt came over and rescued her from the task, a fact she hoped wouldn't come to light. But the maul she was holding now felt several times heavier than she remembered the axes being. It was also solid metal, one piece from the wide head down the shaft to the handle, which was wrapped in cloth.

Hephaestus directed her to get one of the round logs from the stack. "A round without branches or knots for your first attempt, lass," he said. She found a straight one and brought it back over, laying it on end as instructed. "Now, first you look at the end to see if there are any obvious spots to hit it. By obvious spots, I'm talking about areas where the rings bunch up or maybe even run into the center together. There aren't any on this log, which probably is a good thing. So you're going to aim for this spot here," he made a line on the log from the center back toward her, about the same length as the maul blade, "and swing the maul over your head. It's not like swinging an axe, now. That's an eight pound maul, which is one of our lighter ones, but it's still heavy enough to do the job. Use its weight, not your strength, to split the wood. Swing the maul directly overhead like this," he demonstrated slowly, "and bring it straight down. No fancy sideways swipes, mind you, or you might hurt yourself. Just use the weight of the head of the maul to split the log. Got it?"

"Why should I hit the log off center? Wouldn't the center split it more cleanly?"

"The log is going to split down whatever line you hit, since there aren't any knots in it. The center of most logs, the heartwood, is the spongiest. If you bury the head in the center, you'll just get it stuck. You want to split the log toward the center, not starting at the center."

"OK, I think I've got it," Crystal said, taking the maul from him. She planted her feet, focused her eyes on the spot Hephaestus had pointed to, and hefted the maul over her head in an arc that ended right where she was aiming. The maul bounced, creating an eighth-inch divot in the surface of the wood.

"Hmm," she said, turning to Hephaestus, who she was surprised to see was smiling pleasantly.

"Nice first swing, actually," he said. "At least you hit where you were aiming. Now try it again, but actually swing it this time."

Crystal lined up again, standing in the same spot and this time glaring at the divot in the wood. She raised the maul over her head and, seeking to split the wood in a single cleave and impress the god, let out a war cry and brought the maul forcefully down.

She missed.

Her forceful swing took the maul too far away from her body, leaving its shank to hit the opposite edge of the log, the head cleaving the air. The sharp jolt of shaft hitting log sent the maul's handle out of her hands, causing it to flip up and over the round. The maul finally came to rest several feet away in the grass. Hephaestus roared in laughter.

Crystal stomped over to get the maul and then returned, her face glowing red. She lined up to take another swing and Hephaestus paused his laughing with great apparent effort. "Now listen, lass. You've got two choices. You can either do it your way or mine. Your way will take you a bit longer than my way, but it's entirely up to you. Which will it be?"

Crystal rested the head of the maul between her feet and turned to Hephaestus, trying not to glare. "I'm sorry, Master," she said with forced politeness. "I thought I was doing it your way."

Hephaestus chuckled again, raising Crystal's hackles even farther, as he said, "Well, you're doing it wrong, then. No sense melting the forge over it, now, is there? Simmer down and I'll try explaining it again now that you've had a couple of whacks at it." He took the maul from her and lined up on the log. "Now, your pose was just right. You started the swing just right the first time, too, just easy does it over your head to give the maul some speed. What you did wrong the second time was you started swinging it like an axe in the start of the arc, and you'll always miss when you do that. You'll either overbalance yourself and go too far of the log, as you did, or you'll correct your swing and come in too close. Now, if you're gonna miss one way or another, it's better to go too far, as you saw, as that's just embarrassing and a little painful on the palms. Too close, and you'll hit either the splitting surface or your calf. But better than that is to just not miss, right? Start the swing easy, and then when the head is about right here," he held the maul up at about a forty-five degree angle, "put some force into pulling it down. Don't try to use your whole body, just your triceps here, your pectorals here, and your abdomen and back muscles. You're gonna be giving the head the momentum that will power it through the log. Watch. It's like this." Hephaestus raised the maul and brought it down in a perfect arc. The log split cleanly, the two pieces flying a couple feet to either side.

Hephaestus picked one of the halves up and positioned it back in front of Crystal, drawing a line with his index finger before handing her the maul. "Now, you hit this right here, and split the half into quarters."

Crystal did as directed, swinging the maul easily over her head and then pulling it down in the last bit of arc. To her surprise, the maul head bit into the wood, cleaving the half-log into two quarters. She felt like shrieking in joy, but held it in to avoid further derision.

"Good. Now do the other half," he said, and she repeated her swing with the same result. "Good again. Get another log and try it from the round." She did as he commanded again. This time her swing was perfect, she thought, but the maul only split a few inches into the wood and stopped. She tugged on it, but it was firmly stuck. She pulled up on it again, and this time the entire log lifted with the maul. Frustrated, she set it down and looked at Hephaestus, who, to her immense displeasure, was giggling.

"You've never done anything like this before, have you?" he said between guffaws. As she shook her head, he reached over and grabbed the maul handle. He jerked it down quickly and then back up, and the maul head jumped out of the log. "Don't hit it in the same spot the second time, or you'll get the same result," he said, handing her the maul.

I can't give up, she told herself as she meekly took the maul back from him. She aimed at the spot on the other side of center for her second swing, and was relieved when the log split.

"Two hits to split your first round. Pretty good, all things considered," Hephaestus said without a laugh, and Crystal felt elated at the praise.

Good grief, would the whole visit be this difficult?

Crystal successfully split a few more rounds, including one that was knotty, before Hephaestus walked away with instructions for her to stack the split quarters over on the other side of the clearing, standing on end arranged close together. He stopped at the edge of the clearing and called back, "Oh, and lass? Don't ever swing the maul when you're tired. Always let your muscles rest a few minutes instead. Swinging when you're tired means you lose control of the maul, and that's a bad thing." She nodded, and he left her to her task.

Crystal set to work, figuring that it would take her several days to split a mound's worth of wood at the rate she was going. The sun—the illusion of the sun, she reminded herself—traced along the expected arc as she repetitively pulled a log from the pile, set it up, swung two, three, or sometimes four times to split it, then split each half, and then pulled another log. She felt her muscles nagging her to take a break, but she didn't have time for a break. She needed to finish this to get to whatever else Hephaestus would be "teaching" her, blast him. Why on earth did Gaia decide she needed to learn blacksmithing, of all things? She was pretty certain Matt hadn't done much blacksmithing, and she couldn't imagine Apollo or Aphrodite, either one, doing it. And this galling task of splitting wood? The goddess who had thrust her nakedness at Crystal and Matt on their visit to Olympus had never, ever split wood, Crystal was sure. She really wasn't the whining type, but this was exhausting work with no real end in sight.

She lined a round up, holding the maul in shaking hands. The exercise was getting the better of her, but she really didn't have time to take a break. It had only been an hour or two, and she didn't quite have a dozen rounds split. She had to continue, so she took another swing. *Thwack.* Instead of splitting the wood, the maul bounced out of her rubbery hands. Somehow she had been so tired that the maul's head had turned sideways, leaving the flat part to bounce hard against the wood. She cursed herself silently, and then realized she had been so tired she didn't notice her own hand holding her jaw. Not only had she let go of the handle, but she had been so tired she had bent into the swing, and her jaw had been what stopped the maul handle from flying up and around in an arc as it had the last time she'd missed. She felt her face gingerly. Nothing broken. Good. No feel of blood anywhere, either. It would hurt tomorrow, though. She briefly considered using magic to heal it, but decided against it. The pain would sharpen her wits, hopefully, and somehow she felt that suffering through was what it might take to win the respect of some of her fellow workers.

Crystal sat down hard on the very round she had been trying to split. She shook her hands in the air in front of her. Feeling was beginning to return in a painfully tingly way, but it would be several minutes before she dared swing the maul again. A good time, she thought, to see about getting some water. She rose heavily from the log—*have I really been working THAT hard?* She walked ungracefully down the path. As she ambled, her legs began recovering; she started feeling the muscles she had been using lifting the sometimes-heavy rounds and bending down to shift and move the split halves and quarters. Those muscles would hurt tomorrow, too, she knew.

Stretching her chest, arm, and shoulder muscles out as she walked, she made her way back to the forge. She was relieved to see an old-fashioned water spigot on the outside of the building with canteens hanging beside it. Not wanting to take someone else's canteen, though, she went inside and cleared her throat loudly to gain the attention of Hephaestus.

The god's eyes lit on her chin and his face formed a question as his hand pointed. She nodded and pantomimed the maul handle hitting her chin, and then shrugged and held two thumbs up. Hephaestus's face lit up in a proud, brotherly grin as he concluded the nonverbal exchange with a nod.

Crystal moved in closer and yelled into his ear over the noise of hammering, "Master, are the canteens outside spoken for?"

He pulled away and shook his head. In a loud voice, he said, "No, take one back to the clearing with you. We should've taken you one when we first went."

Crystal nodded and walked out, feeling the god's eyes following her out. She got the sense that he was pleased, and that made her muscle strain seem less severe on the way back to the clearing.

She sat again on the round for several minutes, taking long pulls from the canteen and thinking of the work she had completed so far. It was tiring, certainly, and there weren't any shortcuts to be had, but it did seem like the pile of logs to be split was smaller than before, and she could see the logs she had already split starting to make a fair pile of its own. She came up with a plan to help curb the fatigue. Because her muscles needed a break from each of the two very different tasks, she would split four logs, and then move the quarters over to the other side of the clearing, and then split four more logs. She also promised herself that she would take breaks when needed, and then she stood back up and got back to work, pleased at her ability to still be analytical even when in what appeared to be a woodland clearing in the middle of an active volcano while splitting wood. Matt teased her about it sometimes, calling it anal retentiveness or worse, but she knew he appreciated it, too.

As she worked, she began to look for the rounds with knots in them. They were harder, and in some cases much harder, to split than the rounds without knots, because of what the knots, which were what remained of branches, did to warp the grain of the wood. Hephaestus had told her how to judge how twisted the grains would be and how to try to split around the knots, and she was finding the task far more enjoyable than splitting straight rounds. Each one was a little puzzle, something to take her mind off of the discomfort her body was feeling at the unfamiliar exercise.

"Ye gonna work all night, lass?" a voice called behind her, startling her. Peering back, she recognized Angus through the twilight.

"I—I didn't realize how late it was getting," Crystal said, putting the maul head down on the ground and using it as a support. "I guess I shouldn't work too much later, should I?"

"When ye can't see the round, ye can't split the round. It's dinnertime, lass, and I think ye've earned yer spot at the table tonight. It's time to put the maul down and come with me. The logs'll still be here in the mornin'."

Crystal accepted his words and leaned the maul up against the log she had been about to split. She took a step forward, and the depth of her exhaustion hit her. She caught herself, barely, from pitching over, and held her shaky arms out to the sides to regain her balance.

"Need help, lass?" Angus said, and Crystal heard more amusement than worry in his voice.

"No," she said flatly, and then forced her legs to move, one and then the other. Angus watched her strange shamble with an amused quirk on his lips, but the broadly muscled man remained silent till she got to him. "I really am an old woman, you know," she said. He snorted in reply, a reaction that brought a sigh from her. "Okay, are we going to miss dinner if I take a little extra time to walk back?"

"There's plenty to eat, Crystal. Take yer time, and I'll be right here with ye. I've even got an arm ye can use if ye need."

Crystal would be damned before she would let the boy carry her back to the camp, she thought. She set off down the darkening path, still focusing on just putting one foot in front of the other.

"Ye weren't a laborer before the cataclysm, were ye?" Angus asked.

"I was a teacher for a while, and then when the girls got big enough I became a stay-at-home mom."

"So, if ye don't mind my askin', why are ye here? Did ye think it to be easy work?"

"No, I never thought it would be easy. Honestly, I don't know why I'm here. The Earth Mother just told me I needed to learn from Hephaestus," she said, deciding that most of the truth would be easier to deal with than all of it, especially considering how little energy she had at the moment.

"Well, he's a good one to learn from, and if Gaia said it, then ye need to do it," Angus said.

"Have you met Gaia?"

"Aye, she came by once. The Master said that we use more of her resources than most of the other people put together, so he has a special relationship with her. She's a charmin' lady, isn't she?"

Changing the subject to avoid further need to skim the truth, Crystal asked, "So what did your wife do before the cataclysm?"

"Administrative assistant. Worked for the oil companies, she did. I think the last one she worked for was BP, or Balmoral, maybe—that's not an oil company, exactly, but—oh, all that's moot now, I guess. Anyway, she did all the stuff around the office the executives couldn't be bothered to do. I remember, in fact, when she...."

Crystal hobbled back toward camp, listening intently to the lilting melody of Angus's voice. She found that by paying attention to Angus, she felt the leftovers from the day's exertions less severely, and so she kept him going, prodding him for more information when he paused.

"Ah, now I've talked yer ear off, and I'm sure ye wanted to walk in silence, Crystal. I'm sorry," Angus said as the pair reached the door of the dining hall.

"Don't be silly. I loved hearing your tales, and it took my mind off of how badly my muscles are strained, so I'm doubly glad you took the time to walk back with me."

The pair walked in, and Crystal was taken aback by the raucous atmosphere of the dining hall. It was nearly as loud as the forge had been, only this time instead of the orderly clanging of metal on metal, the noise was mostly from the voices of the twenty-five or thirty men, women, and children seated at its tables. Crystal compared this to the other dining halls she had been in recently. Matt's hall had been relatively orderly with some clanking around and talking, similar to the cafeterias in the schools she had served in before returning to the home full-time. Apollo's hall had been disturbingly quiet, so much so that every conversation she had conducted had seemed too loud. The hall of Hephaestus, though, was complete chaos that resolved itself quickly into hard-working men, women, and children who saw this as their time to enjoy life to the fullest each day before going to bed to start the next day anew. Moments after she entered, Crystal felt a kinship with the people in the hall that she knew she'd never be able to explain.

Angus led Crystal over to a table with a single empty chair, and then grabbed an empty chair from a table to the side to add to the seating. A well-built brunette looked up and smiled at Angus, who grabbed an empty mug, filled it with beer from a pitcher, and held it up. It sloshed some, but Angus didn't seem to notice as he bellowed, "Me friends, listen up!"

The hall quieted at Angus's order, and he continued in the same bellow, "This here is Crystal, a new member of our community. She survived the cataclysm at the estate of the god of war, but she's come to us to learn the joy of a day of hard work. She's done a fine job in the charcoal field today. I want you all to welcome her into the family."

A roar answered Angus as he sat down, pointing to the empty chair. Crystal flopped down into it, an exhausted smile the best she could do. A plate filled with steaming beef and vegetables was pushed in front of her, a full mug of ale beside it. The families resumed their eating, but their eyes remained on her as she mustered her strength enough to raise her fork to her mouth with the first bite of roast. It was simple, she found, and relative-ly bland, but it tasted heavenly to her exhausted palate. She chewed, her hurt jaw protesting, and she tipped the mug's contents into her mouth to wash the partially-chewed food down.

It was good. She had never been a beer fan, preferring instead the sweeter mixed drinks, but this beer was nothing like what she had drunk in college. Instead of flat and bitter, its depths held a swirl of subtle flavors. "What is this?" she asked Angus.

"Beer," he said, shrugging.

"No, I mean what kind. I've had beer, and this is way better than anything I've had before."

"The Master makes it. He's got a few of the wives learnin' how to make his ale, but we're still drinkin' what he had barreled when we got here. Ye're probably used to that pisswater that you Yanks called beer, aren't ye?"

"Not used to it at all. I used to drink imported lagers, in fact, not the American pisswater. But this is better."

"Of course it is. You said it—ye drank lagers, and this is a good pint o'British ale."

"What's the difference between a lager and a British ale?"

"One tastes better."

"Yeah, I got that. Why?"

"How the hell should I know? I'm a smith, not a brewer."

Crystal chuckled over the interchange; the straight-talking Angus made conversation interesting. She did notice that food and ale were working together to make her muscles hurt less—or, at least, they made her care less about the hurt she felt. As she ate, she got to know Donna and Robert, their son. Donna was a quiet woman, yet she proved more than capable of holding a good conversation. Crystal learned that she had been an assis-tant to some of the executives at the highest levels of the oil in-dustry, but had always had a passion for sewing and other crafts. Donna loved their new life as a result, since the entirety of her work days were spent with the village ladies at whatever crafts needed doing. The clothes Crystal was wearing had been made by Donna, who beamed when Crystal complimented her on their wear-ability and comfort.

The children left the hall after the food had been eaten, and most of the women left with them. Donna excused herself to go to bed, asking Crystal and Angus to not rise on her behalf. Crystal, who would normally have retired with the women, was finding it amusing to be treated as one of the men. She wasn't ready to make a go for her room, anyway; she no longer felt the pain of the work thanks to the three or four mugs of beer she had consumed, but the side effect of the beer was a head that wanted to spin.

A small glass containing flat amber liquid was thrust in front of her. Looking up, she saw that everyone else—all men, as all the other women seemed to have gone—had one also. "Drink up," Angus said. "It'll warm yer heart and help ye sleep." He lifted his glass with a smile and downed the liquor.

Crystal had tasted Scotch whiskey before and knew how devastating it could be when abused, but this was only a single shot. She smiled, recalling the warming sensation Scotch brought with it. She hefted the liquid to her mouth and swallowed it.

Dirt. It tasted like dirt.

The expression on her face must have been descriptive, as all the other occupants roared in laughter when she set her cup down. Angus, laughing his way to tears, said through the guffaws, "Never had good Scotch before, have ye?"

"I've had Scotch, but that stuff tastes—um, different."

"Ye've probably had highland or Speyside malt, then. Those malts are the ethereal essence of Scotch. Islay malt, which is what ye just drank, contains the essence of the earth, the very heartbeat of what we do for a living."

"That's why it tastes like a peat bog, then?"

"And how d'ye know what a peat bog tastes like?"

"Good point, Angus. But I really do think I'm going to have to get myself to bed before I pass out on the dinner table."

Angus laughed good-naturedly. "Of course, lass. Let me help ye get there, since ye've had a tiring day of it." Angus helped her gently out of her chair, but Crystal made a point of walking under her own power out of the dining hall and back to her room. She turned at her own door and thanked Angus for helping her.

"My pleasure. Between you and me, it's good to have somebody else splittin' the wood for the time being. Smiths and the apprentices have to take our own turns at it, but the Master wants to know ye got the task right down before we get back at it. So," the smith pointed to her bed and pushed her gently in its direction, "sleep tight, and make sure ye get up in the morning, or one of us will have to wake you. Ye won't like that much." Angus shut the door.

Crystal managed to drop her work clothes off of her body onto the floor before she collapsed onto the bed. Her last thought before sleep took her was that she was sure Matt would understand if she didn't call for him on the shard.

Smithing I: The Basics

The next day dawned brightly and painfully for Crystal. She made to get out of bed, and then reconsidered. Every muscle in her body seemed to hurt, as did some of the ligaments, tendons, and even the bones. She thought briefly of using magic to remove the pain, but just as quickly realized that such a concession might disqualify her from further tutelage, and thus would make the pain she suffered yesterday all for naught. She wouldn't, then. Crystal hurt, but she had been through worse pain before. She had made it through giving birth, after all, and she was damn sure she could make it through this.

Her feet hit the floor. At least that part of her didn't hurt. She hobbled over to the window and moved the curtain out of the way enough to peer out. Near as she could judge, it was still fairly early morning. At least they wouldn't need to send anyone after her.

Crystal dressed in the same clothes she had stripped off the night before. She didn't smell bad, though her nose was probably as tired as the rest of her was, but more importantly, as much as she hurt, it really didn't make a difference to her whether she smelled or not. She needed to get out there and finish splitting those logs.

Crystal did some of the stretches she had seen people use. They worked a little, and she felt ready afterward to walk at least as far as the restrooms. Proving triumphant at that task, she entered and splashed water on her face.

"Feel as bad as you look?" a voice from behind surprised Crystal, and she spun around to see Donna there.

"You like to surprise the life out of people as much as your husband does, don't you?" Crystal asked, forcing a smile to reduce the sting in her words.

"Sorry, it wasn't my intent," Donna said, chagrined. "But you do look like shite this morning. Every movement makes you wince. You need a salt bath."

Crystal snorted. "Don't have time for a bath. I have to get out there and finish my work. Thank you for the suggestion, though."

"It's not a suggestion, hen. You can't continue being a useful member of the work force feeling like you do right now."

"Well, thank you," Crystal said, wondering why the woman was pressing so hard. "I'm fine, though."

"Nobody's ever called you hard-headed, have they?"

"Sure, they—oh." Crystal caught Donna's meaning. She turned to the younger woman, smiled, and took her hands. Looking into her eyes, Crystal said, "Guess I'm a little slow on the uptake this morning. Look, I appreciate your thoughts. I really do. This is something I have to endure, though, for reasons that I really can't go into right now. The only way back to my family and my husband is through mastery of what I am to learn here, so I need to get out there and back to it."

Donna nodded. "I get that, petal. But last night your head was about ready to drop to the table. Today you look like death warmed up after getting clocked on the chin. Will you at least let me help you a little?"

Crystal thought Donna's offer over for a moment. Donna had a point. The bruise on her chin was pronounced, and she had been able to see the dark rings surrounding her own eyes. Crystal nodded. "What do you suggest, knowing as I'm sure you do that a bath will take too long?"

"Sit down," Donna said, and pulled over a chair that had been in front of a sink. Crystal obeyed, sitting backward in the chair as requested. Donna moved behind her and started pressing on points through her shoulders and back. Crystal felt her muscles loosen immediately; it felt so good that she had to concentrate to keep from losing tears. Donna's strong hands and fingers worked Crystal's back and shoulder muscles for several minutes. Finally she patted the back with her hand and said, "Okay, that's all I can do for now. It should get you through the day. Tonight, though, or tomorrow morning at the latest, you have to soak in salts."

Crystal rose, moving her shoulders around. She could feel an enormous difference. "Thank you," she said, smiling at Donna.

"You're welcome, love. Now go get breakfast into you and pack a few sandwiches before you head out."

"I'm not hungry," Crystal said, and realized the lie as her stomach growled.

Donna's eyebrow quirked up, and Crystal smiled.

"Yeah," Crystal admitted. "I guess I'll get some food."

In the hall, she ate quickly. Breakfast was hearty, with plenty of ham and potatoes. The men nodded briefly as she entered, but everyone seemed intent solely on fueling their bodies for the day of work. She was pleased that they seemed to have accepted her as a fellow worker.

She arrived at the clearing to find Hephaestus already there. "G'mornin', lass," he greeted her. "Fine job yesterday for a newb. I didn't see any blood anywhere, which really is a welcome surprise, and you've actually got the wood stacking properly. Build it up to the size of the other dome and then cover it in clay from the pile over there. Then come get me. Any questions?"

Crystal shook her head and, not waiting for his response, walked over to the splitting area. Viewed in the more sober light of morning, it wasn't as bad as she had thought. She had split a lot of wood, and the mound was already a couple layers high. Crystal had no idea how many—what was it, cords?—she had split, but she didn't really care. One more layer, and she would be finished with the wood part of the mound.

She got to it savagely, rapidly falling back to the pattern that had proven so successful the night before. She was proud of her progression, too; she split the round in a single swing several times. It really wasn't in the strength but rather in the momentum and aim, as Hephaestus had told her. Thanks to the work Donna had done, Crystal's knotted muscles worked themselves out quickly, and soon she was splitting wood tirelessly.

Midday, Crystal stopped briefly to eat the sandwiches she had brought with her and then walked in to the forge. She cleared her throat loudly and then smiled at Hephaestus when she had his attention. He emerged quickly and walked to the clearing, Crystal just behind.

"A fine job," he said after inspecting the mound. "We're going to fire this up now, and then you'll come out here every couple of hours after to watch for the burn. It has to smolder inside, with no air to fuel it, to turn the wood into charcoal instead of ash. Once we get the fire going, it's your job to make sure the fire burns no holes in the dome. Well, I should rather say, it's your job to make sure that the holes the fire does burn in the dome are patched quickly." Hephaestus opened a spot along the base, digging his way through the moist clay to the wood, and another in the top. He put kindling into a few cracks between the quarter logs and lit them with some coals he had brought out. Crystal smiled, glad at least that she wouldn't have to flounder with flint and steel.

The fire started, Hephaestus directed Crystal to close the dome back up. He pointed to the hole in the top. "Once smoke gets thick coming out of there, close that one too. Don't do it till you see plenty of smoke, since you don't want to put the fire out." She nodded, and he turned and began walking out of the clearing.

When she didn't follow, he turned around.

"What are you waiting for?"

"I thought you wanted me to wait until it was smoking and then close the hole," Crystal said.

"That'll take a bit. I don't want you standing around useless that long. Come with me so I can start teaching you how to make iron."

"I thought iron was an element that came out of the ground," Crystal said, jogging to catch up with the god, who had resumed his rapid pace down the path.

Hephaestus gave Crystal an amused look but didn't slow down. "Girl," he said, "if you're going to be ignorant, that's fine, but take care not to advertise it. Iron ore comes out of the ground. Iron is the result of hours of hard work at smelting."

Crystal followed quietly, embarrassed, as the pair stomped past the forge down another path through the trees. As they walked, Hephaestus explained more. "The thrakkoni and I go out and pull ore from the ground. Magically, of course; it's one of the few things we do using the elemental flows. We bring the ore here in big chunks that contain elemental iron as well as dirt and all sorts of impurities. The first step is to knock them down into smaller rocks to put on the crusher."

They entered a clearing, and Crystal saw large chunks of rock on the left and a pair of horizontal round disks of stone on the right. The disks were about six feet in diameter by a couple of feet thick, and both were held in position by a thick metal screw. Crystal figured it was obvious what the four long horizontal handles jutting from the top of the screw were there for. A shallow tub of murky water and another of clearer water sat beside what had to be a mill.

Hephaestus strode directly to the large rocks, the largest of which were about three feet thick. Most were only a foot or two in diameter. The god picked up two sledgehammers from the side and handed one to Crystal. "First, dearie, we have to make little rocks out of big ones. You learned that with wood well enough, and this is much easier. Just hit the damn things, like this." Hephaestus swung the heavy sledge over his head in an arc, hitting and smashing one of the two-foot rocks into several much smaller pieces.

Crystal nodded and took a swing at a piece of similar size. She was shocked at how much heavier the hammer was than the maul had been—and then surprised when it merely bounced off the rock.

Hephaestus snorted. "That's not...."

"A splitting maul," Crystal finished his sentence for him. "I figured that out, Master."

Her response sent Hephaestus into a full belly laugh so powerful he bent over at the waist. She waited for him to regain his posture, and then she used her full weight to bring the hammer around and down on the rock. It mimicked the rock Hephaestus had hit earlier. Crystal put the sledge down and beamed, proud of herself for splitting the rock so violently.

"Well, that's pretty good," Hephaestus said, still chortling but holding an impressed grin on his face. "Now do more."

Crystal got to it, and the task was over quickly with the help of the god. He took her sledge and set both down beside the pile, then grabbed an armload of the split rocks and headed over to the mill. Crystal did the same.

After several trips, they had the smaller rocks layered evenly between the two flat stones. Hephaestus explained, "Usually I'd send four of the smiths or six or seven apprentices out here to grind this down, as it'll take a bit of pressure. I think you and I can handle it just fine, though. We just have to crush the rocks down. You ready?"

As Crystal nodded hesitantly, Hephaestus reached up and grabbed a handle. She reached for the opposite handle, and together they pushed around in a circle, using the screw's shape to force the stone circle faces closer to each other. At first Crystal found the going easy and rapid, but as the top slab made contact with one, then a few, and then all, of the rocks, it got much harder going. It was easy for her to understand why the god would typically send several out to do this.

Once the stones were about a quarter inch apart, Hephaestus gave a signal and the pair reversed course, separating the stones again. "Now we wash them," Hephaestus said, picking the rock and dirt fragments up quickly out of the dirt chunks that now surrounded them. The pair quickly filled a fine-screened tray with the small chunks of ore, dipped them into the water that Crystal learned was cloudy due to lye, thus getting rid of most of the remaining dirt, and then transported the ore back to the forge to be rinsed. They used running water to rinse the ore before taking it into the forge and dropping it next to a pile of bricks and a pile of charcoal.

"Alright," Hephaestus said after calling Angus over, "I'm gonna get back to me own project. Go check the charcoal mound and get back here so Angus here can teach you how to set up the brick smelter to make a bloom." He walked to the anvil closest to the main fire and picked up his tools.

When she returned, Angus nodded at Crystal. The barrel-chested man put down the tools he held and walked over. "I'm gonna let ye do most of the work, eh, lass?" he said.

Crystal responded with a level glare and said, "You'd better."

Angus guffawed. "Or else what?"

Crystal shrugged, deciding to gracefully accept that her bluff had been called. "Or else nothing. I just want to do the work."

Angus crossed his arms and nodded. "Well, then, work ye shall." He directed Crystal in the creation of a smelter with bricks lining a removable iron shell, a small hole left open through which an iron pipe fit. "Ever used a grand bellows?" he asked, and she shook her head. He held it up in front of her. There were three large flat pieces of wood, one on each side and one in the middle, joined by large bags of leather. Two handles at one end allowed for opening and closing each side, and a spout at the other fit neatly into the iron pipe into the smelter.

Angus put the bellows into the smelter and showed Crystal how to use it. He expanded the right side, filling it with air. He then expanded the other while compressing the first, filling it with air and pushing some air out of the spout. The Scotsman demonstrated how each successive cycle moved one side toward the middle and the other to the outside, and each propelled air into the smelter. Crystal stood, fascinated, over the perpetual air machine that he showed her. "Most shops have it set up vertically, with a food pedal or hanging cable or some other mechanism to open one lung and press the other closed," he demonstrated with his hands moving up and down in sync. "We have a stand that we can do that with, but ye won't need it since all ye're doin' is heatin' the smelter."

They filled the smelter cavity up with charcoal and lit it. "The purpose, now, is to heat the entire mass up to temperature," Angus said. "It'll take several fills of charcoal, since you've got to get the bricks hot too. You'll want to keep the bellows going nearly the entire time, except when you're feeding charcoal to the fire."

"How do I know when it's done?" Crystal said, watching the flames that were growing in the smelting pot. She was too engrossed with the flame to notice that her hearing and speaking were becoming accustomed to the noise in the forge.

"Ye don't, really. Ye give it some time to heat the bricks up, is all. After that, we pour in the iron ore."

Crystal kneeled on the floor to work the bellows. She marveled over how easy it was compared to splitting or hammering.

Not quite an hour later she found herself marveling over how she had thought the task would be easy. It was true that each swing of the bellows' paddles took relatively little effort, but the constant motion back and forth with each arm required a stamina that was foreign to Crystal. She ignored her exhaustion for a time, focusing on the hypnotic whoosh-whoosh of the air flow and the thunk-thunk of the valves inside the bellows. Despite her best efforts at meditation, though, the constant work wore her down and she had to stop.

As soon as she stopped moving the bellows, Crystal noticed a change in the other sounds of the forge. The loudest rhythmic hammering stopped, though the other hammers continued. She looked up and met Hephaestus's eyes, which were staring directly at her. Embarrassed at her show of weakness, Crystal threw her arms over her head and behind her to stretch out the protesting muscles and then picked her rhythmic working of the bellows right back up, eyes still turned toward the god. After a few times of Crystal squeezing each side of the bellows, Hephaestus smiled, nodded his approval, and turned back to his hammering.

Crystal was paying so much attention that she didn't notice Angus standing over here till he cleared his throat. She looked up and he said, "Have ye checked yer charcoal, lass?" She shook her head and rose, looking inside the bricks to see that very little of the charcoal remained. "Ye've got to check it every so often. Charcoal burns quickly," Angus said, and then walked back over to his own anvil and continued work. Crystal shoveled more of the light black bits of fuel into the smelter obediently and then settled back down to continue working the bellows.

Soon the large smith came back over to Crystal's area and looked down in. He took a long rod with a curl at its end and poked around in the fire. Crystal, who had never seen such a hot fire so close, jumped the first time the flames erupted angrily in response to Angus's pokes, and Angus responded with a guffaw at Crystal's expense. "She's ready," Angus said finally. "Time to add the ore." Crystal rose and lifted the nearby tray containing the ore she had crushed and washed earlier, but Angus stopped her and motioned to the leather aprons, gloves, and helmets hanging on the wall nearby. "Time to add some gear, too," he said.

Crystal put on the heavy apron, boots, gloves, and helmet, and walked back over, feeling a little silly. She grinned at Angus through the mask that hung in front of her face, and he chortled in response and stepped back. Crystal carried the tray of ore closer in to the smelter than she had come yet and felt the intense heat. It singed her nose hairs as she breathed, and it made her lungs ache, yet being that close to a tightly-enclosed raging inferno also felt strangely exhilarating. She turned the tray up and dumped the ore down into the smelter, following it with more charcoal by the order of Angus.

"Every several minutes, add more charcoal and use the hook to stir it around a bit," Angus said and then returned to his own task. Crystal settled in, sweeping the lungs of the bellows open and closed rhythmically for a while, and then rose to add more charcoal and stir the massive white-hot fiery sludge in the bottom of the smelter. As time went it got harder and harder to stir, until finally she felt a solid mass at the bottom. She kept going, though, for many more minutes until Angus came over and stirred it himself, looking in to the hot mass in the crucible and somehow making a judgment on its contents. "She's ready," he said simply.

"How do you know?"

"Feel it, and look down inside while ye do."

Crystal did, and saw the subtle change.

"Okay. So, now what?"

"Now ye take it out."

Crystal peered down into the molten mass and said, "Yeah. How hot did you say that was?"

"'bout sixteen hundred degrees, prob'ly. Might be a hundred or two less, or more, but what's a couple hundred degrees when you're that hot?" Angus grinned at Crystal.

"Is that centigrade or Fahrenheit?"

"Does it matter?"

"Well—no, I guess not."

"Good. Flip down the bands that hold on the metal sheeting and remove the bricks, then. The bloom is around twenty-five kilos, and ye'll want the bricks clear before ye try to lift it."

Crystal did as instructed, using a large pair of tongs Angus handed her to remove each of the bricks and set them aside. He told her to hurry once: "Ye don't want the bloom cooling too much." When she got it down to just one row of bricks, Angus signaled for her to watch him as he first used a huge iron beam to pound down into the smelter several times, and then forcefully pried something away from the bottom bricks, going around the circle and levering the mass away. Finally he stopped and handed Crystal the tongs. "It's all yours, lass."

Crystal noticed then that all hammering had stopped. She glanced around and saw all eyes on her. Reaching down into the white crucible, she felt more than saw a massive movable lump and latched onto it. She lifted, and it just rolled to the side. She tried again, and it moved obstinately away. Growling in frustration, she put the tongs around the mass, squeezed as hard as she could, and lifted.

It was heavy.

She was lifting her bloom, she realized with a grin. All the work she had put into the never-ending motion of the bellows, all the charcoal shovels, all went into this piece of—something—she was lifting from the smelter. She squeezed the tongs even tighter and lifted the white-hot mass out of the smelter, grinning. Angus motioned for her to set it down on his anvil and hold onto it with the tongs, and she followed his instructions carefully. One other smith joined with Angus as they used sledgehammers to beat on the bloom she had pulled out. She saw what looked like parts falling away; Crystal considered objecting but decided that the men must know what they were doing.

"It's cooled," the other smith said after a few minutes, and the hammering stopped. He gave Crystal a dark glare before heading back to his anvil, a look both Crystal and Angus caught. Once all the smiths but Angus had bent over their projects once again, Crystal asked loudly, "What's next?" and added more softly, "And what's his problem?"

Angus winked and answered the first question. "Now we cut the bloom. First we heat it back up, so toss it in the fire there," he said, pointing to the main fire in the forge. Crystal did as he instructed, once again admiring the heft of the bloom she had created. It had to weigh fifty or more pounds, she thought.

"What was all the beating on it for?" Crystal asked as they watched the iron heat up.

"Does two things," Angus said. "First, the slag that was around it in the fire had to be beaten off it. Second, the beating settles the ore down, gets rid of any air pockets, and kind of mixes all of the good stuff inside it together to make it what we call wrought iron, which we can later work into tools or turn into steel."

The short explanation opened more questions than it answered for Crystal. Deciding to start with the simplest, she asked, "What is slag?"

Angus turned over the bloom in the fire again before answering. "Slag's all of the stuff that's in the fire that's not iron or carbon. The iron ore never really melts, as ye could feel when ye stirred it. Instead, it makes a hot goop that settles to the bottom. As ye stirred it, the stuff that wasn't iron was displaced upward by the weight of the goop, and it became the slag. It's important to beat it off the iron; ye can't forge an axe head out of dirt or wood ashes."

Crystal realized she enjoyed watching the smith field her questions. He normally was a big, smiling, simple man, but when answering a question his love for the craft showed on his face as his expression took on a radiance that was both serious and joyful. It reminded her of how Matt looked when she visited his classroom or when he was explaining something scientific or historic to the girls.

"Oh," he added, "don't talk about slag back in the village. It has a slang meanin' too, one 'at's not too polite."

"Okay, got it. So, I know I will sound ignorant when I ask this next question, but I always thought iron and steel were two different things. How do you make steel out of iron?"

Angus snorted and once again turned the bloom. He looked at her. "Yeah, that's a rookie question, alright. Steel is iron, mainly. Pure iron has no carbon in it, but that's impossible to get. The bloom you made is wrought iron, with a touch of carbon in it. It's easy to work and solid for building, but it's not hard enough to keep a fine edge for long. Our trick is to add a little carbon to make it into steel. The carbon changes the way the molecules fit together, and thus at just the right amount of carbon, it becomes solid and workable but able to hold an edge."

"Can it get too much carbon in it?"

"Absolutely, though we can't do that here. Wouldn't want to, anyway. Back home, the big industrial setups smelted iron into pig iron with a very high carbon content because of how hot they got the ore. Their task after that was to remove carbon from it, instead of adding it, to get to steel, because pig iron is just a big lump of metal that breaks when you hit it hard. But here, we work on small scale projects, mostly one of a kind stuff, so doing it the old-fashioned way makes sense."

"There," he said, and pointed to the bloom that was once again glowing white-hot. "Pull it out and put it atop the anvil." She did, and he took a stout axe from the wall and held it to the bloom. "We're gonna cut it now, by which I mean ye're gonna cut it now, which means ye take the sledge and hit the cutter to drive it through. Watch how I move the cutter as ye do it, but be as careful as ye can be with yer aim. Don't take a big swing, lass," Angus warned as Crystal started to wind up. "Ye really don't want to miss, not at all."

Crystal took a test swing, hammer contacting the wide top of the cutter's head. She swung harder, her hammer pushing the cutter edge down into the bloom. Angus whooped in appreciation, and his praise made Crystal smile. She worked in earnest at beating on the cutter, which Angus kept moving every few strokes in order to press a crease all the way across the iron bloom. Soon Crystal saw the glow of heat start to fade, and Angus put the bloom back in the fire.

It took several heating and hammering cycles, but Crystal and Angus got the bloom cut down into four similar-sized lumps. While they worked they spoke little, but they shared stories of their past while watching the bloom heat back up. Crystal noticed the smith who had glared at them earlier continue to cast gloomy looks her way, but she ignored the glares for the time being. They took turns beating the four lumps into rough bar shapes, and then stacked them against the wall in a stack of similar bars.

"Ye left a charcoal stack startin', didn't ye?" Angus asked after they had put away their tools and cleaned up the area, and Crystal nodded and explained that on her last trip the mound hadn't been billowing smoke yet.

"Well, it's probably smokin' by now, so let's go tidy that up."

They left the forge, and Crystal was glad for the change. She had grown accustomed to the noise and the heat quickly, and so the evening air felt downright chilly in comparison. Angus smirked at her involuntary shiver. "Feels good, doesn't it, lass?" She nodded; it was an invigorating feeling. They set out down the path toward the woodpile.

"Why was that other guy glaring at me?" Crystal asked Angus as they walked.

"Henry? I'm not sure. Probably just not pleased at yer gender. Women's lib is all well and good, but there's still a fair number of smiths who believe strongly that swinging a hammer all day is man's work. I used to be one of 'em, in fact, in my younger days. I've seen ye work, though, and ye've earned yer spot so far, woman or no, in my book. But it'll take months, or even years, to wiggle into some people's good graces, and maybe never into some. We can ask Henry if that's true tonight at dinner; I doubt he'll react badly in the group."

"Let's do that, then. On a different note, why do we bother with charcoal instead of regular coal? Did you use charcoal where you worked before the cataclysm?"

"No, we didn't. Charcoal, as ye can see, eats up trees at a massive rate. That's why the industrial world switched to coal as soon as it was discovered. Well, that, and the amount of effort it takes somebody like you to make charcoal. But we're a small smithy here, with a minimal impact on the forestation, and charcoal is better to work with besides. Steel slides over charcoal as though it was silk, while coal roughs up the blanks if ye're not careful. Ye'll see how good charcoal is to work with soon enough."

They arrived at the clearing to see thick smoke billowing from the hole in the top of the mound. "Nice work," Angus said, and Crystal grinned again in spite of herself; she was tired of grinning like a schoolgirl every time they said something nice to her. Still, this was a much more pleasant experience, despite the hard work, than what Apollo had put her through.

Crystal climbed up the outside of the pile a little and pressed the top closed. She patted it down hard until no more smoke came out, and then looked at Angus, a question on her face.

Angus went around the hillock, surveying Crystal's efforts critically, and after a full circuit proclaimed them satisfactory. "Ye'll want to come out every few hours, now," he added, "and make sure there's no smoke coming out of any new holes. If a hole develops and lets air in, yer charcoal will turn to ash, and that'll be no good for anything but soap-making. Anyway, it's a fine pile, and in a few days there should be plenty of charcoal to bring to the forge."

"Excellent. So, back to the forge we go?"

"No, lass, it's too late to begin another project tonight. We'll go back to the village and give ye some time to relax and chat with that husband of yours."

"As much as I love a chance to chat with my husband, that's not going to get me in trouble with Hephaestus, is it? I don't want him to think I'm slacking."

Angus started back to the village, Crystal following, and then he answered. "Lass, I can't imagine anybody who's seen ye work might think ye're slackin'. But more than that, a smith's life is like this. The projects we work on aren't five-minute quickies. They're typically done over the course of hours. Ye have to manage yer time. If ye get into something that will take a few hours just before dinnertime, ye're gonna be eatin' cold bread and meat or nothing at all. Sometimes we end up workin' very late, and sometimes we end up breakin' a little early."

"So what's on the schedule for tomorrow?"

"Dunno. That's for the Master to decide."

"Well, I appreciate your help learning his lessons of today."

"It's my pleasure. I used to teach classes at secondary schools around Aberdeen. I heard a quote once: by learnin' ye will teach, by teachin' ye will learn."

Crystal nodded and said, "Docendo discitur."

"Eh?"

"The original, as far as I know. A Latin phrase. 'Docendo discitur' is Latin for 'teaching others teaches yourself'."

"Oh. Ye speak Latin?" he said.

"I was a teacher by education and by profession for a while. That is the kind of pithy phrase they teach in teaching school. That, and I did take a semester of it. Long semester, that was."

Their strides had taken them to the village, and Crystal excused herself to go back to her room. She was missing her family greatly, she realized.

The blue shard crackled obediently to life as she called Matt's name. "Hey, love!" Matt's voice called out of it, and Crystal's heart sang at his cheerful greeting. "We sure have missed you." The girls joined in the greeting, delighting Crystal further.

They talked for a long time, of Crystal's new physical exploits, and Angus's jovial assistance, and the skillful healing Donna had administered. Crystal heard all about the twins' latest exploits with the boys. That foursome seemed to really be growing closer, and she worried whether, at the girls' age, she should still be assuming the time together was innocent fun. Soon the girls excused themselves to get ready for bed, leaving Matt and Crystal to speak alone.

"Matt?"

"Yes?"

"Something the girls just said…it's bedtime there?"

"Yes, it is. Why?"

"It's not quite dinnertime yet here."

"Of course. We're in different time zones, or at least what would have been called that before the cataclysm."

"The trips I've taken earlier just always seemed to be in the same time zone, so I just wasn't even considering a possible difference. Silly, I know. But Hephaestus told me that his estate is on the island of Sicily, so if you're several hours ahead of me—your estate isn't in the Western Hemisphere, is it?"

"No, love, there aren't a lot of truly inaccessible places over there, and when you can teleport anywhere instantly and recreate terrain pretty much at will, inaccessibility for others is the only real consideration."

"So I assume Apollo's estate is in roughly the same area?"

"Pretty much, yeah. Most of us are here. You're at the estate of the only major exception, and that's mostly because Hefe loves his volcano."

"So where's Olympus, relative to you? What time is it there?"

"It's not. Olympus is in an entirely different phase of existence, remember? It's always whatever time you wish it to be. Didn't we already talk about that?"

"Oh," Crystal said, digesting the new information. "Yeah, we did, I remember now. That was just such a stressful and amazing night, both at the same time, that I'd forgotten. Hey," she said, getting around to the subject that worried her, "should we be okay with letting the girls spend hours of unsupervised time with two slightly older boys? They're not little girls any more, and I—I just worry."

"Oh, I think it's still okay for now," Matt said with a chuckle. "I've been thinking the same thing, though, so I've already asked a couple of the thrakkoni to monitor them and let me know if they get too far away from everybody else."

"Great. So now we're spying parents."

"No, no. Spying would be watching everything they do. We're just monitoring, making sure I kinda sorta know where they are."

"You're rationalizing, Matt."

"Yeah, it's what dads do. I think."

The couple spent several more minutes talking over trivial matters of the estate. Crystal wasn't interested in the slightest in most of the details, but she loved hearing Matt's voice so much that it didn't matter what he was talking about. Finally, though, her stomach growled loudly enough for Matt to hear it across the link. He sent her to eat over her protests, reminding her that she needed to fuel her body for the work she was doing, and promising to be available later.

Crystal got to the dining hall late. She was glad to see that Angus and his family had saved her some food as well as a seat. She was also relieved that the smith who had glared at her all day was absent. "He ate and left, lass," Angus explained. "I talked to him a bit, as did some of the other boys, and we managed to convince him that ye deserve a spot in there as much as any man might. I think he'll be more civil toward ye tomorrow."

"So you were right, and he was just being sexist?"

"Traditionalist is more like it," Angus said. "It wasn't that long ago that a woman in a smithy would certainly be there to bring her man dinner and a beer. Matter of fact, back in those days, dinner and a beer would've likely been the same thing. It's not so much sexism as reality. In a simpler life like ours, everybody has an important role to play, and choosin' which role isn't always a luxury we can afford. Henry actually thought that yer bein' here might mean yer husband had to fetch for himself while ye played at men's work, as he called it, but I set him straight that yer husband, bein' the god of war and all, probably had hundreds of beautiful servants fetchin' dinner for him."

Crystal smiled at Angus's contrived image and corrected him. "Just one beautiful servant, actually. Sorscha is her name, and she's a pretty awesome thr... . Person."

"You were about to say thrakkona, weren't ye? She's one of those dragon humans ye told me about?"

Angus's son's ears perked up. "A dragon? Where?"

Donna shushed the boy, chuckling. "There's no dragons here. You'll have to grow up a bit before you learn to fight them, anyway." Her eyes measured Crystal's demeanor, and she said, "You look better tonight, sweetie, but you still owe it to me to take a bath in salts tonight or tomorrow morning. You won't forget, will ye?"

Crystal shook her head, though she was certain Donna hadn't been asking a question. She finished her dinner quickly, and downed another ale. *Man, this stuff is good,* she thought as she drank the last gulp. Angus passed her another small glass of whiskey, but she held it off. She'd have to be a lot worse off than she was tonight, she thought, to brave another sip of that liquid dirt. She excused herself, and ambled back to her room where she found a large towel and a small bag of salt crystals laid out on her bed. Smiling, she decided that a bath really would help deepen her sleep, so she ambled down to the bath, soaked her body in hot mineral-laden water until it cooled completely off, and then dried her refreshed body and returned to her room to settle in for a night of sleep.

Smithing II: Advanced

The next several days flew by. Crystal spent most of her time in the forge learning from Angus, Hephaestus always watching out of the corner of his eye. She smelted several more blooms, and learned how to hold and cut the blooms by herself, a task that took not only strength but also dexterity. After a few blooms were made and cut, Angus showed her how to convert the wrought iron to steel in a similar contraption by packing charcoal around the iron bars they had made and heating the mixture up. The smith also taught her what to look for in the cut to tell when the bloom had been made well, and he showed her how to gauge by color when the steel was ready.

Five days after Crystal had lit her first woodpile to make charcoal, Hephaestus ordered her to go make another. "You need the practice, and we need the charcoal," he said. "And Angus needs the time to work on his own projects, too." Angus, standing by his anvil, shrugged a rueful smile Crystal's direction and put a steel bar into the fire to begin.

Crystal surprised herself in the ease and speed with which she split the logs this time. She hadn't noticed the changes in her body, but now that she was swinging the maul again the difference was clear. Her muscles were already better toned than before, but more than that, her control over her own body was now more solid, more agile. She wasn't that much stronger, she proved to herself by trying and failing to lift a round that had denied her earlier as well, but the hours of pounding big and little sledgehammers in various situations left her significantly more aware of her body and its motions.

It only took Crystal and her new body a few hours to construct and cover the wood pile to burn. She stepped back, and, deciding to keep Hephaestus from having to come out, gathered a flow of fire to light it.

"What are you doing, Crystal?" Hephaestus's voice from behind her startled her into releasing the flow. She turned and wondered whether he had been behind watching the whole time or had teleported when he sensed her preparing to use magic.

"I was going to light it for you, Master, so that you didn't have to leave your project to do so," she said, smiling brightly.

"I'm glad you want to light it yourself," he said, crossing his arms across his chest, "since I want that too. But there's embers back at the forge to use for it. What I thought I saw was that you were about to take a shortcut."

Crystal bowed, knowing there was no point doing anything other than admitting what Hephaestus already knew and accepting whatever punishment he had in mind. "I was, Master, though I didn't think of it as a shortcut. Since the time I first learned to control the flows of magic, that's the way I've lit fires. I realize my error now, though, and won't do the same again."

Hephaestus grunted and nodded, accepting her explanation. "See that you don't. You're here to learn to work like a smith, not slack like a mage. Now go get some embers and start the fire the right way." Uncrossing his arms, he turned and tromped back down the path.

As the days passed, Crystal made two more piles of charcoal and harvested the charcoal out of the two she had already made. While she wasn't working over the woodpile, Angus showed her how to do other smithing tasks: drawing down a piece of ore, punching a hole, bending a rod, all things that Crystal would have imagined easy to do back when she could only picture machines doing this work. Now, though, she very much appreciated the effort, the skill, and the finesse that went into the art of forging a piece of iron into whatever shape was needed.

One night over dinner Angus commented on how quickly she was learning. She asked how long he had been an apprentice.

"There was no apprenticeship for me, lass. Most modern smiths learned the art the same way I did, I think. I took a class at a local trade school, and then I went to work for an oil company doin' it. In the very old days, it was different. Then, an apprentice would spend months just carrying water and charcoal for the journeymen and the master, and the apprentice'd be the one to start the fires and clean out the forges at night. After many months, maybe a year, he might get to swing at a piece of metal once or twice on an unimportant project like, say, a nail or a hairpin. What ye're doin' is more like the modern way than an apprenticeship."

Once Crystal had made, unmade, and remade the same short curved blade several times out of wrought iron, Angus brought out a piece she had made earlier that looked a little like the head of a splitting maul, only narrower and blunt-tipped. "I'm gonna teach ye one of the most challengin' things in smithin' now, but we'll start easy. That blade ye just made goes onto this head to form the head of a battle axe. It's too difficult to make the entire head out of a single piece of metal especially since the blade and the rest of the head need to be different hardnesses, so we make two separate pieces and weld them. Ye're gonna learn to weld now." He heated the end of the head and split the blunt spot where it would join the blade, pressing the newly-created flanges apart by a quarter inch.

Angus turned his attention to the forge, building up a huge and deep pile of charcoal. As he worked, he explained to Crystal the basic process of welding, which, he said, was much easier with two pieces of wrought iron than with any other metal or, especially, two dissimilar pieces of metal. He told Crystal how the pieces to be welded had to be heated to very hot, to where they glowed a yellowish color for wrought iron. A journeyman smith needed to know to heat other metals to different temperatures based on experience. Speed was crucial, since the pieces only stayed hot enough to weld for a short period of time. Patience was also vital, though, because heating the fire too fast would pump oxygen in faster than it burned up in the flames, and that would oxidize the surfaces to be welded, the oxygen then preventing a solid weld.

She nodded at his wisdom and went to fetch a couple more buckets of charcoal. When she returned, Angus put the two pieces onto the charcoal and covered them with several more inches of charcoal, directing Crystal to pump the bellows. She did, slowing down to the pace he described, and watched the fire slowly glow to life.

Angus used a rod to push a small hole through the fire to where the pieces must have been and tapped. He shook his head. Minutes later, he tapped again, and once again shook his head. The third time he tapped and twisted the rod, and then he smiled. He took over pumping the bellows to have Crystal tap the rod, and he pointed out as she was doing it that the rod stuck to the welding surface, thus proving it to be the right temperature. It was hard for Crystal to look; the heat seemed to burn through her eye all the way back into her brain. Still, she saw what he was talking about, and relinquished the rod to go back to pumping.

As she pumped the bellows deliberately, Angus explained the next steps in detail, saying that they had to flow quickly or else the weld would be ruined. Angus would take the part of the apprentice, grabbing the two pieces out of the fire with the tongs, and Crystal had to be ready to hit the two pieces hard with her hammer right at the join spot when Angus had them positioned. He pointed to the exact spot on the anvil where he would put them, cautioning her that he wouldn't actually set them down on the anvil for fear that its coldness would sap heat from the pieces.

"So when I say go, you stop pumpin', stand right there, and grab yer hammer and prepare to swing, all right?" Crystal nodded, feeling the tension and excitement of the moment. "Well, then, go!" Angus said, shoving the charcoal out of the way and grabbing each piece in a pair of tongs. He spun around and held the pieces together a few millimeters over the anvil, and Crystal was ready with a well-aimed blow. It was exhilarating, feeling the two pieces joining, and Crystal felt like leaping around the forge.

"Don't just stand there, lass!" Angus yelled, his voice whooping over all the noise in the forge. "Hit it again! Ye've joined them, now ye've got ta form the edges."

She did as he directed, her excitement building. Crystal hammered the new axe head over and over, watching her efforts smooth out the join between the two pieces and create a classic blade shape. He turned it over, and she beat the other side into the same basic shape.

She looked a question at Angus when she thought it was done, and he nodded. "Good job," he said, pride filling his voice. "Ye've done it."

Hephaestus appeared at her side with his own tongs and lifted the axe head, examining it on both sides. He took a small rounded hammer from his belt and tapped the weld several times, listening to the ringing sound each tap created. Setting it back down, he nodded appreciatively. "Aye, good job. Good job, both of you. Welding is tough to do, and it's even tougher to teach." The god slapped Angus on his shoulder in approval and then walked back to his forge and bent back over the piece he was working on.

"So, can I put a handle on that and take it home when I go? It's the first useful thing I've made here." Crystal said, holding up the axe head with tongs.

"I don't see why the Master would mind, but it's not ready yet. Ye've still gotta learn to harden it and temper the edge."

"Tempering is where we heat it up and quench it in the bucket, right?"

"Sort of. First thing first, though. Let's make a few more axe heads to make sure ye've got the work up to this point down."

They made half a dozen more axe heads, in a few different shapes, before Angus pronounced her ready for the next step. "Let's go make more iron bars while I talk, though," he said. "We can still do some work while I lecture, aye?"

They went back outside and around the forge, where Crystal noticed that more chunks of iron ore had been left. "Where do the chunks come from?" she asked Angus, wondering if he had ever considered the question.

He shrugged. "I assume the Master goes and gets them. Did ye know that he can teleport? Oh, of course ye did—it's how ye got here, isn't it?"

Crystal nodded and let the topic go. As they worked on crushing the ore with several apprentices Angus had called to help, Angus explained the science behind hardening and tempering and how, just as in welding, the appropriate temperatures and associated colors for each of the metals were different. He then went into the processes themselves and why they worked.

"Let me see if I have this down," Crystal said as his lecture wound down. Angus nodded and continued his task of rinsing off the crushed pieces of ore. "As we heat up wrought iron, it becomes Austenite, which is not only malleable enough for us to work it, but it's also receptive to the carbon that makes the iron stronger. Then if it cools down at a normal rate, the carbon atoms leave and it becomes iron again. But by quenching it quickly we make it into, um, Martensite, wasn't it?" Angus nodded. "And Martensite is much tougher than iron because of the carbon that's trapped in it." Angus nodded again. "I'm still not sure I get the part about body centered versus face centered."

"Have ye ever seen a stack o'cannon balls?" Angus asked, and when Crystal nodded he lifted the rinse screen out of the lye water and set it down to drip. He held up his fists to demonstrate. "Cannonballs stacked the normal way ye see them, with one row like this and the next offset, are in body centered cubic structure. It's a very tight, compact, and strong structure. That's Martensite. Take that same stack of cannonballs, though, and balance each one atop the one under it, and what do ye get?"

"Falling cannonballs," Crystal observed drily.

"Yeah. Yeah, exactly. But that's just due to the weight of each one. In a crystal structure, that's face centered structure as in Austenite. It's called tetragonal instead of cubic because one dimension is stretched a little, but ye get the idea. Face centered is more open, and a coarser structure. Body centered is tighter and stronger, and it's what we want when we're hardening the iron."

"So what's tempering?"

"Reversing the Martensite transformation. Softening the metal, in other words."

"Why would you do that?"

"An axe blade that's just regular iron will slowly deform as it's used. The same blade after ye harden it won't deform, but will instead break. By hardening most of the blade and tempering the edge, ye get a solid axe head with an edge that slowly deforms and can be re-sharpened."

"So you heat the edge back up and let it cool normally, then."

"Sort of. It's a bit of a trick since the edge is still connected to the rest of the blade."

"I see," Crystal said.

Angus explained how tempering could be done in several different ways, sometimes by heating the whole piece up from the edge farthest from the cutting blade, and sometimes by quenching just the edge and allowing the heat to spread back into it. They rinsed the ore they were working on with clear water and set it into the hopper to dry, and then walked back into the forge.

"Now, ye try it with the first axe head you made," Angus said. "It's wrought iron, so just use a dull red temperature as the temperature to heat it to. Quench the cutting blade, then allow it to re-heat to a blue-ish color, and then quench the whole head."

Crystal did as instructed, working carefully. She finally thrust the whole head into the quenching bucket and pulled it out, and Hephaestus, whom she hadn't heard come up, pulled it from her hands and looked at it closely.

"Another nice job," the god said, nodding his appreciation for the second time that day. "A few dozen of these, and you'll be ready for some real smith work. Capital job, Angus," he said, and then returned to his own anvil.

Crystal and Angus called it a day, returning to the village for dinner. Crystal was rapidly becoming fond of Donna as the woman's matter-of-fact attitude and quick wit won her over. As usual, dinner was a hearty fare of meat and potatoes washed down with ale. Crystal again asked if she could help with the dishes or with the food preparation the next day, and once again Donna refused her. "Your place is in the forge, darling. We all have a job to do. You do yours, and I'll do mine, and the rest of the village will do theirs."

The next several days Crystal made more axe heads, the first bunch out of wrought iron entirely. Angus explained the difference between working with steel and working with the iron, and then gave her her first experience welding steel to iron. It didn't work; Hephaestus glanced over and shook his head. Angus, seeing the god's response, shrugged. He took the axe head, put the hole over a spike he had inserted in the anvil's hardy hole, and smacked the top end of the blade with his hammer. It detached neatly from where it had appeared solidly welded, and Crystal was chagrined to watch it hit the floor.

"Close, but the temperature wasn't right," Angus said. "Ye tested the one piece, but not the other. Try it again." Crystal realized she had erred in assuming that if the two pieces were the same color, and thus the same temperature, they were both at the welding point. Angus had warned her, she admitted to herself, and now she had seen first-hand what he had meant.

Her second attempt was successful and drew a satisfied nod from the god at his forge. Crystal whispered to Angus, "How does he know it's a good weld from over there?"

"I have the ears of a god, and I've been doing this for millennia," Hephaestus answered her from his forge without even turning to look at her.

Angus shrugged, a mischievous grin on his face as he picked up a rod from the stock she had used to make the blade. "Ye've got to harden differently because it's a different metal." He held the end of the rod in the fire, heating it till the end was glowing white. He held it up in front of her and pointed out the variations in color, telling her to remember where they were. She nodded, and he plunged the rod into the quenching bucket. He laid the rod across the anvil with its end sticking out and hit it, breaking a half-inch piece off. "See? Coarse structure," he said, and then repeated the break a little farther down. "See? Still coarse structure." He repeated until the break became significantly different. "See the fine structure at the break? That's Martensite. Remember the color it was here?" She nodded, and he continued, "Ye need to heat the blade to the same color, then, to harden it. Heat it too much, and ye'll make it brittle like ye saw at the end."

"There's a lot to know to get this right."

"That's why it takes years of experience, Crystal."

Crystal followed his directions, first by heating the blade to the correct color, and then by quenching the edge, and after letting the edge warm back up before quenching the entire axe head. Hephaestus came over this time and pronounced her work perfect. He explained, still looking at the blade, "A good smith can hear when a weld goes bad. But all quenches sound the same, so I have to look at it. This is a good hardening and tempering job. You're progressing extremely quickly."

Crystal's chest swelled with pride as she turned back to work. She noticed that Henry had been casting looks her way that were more admiring than resentful, one of which he directed at her now. "So now what?" she asked Angus.

"Now ye do it again, lass. Ye've got to make enough of these that yer body knows how to do it without yer brain being involved."

She launched herself at the task, and over the next few days brought two dozen axe heads of various compositions into the world, creating another charcoal burn hill during that time as well. Angus showed her the different types of steel available to them in the forge, explaining the differences in his easy-going lecturing fashion to her. He turned his nose up at the topic of stainless steel, a metal that a group of people who knew how to take care of metal didn't need much of, he opined. They had a wide variety of alloys available in the forge, though some required heat and processing that couldn't be obtained with their limited equipment unless Hephaestus himself stepped in. The smiths, and their families as well, loved the god, she learned. He was all things to them: ruler, disciplinarian, healer, teacher, and most often a hands-on co-worker.

After making the axe heads and a few standard short swords, she spent another tired evening in the dining hall and took another mineral bath. Though her muscles had long since stopped protesting and, in fact, were shaping up very well in the mirror when Crystal had a vanity moment and flexed them, she still enjoyed her nighttime soaks greatly. Afterward, she settled into her bed and had a long and loving conversation with Matt, whom she realized she hadn't seen in nearly a month. She loved him greatly, and missed his soft touch, but she was also invigorated by the physical and mental changes she was going through, and she told him that. They exchanged their good night wishes and closed the link, and Crystal settled her head into the pillow to sleep.

Her head popped back up as she heard a rustling noise outside. It was the first noise outside her room she had heard since she got to the village, she realized, and so she quietly rose and peeked out the window. A little donkey was nibbling on the bush just outside.

She spent several moments gazing, mesmerized by the cuteness of the scene presented through the window, before its impossibility struck her. She was, after all, inside a volcano. With dragons, at that. Where would a donkey have come from, and how would it not have been eaten for dinner already?

Crystal dressed quickly and stepped out of her room. The donkey looked over its shoulder at her and nickered quietly. The animal then began walking, following the tree line around the village and back toward the forge. The donkey kept a slow and steady pace, walking purposefully just ahead of her as though leading her somewhere.

Arriving at the forge, the donkey touched the leather flap hanging over the entrance and walked a few feet away. Crystal looked at the donkey to see if it was headed anywhere else, but it just looked at her and then at the flap. She shrugged and then entered the forge quietly.

Hephaestus was there alone. He gave no indication of seeing her, but instead continued beating on a project. He held it up head-high, and though most of it was still hidden by the god's massive body, Crystal could see the head of what must be a war hammer. Crystal guessed from the fact that a pair of tongs were laying haphazardly on the floor to the right-handed smith's right side that he had just finished welding something, likely the face of the hammer to the body since she knew that the faces of hammers were often made of different steel than the body.

"Can you see flows of ka?" Hephaestus asked, still closely examining the head of the hammer.

"Yes," Crystal said simply, walking over to the smith's side.

"Figured you could. The Mother wouldn't'a sent you to me if you couldn't at least do some basic magic. None of my apprentices can even see elemental magic flows, which is just fine by me, but the wife of Ares might wish to see how this is done."

Crystal watched closely as Hephaestus, satisfied with his welding work, set the hammer's head down on the face of the anvil. He picked up the pair of tongs on the floor and put both pairs away neatly, and then took out his smith's hammer and a chisel.

The god bent over the piece and began striking a pattern into the iron at the center of the head of the hammer. As he worked, he hummed, and Crystal saw tendrils of white essence swirl around the project. His fingers moved nimbly over the surface, directing the sharp chisel to inscribe a sort of rolling design. The magic, on the other hand, was doing something entirely different; first, what looked like individual strands of essence wove together into a rough fabric and then settled into the hammer's head. Crystal opened her mind further and realized she could sense the purpose of the spells; the current weave was for self-healing for the hammer in case it got dented or broken. Another spell that looked like a large infinity symbol embedded itself inside; Crystal sensed that it was there to require the hammer to return to its owner.

The hum changed pitch, and Crystal watched tendrils of magic start at the hammer's head and slowly wrap around and make a handle. It looked to Crystal like the handle was actually grow-ing out of the head as it formed.

Hephaestus finished the pattern he was working on and stopped humming. The glow of magic surrounding the hammer faded away, leaving in its place a beautiful but ordinary-looking hammer.

"You'd think that a magic hammer would glow," Crystal said.

"The guys with the glowing hammers are always the first tar-gets of archers on the battlefield, dearie," Hephaestus said. "'Glowing' is therefore usually the least popular enchantment of the ones I offer."

"Why did you hum?"

Hephaestus turned toward her, hammer held out in his hands. She took the hammer from him and admired his work up close as he said, "It's how I connect with the essence. I was a smith for so long that it proved impossible at first to un-focus enough to touch ka. Have you reached the point where you can touch it yet?" She nodded. "Figured. It wasn't happening for me till I started working and humming one day, and suddenly then I was able to form whatever weaves I wanted."

Crystal nodded absently, looking at the beautiful curved han-dle made out of what appeared to be a dark wood but was as hard as stone. "Ironwood," the smith said. "There's a lot of trees called black ironwood and white ironwood and southern iron-wood and Irish ironwood, but true ironwood can only be grown from the essence of magic. It makes a handle that'll never break or loosen. Go ahead, swing it."

She did, experimentally at first and then harder. Curious, she hefted an iron bar onto the anvil and brought the hammer down on it. She lifted the hammer, amazed—the iron had been flat-tened.

"Throw it at Angus's anvil."

She aimed and threw the hammer, and it knocked the anvil right over onto its side...and then disappeared. She blinked at her hand; the hammer was in it again. She had watched the enchantment and knew it would happen, but actually feeling the hammer return jarred her senses.

"Wow. How often do you make a special project like this?"

"Nearly every project I do is special in one way or another. I've got journeymen to do the boring stuff, after all. I get requests from the other gods all the time, and when I'm not filling one of those I'm usually making something special for myself."

"So whose hammer is this to be, Master?" Crystal asked, marveling at the beauty of the design on the side and the overall heft and craftsmanship of the hammer.

"Yours, dearie. You've done a lot for us around here, and this is meant to thank you. You've still got an awful lot to learn if you ever want to be a master smith, but I think that your time here will be coming to an end soon. I sent my projection to bring you here so you could watch me enchant your new hammer."

The reality of Hephaestus's words sank in slowly as Crystal's eyes followed the beautiful wavy scrollwork inscribed into the new hammer. Her new hammer. Finally she looked up, tears just beginning to form in her eyes. "Did you say mine? This is—beautiful. It's amazing. I love it! Thank you, Master." She moved over and hugged Hephaestus as firmly as she could.

"Alright, lass, now I'm a god and so I can handle it, but before you go unleashing that hug on anyone else, keep in mind how much all this good hard work has changed your muscle composition," Hephaestus said, chuckling, as he disconnected himself from her arms. "And while you're busy flexing those muscles, go pick that anvil back up."

She obeyed, righting the anvil onto its base. Hephaestus was right; before she had come to the smithy, she wasn't certain she could have lifted the anvil at all. She smiled at him and flexed her arms playfully.

"Yes, you're stronger, dearie. Now quit acting like Stacy."

The words hit Crystal like a bucket of ice water. She struck a neutral pose and gripped her hammer. "Have any other people come through your forge on the way to becoming a god or goddess?"

Hephaestus shook his head. "Nope. Not mine to tell that. Then again, the rise to goddess status is a bit decentralized. Better to ask your husband."

"I'm going to have to fight her, aren't I?"

Hephaestus peered at her intently before answering, "You'll have to prove your worth. Whether that means fighting Stacy or not isn't mine to say."

Crystal sighed and then hefted her new hammer again. "So, why a hammer?"

"You mean as opposed to a long sword or a mace or a flail?"

She nodded and added, "Or a splitting maul or a garden rake or a really excellently-made butter knife, for that matter."

He snorted. "Your husband can conjure butter knives all day long, and so, I think, can you. Once you leave here you'll never look at a splitting maul again, I bet, and a garden rake is a tool for thrakkon to use back in your world, right? As for what type of weapon, I just think you're more a hammer person. Swords are fine but they get pretty messy in combat, and to be a sword or dagger master you have to work on the skill for years. Hammers, though, can be used effectively with relatively little training. Maces and flails are, to me, barbaric instruments of head-bashing, and not very ladylike at all. I just think that a hammer is the weapon that fits you best."

"Well, thank you, again. I will cherish this hammer."

"You're welcome. And no, I didn't make Stacy a hammer."

"How did you know I was wondering that?"

"I guess well."

"So what did you make for her?"

"Nothing. She was a bitch. And she played me, the same way she apparently played Matthew and—others. You're so opposite her, it's refreshing."

"I appreciate your telling me that. I think, though, that I need to get some sleep if I'm going to get up and work in the morning. I'm not a god who can keep going indefinitely without rest."

Hephaestus nodded and walked over to the metal stock. "Good night and good dreams, Crystal."

Crystal cradled her new hammer possessively all the way back to her room, where she stowed it carefully in her wardrobe cabinet, climbed back out of her clothes, slid into the covers, and immediately fell asleep.

Home Again

Crystal woke the next day and returned to work, telling no one about the god's gift the night before. She really didn't want to seem his favorite, for one thing, but she also wasn't certain how much he wanted his journeymen to know about his magic. Regardless, it was his to tell. She went back to task, then, learning to forge swords. Angus introduced her to the task of combining different types of steel into the same blade. A simple sword, he showed, had a core of iron sandwiched between layers of springy steel so that the blade remained light and supple while being able to hold an edge. He told her of a type of steel called Wootz steel, which was usually approximated by folding two types of metal together many times, but the actual manufacture of which was legendary and extremely complex. He shrugged off most of her questions, explaining that bladesmiths typically specialized for years on the topic, and that he wasn't one, and that she couldn't hope to be one till she had practiced the basic blacksmithing skills for a few more years first. Finally she gave up and went back to the clearing to split wood.

She finished the work in just a few hours, and so she ended up back in the forge before lunch. She looked around to see what project to work on next, and then she came to a decision.

"You were right, Master," she said.

Hephaestus stopped his work and turned around, nodding once. "Indeed. You have come as far as you can without actually becoming a smith, and that's not what your path holds for you, is it?"

She shook her head. Angus, sensing the importance of the conversation, walked over. "What's up?"

Crystal looked up at the barrel-chested smith whose acceptance, and whose wife's massaging fingers, had made her entry into his world so bearable. This was the hardest part, she thought. "The time has come for me to return home, Angus," she said softly.

Angus nodded briskly, his face neutral. "We knew the time would come, aye? It's been a right pleasure teachin' ye and workin' beside ye, but ye have a family and an estate to get home to. Servants and mythical creatures and all, I guess. Ye're goin' to wait till tonight so we can all say goodbye, aren't ye?"

"I will," Crystal nodded. "I'd love to have one last round with all of you. You're such amazingly good people."

"I need to go back to the village, Master, and let the women know to plan an event, then," Angus said. "Crystal, are ye coming back with me? I don't think ye have any projects undone to finish up, do ye?"

Crystal shook her head. "Master, is it all right if I go exploring a bit?"

"I should probably go with you," Hephaestus said. "There are some dangerous areas. Nothing you can't handle if you know they're coming, but I'd hate for you to get surprised. Besides, there are some places I need to visit that I haven't been to in a while, and on top of that, it's my pleasure to escort the wife of my friend Ares around my humble estate."

They stepped out of the forge, Crystal following Hephaestus closely. They continued through the clearing where the iron ore was processed into the tree line beyond. As they walked, Crystal started feeling uncomfortable. At first she felt itchy, but soon her stomach was upset and her sinuses were hurting too.

Hephaestus stopped and spun around, but she was paying so much attention to her discomfort that she missed it and walked into him. "Can't you see the wards?" he asked.

Crystal looked, unfocusing as much as she could, and saw the wards spread out in a wall a few feet in front of her. "Uh huh." She sniffled as her nose began to run.

"So neutralize them in a zone around your body. It should be easy for you."

She was surprised she hadn't thought of that herself, but she found it awfully hard to use the mental tricks necessary to grab the essence of magic while her stomach was tying itself in knots.

"It might be easier if you stepped back several feet, but then again, doing it here is a useful exercise," he observed. "You won't always be in ideal conditions to use magic, and it won't do to lose a battle because you're feeling sniffly and weak at the time."

Crystal nodded, and then thought back to her time in the itchy robe during Apollo's test. She had concentrated there, and that robe was far worse than the wards she was facing now. The thought brought her new confidence, in the midst of which she drew in a calm breath, unfocused her attentions once again, and grabbed the threads of magical essence that were swirling around her. She recognized the patterns pressed outward by Hephaestus's wards, and assumed that casting her own identical patterns would neutralize his. It worked; as each pattern she cast snapped into place in a small area around her, one of the discomforts slipped away into her memory. Soon she was standing comfortably again, able to see the wall and its wards but no longer being tortured by them.

"You know, you've got to learn to think of these things yourself if you're going to be one of us," Hephaestus said drily. He turned on his heels and continued walking toward the wall. Crystal followed, chagrined and silent.

They stepped through the wall, and Crystal gasped at the complete change of scenery. Where there had been lush trees and bushes, there were now dark rocks. Beautiful blue sky was now black cave ceiling. Worse, the green ground carpeted in thick grass was now bare rock that shimmered in heat; Crystal felt it immediately through her boots. She looked at Hephaestus, who was glaring at her with an expectant eyebrow raised.

"Oh, duh. Magic," she said, and built a flow of air beneath her soles that raised her millimeters above the ground and insulated her against the heat.

"Not the ideal solution, but better," he said, and then motioned behind her.

Crystal turned and gaped. From this side, it was obvious they had been living in an illusion. She could see the piles of ore and equipment set up to process it. She saw, a little farther away, the forge building, and past that was the wood pile. The village itself was a bit farther down and was partially concealed behind a rock outcropping.

"I like the illusion much better," Crystal said.

"Of course you do," Hephaestus replied. "Come, let's see the thrakkoni." They walked farther down, finally rounding another outcropping and entering a second lobe of the cavern. In it were huts, and a group of thrakkoni milled around. As they approached, a few rose and came over to greet the god.

"Master," the largest thrakkon, a male with glistening gold hair, said, "is everything all right?"

"Absolutely," Hephaestus said. "I'm just showing a friend around. Is anybody up top?"

"Not at the moment, but I was thinking of heading up to eat soon, and a few others will likely go with me."

"Well, I won't keep you then. Thank you, and good hunting."

The thrakkon nodded. He walked back over to the camp, removed his clothes, and then walked out onto the ledge. He transformed into a huge gold dragon and lifted up, flying straight up faster than Crystal would have thought possible. Some others, including a silver as large as Sorscha as well as a massive red dragon, followed.

Crystal watched with interest. "Don't their feet get hot like mine?" she asked Hephaestus.

"You must work on that goddess knowledge, dearie. Thrakkoni are cold-blooded."

"I knew that already, but what does that have to do with their feet?"

"In their case, it means they don't feel temperature variances. They're just as comfortable in a hundred degrees below zero as they are in several hundred degrees above. They were made to withstand those temperatures, so why should they be uncomfortable in them?"

"So a fireball doesn't touch them because it's magic, but its heat doesn't touch them either?"

"Right. Why, were you thinking of casting a fireball at my thrakkoni?"

"No, just thinking back to a battle I watched some time ago."

"Oh. Okay, I guess that goes with being the wife of Ares. So, are you ready to head back into comfort?"

"This is comfort now, isn't it?" Crystal said with a wicked smile.

Hephaestus smiled, tipping his head. "Well done, lass. But I suspect you want to get back to the party area before it happens."

She nodded, and they walked back through the wall and into the Scottish forest of Hephaestus's illusion.

The party that night was nothing especially grand, but Crystal was touched more than she ever would have thought possible. The women pulled out not only a cake but also all sorts of sweets, and the whole village joined together to sing and dance. Hephaestus himself even jumped in.

Crystal managed, over the course of the party, to say farewell to all. Even Henry wished her well. She would truly miss these people, she realized as the evening wore down.

Hephaestus accompanied her back to her room to get the blue shard and her new hammer. She turned and wrapped her arms around his neck. "Thank you, Master. You've taught me so many things."

The god smiled back at her. "You've been a grand pupil, Crystal. Whatever happens in the coming days, I wish you well. Now, time to get back to your family. Ready?"

Crystal nodded, and after the lurch found herself back in Matthew's throne room. Matt rushed up to her, pulling her into a hug. "I've missed you so much, my love," he said into her hair.

"I've missed you too," Crystal said, squeezing her husband. He pulled away and felt her arms.

"Impressive musculature. Quite sexy. Adds to your other charms." He stepped away and leered at her body from neck to shin and back.

She smiled and held out her new hammer. He took it gently, holding it up in the light in front of him, looking closely at both sides silently for several long moments. When he finally opened his mouth, the first thing he did was whistle in admiration. "Love, the work of Hephaestus is prized among the gods, and this looks to be one of his best pieces. It might even rival Thor's hammer." He stepped away from her, turned and swung the hammer in a figure eight in front of him. The god of war flowed through several martial poses, each time bringing the hammer around rapidly. Crystal was amazed to hear the air actually whistle as the heavy hammer's head pressed it aside at high speeds. Finally Matt turned and nodded, reverently returning the hammer to Crystal. "Did you watch him inscribe this for you?"

"I did, last night," she said. "How do you know he inscribed it for me, though?"

"It's what he wrote. This writing font is an ancient script that we gods still use when we're writing something impressive or when we're trying to screw with humans. I suspect he meant it the first way, of course. It says 'For the beautiful and mighty goddess Crystal.' If you ever get the chance, don't show this to Thor, by the way. It'll probably piss him off, as stunningly as it rivals Mjolnir."

Crystal thought back to when she had met the giant whom Matt had introduced as Thor in Olympus. No matter how much stronger she felt now than she had been then, she still didn't imagine she wanted to see Thor pissed off.

"I'll take your word for it, Matt."

She looked in his eyes for several more long moments, and then she leaped into his arms. They continued their tight embrace as he carried her down the stairs into their bedroom, stopping first to remove her clothes and then gently laid her in the soft bed she had missed so much. He stood over her, looking down at her naked body lying in front of him, and shook his head. "An amazing transformation, Love," he purred. "You have always been the most beautiful lady in my world, but now you have a power and agility about you that take my breath away." He pulled off his own clothes, ripping his shirt off of his torso, exposing a muscular frame that Crystal hadn't seen since her twenties.

Crystal saw the tendrils of energy passing around his body as the clothes came off but had missed the actual composition of the spell. She cataloged it away as something useful to learn for later, but for now, she really didn't care. She was finally back home and in bed with her lover, and she wanted him as badly as he obviously wanted her.

It was a magical night, literally. Matt wove a symphony of energy around Crystal's body, adding nerve stimulation atop physical stimulation to carry her to heights she had never felt. Crystal, in turn, experimented with her lover's body, attempting the same effects. Once it sent the god of war into a fit of giggles, but he good-naturedly instructed her in how to do it properly, and she eventually succeeded in arousing him to new heights as well. Belatedly she remembered how tiring wielding the essence of magic could be as she collapsed into his arms, physically and emotionally spent from the mutual pleasuring.

She woke to the quiet whisper of slippered feet on the floor. She felt Matt's strong arms still around her body and smiled contentedly, happy that her lover was still in bed with her, and then the sound she had heard caught up with her thoughts. She opened her eyes and sat up quickly. It was Sorscha, she saw, carrying a tray of food.

Matt sat up and chuckled. "Good morning. I let Sorscha know you were home, and she wanted to bring you breakfast in bed this morning as a welcome home present."

"Oh—why, thank you," Crystal said, and then remembered what she had promised herself to talk to Sorscha about. "Oh, Sorscha, did you know that the followers of Hephaestus don't even know that thrakkoni exist? That the god of the forge keeps his servants outside of the illusion in a nook in the volcano?"

Matt chuckled. "The only variance this cycle is the illusion. Most of the time the followers of Hephaestus are from a warmer climate and get to live in the volcano with him."

Sorscha also chuckled, a dry throaty sound from a thrakkon. "His servants are, I assume, well taken care of and comfortable. My race was created to withstand a much greater temperature range than yours, Crystal."

Crystal nodded and said, "That's pretty much what he told me." Her senses were waking up too, and Eggs Benedict made her mouth water. She dove in.

When she finished with breakfast, Sorscha took the tray and walked out, leaving the door open. The girls ran in excitedly and leapt in bed with their mother, both starting to talk at the same time.

Matt laughed and joked that he was no longer the star of the conversation, so he needed to leave. Crystal panicked momentarily as he threw off the sheets and rose, but she again saw a flash of energy just prior to the movement, and Matt rose with pajamas covering his frame. He left the room, leaving Crystal to the incessant questioning of her daughters. Crystal spent several minutes answering, and then asked a few of her own, trying to determine the extent of the girls' involvement with the boys.

"Where's Matt?" Crystal asked Sorscha when the girls finally finished their inquisition and left.

"Down in the sorcerer's chamber," Sorscha answered. "He's working with the new initiates."

"Thank you," Crystal said. She rose and put on the clothes Sorscha laid out for her and marveled at how nice it could be to have a servant when compared with the last several weeks she had spent in the village. She also noticed that the blouse fit a lot more snugly than she remembered.

"You probably can't tell, Crystal, but your physique has changed quite a bit," Sorscha said, noticing the way Crystal was moving her shoulders around in the shirt. "You have well-defined muscles in your shoulders where there used to be no hint of any. Your back is also wider by a couple of inches. The transition is quite impressive, and I'm sure the Master approves."

Crystal grinned wickedly, remembering Matt's expressions of approval the night before. She flexed playfully at Sorscha, and in that motion noticed muscle tone on herself that she hadn't seen before. "Wow. You're right that I didn't notice it as it was forming. I was moving too much, always hammering or smashing or splitting something. But now, yeah. Yeah. I just have to figure out how to keep it."

"Come with me, then," Sorscha said and led her through the sitting room into a side room she hadn't seen before. "There was nobody in the suite to this side, and so the Master took away one of its rooms and made a workout room for you. I helped him find some equipment to recycle." It was quite a room, Crystal saw, complete with barbells and workout machines. Crystal imagined that there must be thousands of abandoned gyms around whose owners wouldn't care one way or another what had happened to their equipment.

Remembering the change she had seen Matt undergo last night, she looked down at her own leg briefly. She touched the thigh with magic and smiled as the muscles bulked up even further. She touched the muscles again and watched them return to the size they had been.

She thanked Sorscha again and left, taking the halls toward the sorcerer's chamber. She didn't go in, though, instead opening the hidden door to the side and going into the war room. For the first time, she devoted her attention to the arsenal along the side wall. She had never really noticed that it contained several types of hammers: one with a broad head and short spike and handle like hers, and others with longer handles and narrower heads. She took each one off the wall, swinging it experimentally to feel the differences.

Wanting to see them in action, she chose two figures that looked like medieval knights from the desk and brought them to being. "Stop!" she said forcefully to prevent them going at each other with their already-equipped swords, and when they obeyed she handed each a type of hammer.

"My lady," the knight to whom she had handed the longest-handled hammer said, surprising Crystal in his ability to speak, "I shall fight with whatever weapon you deem most suitable, but you must know this hammer puts me at a disadvantage in close combat."

Oh, of course. "What's that hammer used for, then?" She almost added a term of politeness, but being polite to projections seemed silly.

"My lady, the crow's beak is meant to bring down mounted opponents or to reach through shield walls. Once the opponent is squared, it's normal to drop that hammer and draw a sword."

"Oh, right." Crystal had meant to see a hammer versus sword fight anyway. "Draw your sword, then, and let's see which of you is the more—um, valiant."

The knight complied, and Crystal was thrilled as she watched the battle unfold. Both combatants seemed very skilled with their weapons. Crystal immediately saw the advantage of the heavier hammer, as it staggered the other knight and crushed part of his armor with every blow landed. She saw the disadvantage too, though, as the sword-wielding knight got in two blows for every blow of the hammer, and he was also able to duck out of the way of most of the slower hammer swings or at least redirect them to solid areas of his armor or shield.

The battle continued, and Crystal was surprised at how long it lasted. Sword Guy landed blow after blow, but most of them didn't seem to matter against Hammer Guy's armor. He got in a solid blow to Hammer Guy's head once, causing a ringing that was loud even to Crystal several feet away, but his seasoned opponent shook even that off.

The battle finally turned when Hammer Guy skillfully spun the hammer around mid-swing. Sword Guy shifted to let the hammer's face hit on his heavily-armored shoulder, but instead found the spike of the hammer lodged through the joint on the back of his shoulder. Hammer Guy used the spike to pull a winded Sword Guy forward, toppling him onto his knees. Sword Guy made to scramble back up, but he clearly had very limited agility in the heavy suit of armor he was wearing. In one smooth, strong motion Hammer Guy pulled the spike out, spun the hammer overhead in an arc, and crushed Sword Guy's helmeted head. Sword Guy disappeared as he fell, and Hammer Guy tossed the hammer onto the floor and vanished also.

Matt chuckled from the doorway. Crystal had noticed the movement as he entered, but her concentration had remained on the combatants. Now she looked at him, a smile on her face.

"So now you've seen how effective a heavy war hammer can be against an armored opponent." Matt said. "Replay the same battle with unarmored combatants, and the outcome would be less predictable, with just about even odds."

Crystal smiled at her husband; she had already come to the same conclusion. "I need to prepare to fight Aphrodite," she said bluntly.

"Yeah, that's looking more and more probable as a future event. Still, you should ask Mother for her direction."

"A goddess would make her own path, though," Crystal objected.

"You're not a goddess yet, Crystal."

"You always told me I was one," Crystal pouted playfully.

"Sure, to me, you are like a goddess, but that only counts for so much. You still need something from Mother to get from here to there."

Crystal looked at him suspiciously and asked, "You know the path, don't you?"

Matt shrugged. "I may. I may be wrong, though. It's not like there's a textbook out there describing what to do. For me to tell you what I suspect would prejudice you toward a course of action, and that would be a disservice. You do need to make your own path, and Mother is the one to guide you along it."

"Let's go, then."

"Not even gonna take some time to get to know your poor hubby first?" Matt asked, a playful pout covering his face. "I built you a special room while you were gone."

"Sorscha showed me, actually. Thank you, Matt. It does mean a lot to me, and your company does too. I just...." Crystal ran out of words to describe her dilemma.

"I know. I was just teasing. Of course we miss you when you're gone, but this is something you have to do. I get that. Besides, a trip to Mother won't take long."

Crystal grinned and skipped out of the room, not even attempting to hide her eagerness to make the trip. Matt caught her arm as she started skipping down the hall. "Teleport, remember?" he said as the familiar jerk in her insides told her she was moving through space. She stood momentarily with Matt on the gold circle and then was jerked again. She found herself looking once more at the breathtakingly beautiful figure of Gaia, the Mother goddess.

Gaia strode over and lifted Crystal's arm, shaking it to get Crystal to flex slightly. She nodded approvingly. "Nicely done, child. You do pay attention, and you're smart, and you're resilient, too. You just might have a slight chance of success."

"Thank you, Mother," Crystal replied out of a desire to be polite, though she was less than completely grateful for the mere 'slight chance.' "I found the work with Hephaestus to be satisfying in many ways, and so I'm very glad for the opportunity."

"And a nice new war hammer to be glad for, as well, right, child?" Gaia said, surprising Crystal. "Oh, don't look so shocked. I'm not just the earth goddess. I am the earth. I see most of what goes on most of the time. Hephaestus gave you a truly amazing gift, one that will serve you well in the coming trial."

"I must fight Aphrodite," Crystal stated, a tentative question in her voice.

"You must prove your worth, yes, and that means you must defeat another god or goddess in a battle to the death. It's not surprising that you would choose Stacy, but it is your choice."

Crystal shivered from the chill she felt at hearing the pronouncement that turned her suspicion and fear into her future reality. "To the death? But Mother, I'm the only one of the combatants who can die."

"Anyone can die, Child, given the right circumstances. You've seen the effect that Stacy's sword had on your husband—or I should say, the effect it didn't have. But there exists a special blade, made of a very special metal. It is the very blade that was used by the titans to disembowel Uranus. Once you are worthy of wielding it, you may carry it into battle to even the odds against any deity, including Stacy, should that be your choice."

Crystal blinked and heard Matt's gasp behind her as Gaia opened her hands and a sword with a curved end appeared in them. It was strangely dull, made of a grey metal that reflected very little light. The handle looked like ironwood, but it, too, reflected nothing. Along the outside curve of the blade ran the same wavy lines that Matt had said was ancient script on her new hammer, and she longed to ask Matt to interpret it. She couldn't open her mouth, though; she stood speechless, looking at a god-killing weapon that emanated power and, Crystal sensed, malevolence.

"Take it," Gaia said. "Don't worry, you won't be able to swing it until you're ready. Its fibers hold ancient and powerful enchantments, and it will serve you only if you impress it."

Crystal took the sword's handle from Gaia, feeling its weight as she moved it. She experimentally tried to swing it, but—it resisted, somehow. Crystal found through more testing that she could move it slowly, but anything fast enough to be considered a strike was stopped by some sort of internal magic of the blade itself.

"Once you're ready it will comply," Gaia reminded her, a smile beaming on the goddess's face. "I suggest that you go see Thor to learn to use it."

"I'd think Matt could at least teach me the battle arts," Crystal objected.

"Can you, Matthew?" Gaia asked, gazing over Crystal's shoulder toward the god of war.

"Yes and no, Crystal," Matt directed his answer at Crystal, and she turned to hear it. "My interest, my area, my specialty, if you will, has always been war, battles played out across fields and sometimes continents. I stand fascinated at the perspective of the general, who directs units and strategies. The art of solo combat, champion to champion, is part of that, true, but it's not my specialty. That is the world Thor lives in. Long, long ago, he lived as a mortal in that world, a barbarian king who won his place through mighty feats in the combat arena. That's why, also, he didn't ever bother to play with the Greeks and Romans in the last magic cycle, since they were mostly interested in combat by units and armies. Short answer, I guess, is that while I can teach you, Thor should teach you. Besides, I think you might find Valhalla interesting," Matt finished with a smirk.

Crystal shrugged. "OK, then, to Valhalla I shall go," she said, trying to sound more lighthearted about it than she felt. "I suppose, after Hephaestus's forge, I can survive anything, even Thor's training grounds, right?"

Matt and Gaia both chuckled, and Crystal turned to Gaia and bowed. "Thank you once again for your guidance, Mother. I will do as you say and prepare for battle against Aphrodite."

"Prepare well, child, for Stacy was trained in the same manner as you are, and she's had much more time to improve at it. Don't summon the fight until you are ready."

Crystal nodded, and felt herself plunged back through the dimensions to Matt's estate. She stepped out of the alcove into the throne room, Matt just behind, and was greeted by the one being she least wanted to see.

She sensed Matt grabbing hold of magical energies as Aphrodite's laughter pealed through the room. "Oh, relaaaaaax, Matthew," the goddess said. She shifted poses, and suddenly her green dress became a see-through gown of black lace that fit her perfect curves tightly. "I'm just here to wish your darling well in her futile little quest. What would be the fun of killing her before she suffers through Thor's training? Little girl, I see you hold a mighty weapon, one that I once wielded. I want you to work hard and train well so that you'll at least give me some game, you hear? I'll be disappointed if killing you is too easy."

The goddess laughed merrily, and then directed her gaze at Matthew. "And you, Mister War God. I expect you already know that you are the victor's spoils for this battle, right? I will claim you as my own once more as I stand over this child's corpse." She looked back at Crystal and waved her hand as though she had won a beauty pageant. "Good luck, and toooooodles!" The goddess disappeared, her evil-sounding laughter lingering in the room.

Crystal heard Matt's harrumph behind her and was glad he was there.

"She's scared," he said. "She wouldn't bother trying to intimidate you if she weren't."

Crystal turned to her husband and wrapped her arms around his neck, carefully keeping the god-killing blade away from him. "I love you, Matthew," she breathed into his hair. "I need to get to Valhalla so I can wipe that smile off her face that much faster, but for now I just want you to hold me tight."

"I think I can manage that," Matt said and lifted her body so her feet didn't touch the floor. He carried her that way down the circular stairway and into the bedroom. He disengaged then only long enough to have her put the god-killing sword down on the opposite side of the room, and then he carried her to the bed, undressed them both, and held her for a long time.

The Future

Crystal skipped lunch, happily entombed in Matt's arms as she was. Dinner, though, proved a little more persistent as her stomach started and then wouldn't stop growling. She met Matt's eyes, a combination of sadness and hunger in her own.

"Frankly, I'd be surprised if your appetite weren't far greater than when you left," Matt sad, tickling her side. "Oh, look, I feel an empty spot down here that needs sustenance."

Crystal stuck her tongue out at him and then sprang out of his arms to a standing position beside the bed. "You better watch it, Mister. I'll have Thor teach me how to karate chop you," she said, holding her hands up in what she imagined was a danger-ous-looking stance.

Chortling, Matt replied, "You'll have to ask the big ox when the last time he karate chopped anybody was. Remember, he taught the Vikings, who weren't exactly known for their ninja skills." Matt rose and came around the bed to her, grabbing her hand. "Anyway, Sorscha tells me the girls are ready for dinner too, so let's go fill that empty spot."

They were greeted by the twins and Sorscha when they exited the bedroom. Sorscha bowed and the twins ran over and hugged their mother. "Mom," Heidi said, "Sorscha told us that Aphrodite came back. Are you okay?"

Crystal laughed a far brighter-sounding peal than she felt. No point, she reasoned, upsetting the twins as much as she was. "Of course I'm okay," she said. "Aphrodite knows that I'm going to have to fight her to finish becoming a goddess, and she's trying to intimidate me because she's scared I'll beat her."

Linda asked, "Can you beat her, Mom? I mean, she's a goddess already, and has been for a long time. She almost killed you last time you fought, didn't she?"

"Your mother probably didn't need the reminder, kiddo," Matt said, but Crystal brushed him off with a hand.

"Yes, she did almost kill me, Linda," Crystal said, growing somber. "She would have, in fact, if not for your father and Sorscha. But I'm much stronger in magic now than I was, and I'm physically stronger, too, and by the time Thor is done teaching me I'll be able to fight. Gaia gave me a special weapon, too."

"Well, all right, Mom. I didn't mean to scare you."

"You didn't scare me, Linda. The coming battle scares me a little, but it should scare anybody. And it's important that we not kid each other. It's going to be hard to win, awfully hard. I think I stand a pretty good chance of winning, as hard as it might be, though, so you shouldn't worry."

"What happens if you don't win, Mom?"

"I don't know, Linda," Crystal said, figuring the lie was justified. "I don't plan on losing, though. How's that for an answer?"

Linda closed her arms around Crystal's chest and hugged her mother tightly. After several long moments, she detached herself and, in her characteristic solemnity, said, "Is everybody else as hungry as I am?"

"Yes, I am," Crystal said, and she led the family down to the dining hall. They found most of the original crew of battle mages up at the head table; Birch and his wife had just sat down, and RJ and Krista were halfway through their meals. Phoenix was the only one missing. The family took their places to cheerful greetings.

"Where's Phoenix?" Crystal asked, surprised that her friend wasn't there. Typically Krista, Phoenix, and Birch were so devoted to their mutual studies that they were inseparable except when they went back to their families at night. Well, Birch and

Krista were, Crystal thought; Phoenix, being perpetually single, remained devoted to her studies nearly all the time.

"She found a guy on the grounds crew to hang out with to-night," Birch said. "She liked his smell. She's probably riding him to his exhaustion right now; later she'll remove his soul through his nostrils and come down here for an evening snack."

Crystal giggled; Birch and Phoenix's relationship had always been playfully caustic, but there was a ring of reality in Birch's words. The Phoenix she had known before the cataclysm had been a devourer of men, though thankfully not literally, and it actually was good for Crystal to hear that her friend was return-ing to her old habits. It also meant RJ might need another groundsman, but she imagined that the former college president could manage.

"I was going to ask where you've been for the past several weeks," Krista interrupted, "but it's pretty obvious you were liv-ing at some sort of heavenly gymnasium. You are ripped, girl."

"Thank you," Crystal said, glowing in pride. "Not quite a hea-venly gymnasium, though. I was at the forge of Hephaestus."

"Vulcan!" Birch said, always ready to show off his knowledge of mythology—history, he enjoyed calling it now that Mars had turned out to be a real person. "You lived in a volcano for over a month?"

"It's in a protected area in a volcano, off the main chute, ac-tually," Crystal said. "His thrakkoni fly up Etna's chute to gather ore and meat for the humans in his forge to work with. The fun-ny thing is that the humans don't know the thrakkoni exist. He-phaestus has his enclave wrapped up in a magical illusion that they're inside a forested glen."

"Did you actually get to make things?" Krista asked.

"Yeah, well, I spent my first several days just splitting wood to make charcoal. Then I learned to crush and then smelt iron ore. Finally, they did teach me some basics of smithing. I can make some basic tools and weapons now."

"But what's the point?" Krista asked. "It's not like you're going to do much smithing now."

Crystal hadn't found the time to tell her friends what she was after. This wasn't the time for that, either. "Oh, it was a strengthening exercise that Matt thought would be good for me," she said. "He was right, yes?"

"Yeah, I guess so," Krista said, sounding unconvinced. "So what's next?"

"Well, next I'm going to be trained in the art of battle by Thor," Crystal said, trying to make it sound as though she were going for a walk around the estate.

"Thor?" Birch asked, his face beaming in excitement. He reached to his neck, around which hung the hammer-shaped pendant he had worn every moment Crystal had seen him.

"Yes, Thor. Why?" Crystal asked.

"Oh, he's the god I'd have to admit to always having wanted to meet, if you made me admit anything of the sort. No offense, Matt, but he's amazing. He's the god who was willing to dress up like Freya to trick the giants into giving him his hammer back, for one thing."

Matt sat back and crossed his arms over his chest, a wry grin on his face.

Birch continued, "If you get a chance, make sure you touch Mjolnir and tell me what it's like. Thor's hammer is what my pendant is based on. I'd ask you pick to it up and tell me about it later, but nobody, not even Thor himself, can pick up the hammer without Thor's magic glove, Jarngreipr."

"Mm hmm. Now why would a god have a hammer he can't pick up without special gloves?" Matt asked.

Birch looked confused. "Well, that's what the legends say. Jarngreipr is a special dwarf-made set of gauntlets that are used by Thor to handle Mjolnir. I assumed that meant he couldn't handle the hammer if he didn't have the gloves on."

"That was before you knew magic as a viable and touchable energy, Birch. What do you think the gloves might be, now that you know something of the flows of elemental power?"

"I—I honestly don't know, Matt. I guess they're just props, there to help people see him as mighty."

"No, Thor's gloves do have some power to them. It's possible to embed elemental energy into objects through something called harmonic resonance. But surely you recognize that there's no way a self-respecting god like Thor would have a hammer that he couldn't lift without a special pair of gloves." Matt mimicked trying and failing to pick up an unseen item, his face set in a pathetically sad expression.

"Well, okay, I guess. So what power do the gloves have?" Birch asked.

"Not mine to tell. Crystal might find out while she's at Valhalla, though."

"Well, but Valhalla is..." Birch started to object, and then he eased off. "I mean, isn't Valhalla ruled over by Odin?"

"In Norse mythology, yes it is," Matt said. "Odin was the father-god to the Norse, and Valhalla was pretty much the ultimate heaven to them, so it made sense to their mythology that Valhalla was ruled by Odin. But that was the world and the heavenly universe according to a warlike people. Yahweh, the real God Father, really isn't all that much into war as Odin was reported to be. He's not really the type to open his—what was it, five hundred doors?—and have eight hundred men pour from each to battle a mystical beast. The God Father has enough power to defeat a wolf, even a very large wolf, by himself, trust me."

"But it..." Birch said, and was cut off by Matt.

"...makes a good story? Indeed. Especially to a drunk Icelander," Matt said. "But here's what really is. Valhalla is a hall of heroes. It's ruled over by its chief hero, Thor, now that Odin is apparently no longer interested. That it would gain the exalted status of a sort of heavenly place, ruled over by the Father God, isn't surprising when you consider the men of the north and what they held to be important, but you have to keep myth and reality separate."

Birch settled into a gloomy mood and finished his dinner silently. Krista took over the conversation, asking Crystal more about her time with Hephaestus. A few comments about the blacksmithing work peaked RJ's interest, and he questioned Crystal at length.

Birch and his wife and Phoenix were the first to leave as dinner wound down. Crystal watched Birch stump out of the dining hall with a worried expression on her face. Matt noticed and said, "Love, Birch will be fine. He's just dealing with the fact that everything he thought he knew about Norse spirituality—a myth to some, but a religion to him—is a skosh off from reality. He'll get over it and ply you for details for hours when you get back."

"Reality? You keep talking about reality. What is it?" Krista asked no one in particular. She continued, "Ever since we came here it's been like living in a fantasy book. There are dragons that can change into humanoids, and magical spells that we can cast, and a god to rule us. That's a strange collection of things to call reality."

Matt turned and met Krista's eyes for several long moments. Then he shrugged, saying, "Welcome to my world. Would you rather have died in the cataclysm?"

Krista sighed and said, "No, of course not, Matt. Life is just so different now. Look, we've been through this before, and it's really not that important. I'd say that you have to accept that we're only human, but you really don't. You're a god, after all. But we mere humans had a life lined out, with stuff to do, and now we're just guests at your estate, helping to keep the grounds nice or working the kitchens or learning to use magic, and it doesn't seem like there's anything to—well, to live for any more."

Matt nodded, still fixing his eyes on Krista's face, ignoring RJ's fierce expression as the man wrapped his arms protectively around his wife. After several long moments passed quietly, he said, "I suppose it won't help much for me to tell you that every group I've brought here has reacted the same way, will it?" As Krista snorted and opened her mouth, he interrupted, "No, hear me out. Your entire world stopped existing several months ago, replaced by a world that is foreign to you. I trust you've taken the thrakkoni up on their offer to fly you back to your homes, right? You've seen the devastation, the destruction. The fabric that held your world together no longer exists. The world out there now requires different skills than the ones you had when I brought you here. Could you survive in it? Probably, but what you've been doing here is building the tools within yourselves that you'll need to someday go out in the new world and thrive. You're not ready yet, but when you do leave, it will be to go out there and rebuild civilization. And you'll be doing it alongside the wizards that Apollo is training, the steelworkers from Vulcan's group, the warriors from Thor, the hunters of Artemis, and so on. Each of us trains our followers on our own particular interests, and each of you will play an important associated role in the rebuilding of civilization in the coming years. But to get there from here, you need to quit worrying so much about getting there and instead concentrate on the lessons of today."

Matt chewed on a green olive for several seconds, watching Krista's face as she digested his words. Finally her face lightened and she opened her mouth to speak again, but Matt interrupted once more, shifting his gaze to her husband. "RJ, you seek to protect your wife, and that is noble of you. You've grown as much as anyone here over the past several months. Do you know why I say that?"

RJ looked confused and said, "No, not really. I've always been protective of Krista."

"I know," Matt said. "That wasn't what I was talking about. Before we came here, you were the most pompous man I knew. You gave orders with no regard to those who would carry them out, for one thing, and you bragged to us about the gardening work you did at home as though you seemed to think that your stories of getting your hands dirty made you more human. But they didn't, and I trust you can see that now. You've dived in, here, and done the work that needed doing because it needed doing. You haven't sought to tell us about how many bushes you planted today, have you?   You just do it. The humans and thrakkoni on the work details love working for you, don't they? You, my friend, have changed from a man who used to pride himself on what he could push others into doing into a true leader."

RJ sat back, visibly struck by Matt's words, and apparently speechless as a result. Matt shifted his eyes between each member of the couple and said, "So, RJ, at some point, when you're ready, I'm going to pull you off the work detail and set you to learning some martial skills. You don't have to be an expert warrior, but you do need to be good enough to defend yourself and your wife. Krista, you will need the same training. Once you've got that figured out, you'll make one of the most potent husband-wife teams ever to go out there and build something."

"What will we build, though?" Krista asked.

"Whatever you believe most needs building," Matt said, ending the discussion with a warm smile.

Thor

I really don't want to do this, Crystal thought as she stood on the gold inlaid circle the next morning. She had spent the night before in the pleasant company of her family, a company she knew she would now miss for several weeks, if not months. She had been surprised that the girls hadn't brought Steve and Corey along, but their explanation that they had missed her a great deal, and that the boys could wait, had warmed her heart.

She smiled as her body remembered the night of lovemaking. The newfound power running through her muscles she had put to good use as the couple tried some positions they never would have before. She had also experimented more with using tiny elemental flows to magically enhance Matt's sensations, and he had responded with great enthusiasm.

Matt shattered her waking dream by asking, "Ready, my love?" She was. When she woke, Sorscha had given her a leather belt with a loop on one side and a scabbard on the other, and now the magnificent war hammer and the god-killing blade both hung ready, more or less, at her sides. She had no idea how, or even if, she would be able to wield both weapons at the same time in a brawl with Aphrodite, but she knew that Thor, if anyone, could teach her.

She nodded, and the world blinked once again. As her eyes readjusted in the bright sunlight, she heard massive sounds of battle behind her. *Go figure—sounds of battle in Valhalla*, she thought. She forced herself to keep her eyes forward, confident Matt would protect her if needed, and not willing to appear skittish.

The massive shape in front of her resolved itself into the rising form of a hairy-armored giant as his booming voice greeted them. "Tyr! Good to see you again, old friend. And you've brought your lovely bride for a visit, too." Thor was as big as she remembered from her trip to Olympus, and seemed to be wearing the same armor, with even the same smell. He clasped Matt's hand in his bear paw and smiled.

"It's not exactly a visit, Thor," Matt said.

"I know, old friend. I can feel the power radiating from what she's got dangling from her belt. Those aren't toys, girl."

"I know," Crystal said, concentrating on keeping her voice level and strong, even though she felt nothing of the kind. Thor was huge, and seemed intent at the moment on proving that his glare could intimidate a stone cliff. "I've come to you so you can teach me how to use them."

"Why would I do that?"

"Um," Crystal stammered briefly, and mentally cursed herself for it. Steeling herself again, she met Thor's gaze and said, "Gaia said you needed to."

Thor snorted. "Gaia said *you* needed to, you mean. I have over a hundred men here that I need to train. You're not one of them." He turned back to Matt and said, "So, Tyr, old friend, would you like a tour for your lovely bride before you take her back home?"

Crystal started to panic. She had never considered that Thor might say no; Apollo and Hephaestus had both agreed when they heard the request was from Gaia. Calming herself back down, she forced herself to think. The giant god of battle and of thunder would appreciate only one approach, she knew, and timidity wasn't it.

She took a deep breath and stepped between Thor and Matt. Looking up to stare him directly in the eyes, she said, "This bride isn't going back home. I'll gladly work in your kitchens or serve in your dinner hall to pay for it, but the only way I'm going to be able to stand up to Aphrodite is with your training. Name your price, then, Master."

"Bah, I have all the serving wenches I need, and I won't see Tyr's wife reduced to that in any event. And if it's Stacy who's bothering you, I'll happily stand beside your husband to protect you. Who do you think taught her how to fight? But I'm not going to do it again. The answer is no."

"Thor...." Matt interjected.

"Don't try it, Tyr."

"Try what? Look, old friend, you're the best fighting trainer in the universe. She's put up with Apollo's peevishness and Hephaestus's gruffness so far, and come away stronger for it. Won't you give her a chance?"

"No."

"Did I say no when you needed help getting ready for your trip to get your hammer back?"

"Now, that's not fair."

"Yeah, yeah. *That's not fair*," Matt said in a peevish voice and then continued, "When has anything ever been fair to us? Did I balk when you needed that huge cauldron from Hymir's place?"

Thor groaned, his huge voice grinding like thunder. He looked back down at Crystal, who was still standing defiantly between the two gods. "So be it, wife of Tyr. Your husband has the right of it. Your training has been purchased by his deeds. It will be hard, but I'm sure you've heard that before. You might wish to have a few changes of clothes, because you'll be here a while."

"With your permission, old friend, I will have the trunks she already packed teleported to her room," Matt said.

Thor glared over Crystal's head at her husband. "Fine. You know what you've gotten her into, right?"

"Yes," Matt said. "I wouldn't do it if she didn't desire it to the depths of her soul. Or if I didn't think she was up to it. But she's as close to my equal as I've found in many eons, and so my money is on her when the time comes."

"Stacy has gotten stronger," Thor said. "That's a risky bet you're making."

"In more ways than one, I know. But I trust your ability to even the odds."

"I'm not the one who will have to battle Stacy," Thor said with a snort. "But that die is cast already, I guess. Matt, you're welcome to stay or to go, and of course you may visit at any time. Wife of Tyr, I will have a valkyrie show you to your quarters."

"Call me Crystal. Would you prefer I call you Thor or Master?"

Thor's harrumph gave Crystal the answer even before he said, "Crystal, then. Tyr's wife can call me whatever she wishes. Only the valkyrie around here call me Master, though, so you might wish to stick with my name." A thrakkon walked up, glaring toward the party, and Thor jerked his head toward her. "Hildr will take you to your room. Stay there long enough for your husband to teleport your stuff to you, and then change to some good workout clothes and come meet me in the main hall. Leave those fancy weapons in your room. You need to start with some basics, and it'll be hard to tell your abilities from the skills imbued in a Hephaestus-made hammer."

Crystal kissed Matt good-bye to Thor's amusement, and then followed Hildr up the hill into a short, squat fortress. On the way, she said, "I didn't expect Valhalla to have any thrakkoni. Are there many of you?"

Hildr smiled pleasantly. "I haven't heard the word thrakkoni in a long while. We residents of Valhalla prefer to be called the Valkyr, or Valkyries as some say. We're a little different from most of our kind at the estates of the other gods."

"Really? In what way?" Crystal wasn't sure if her question would be taken as prying, but she was genuinely curious.

Hildr stopped and turned to Crystal. She held the folds of what Crystal now saw was a riding dress out away from her legs and then transformed. Instead of a dragon, though, Crystal faced a woman mounted on a winged steed, white feather-covered wings folded against the wind. Crystal moved closer and looked where there should be a gap between human body and horse body. She gasped; what looked like two beings was actually one.

Hildr transformed back into a humanoid shape and said, "Normally I would have my armor close by to put on. The effect is much more beautiful if I'm wearing gleaming battle regalia."

"Oh, I don't know. It was pretty stunning without armor," Crystal said, still awed. "Do you shift into dragon form too?"

"I can, but I don't except to eat. That is my kind's natural form. We all prefer the winged horse maidens, though. We were made a little different from our kind elsewhere, I think."

"Clearly," Crystal said. "Are there male Valkyr?"

"No." Hildr started walking again, leading Crystal into and down the central path of a huge inner courtyard that was filled with men sparring. She raised her voice to be heard over the noise of battle and said, "All the Valkyr are made in female form, but gender is superficial and somewhat meaningless for my kind."

"Oh, of course," Crystal said. As she walked, she looked around at the sparring warriors. "Are all of the humans here, except me, of course, male?"

"All of the warriors are. Their wives and children help to run the keep, if they have wives and children. And there are some tradesmen here as well. The quartermaster and blacksmith over there, for example." Hildr pointed to the right, and Crystal realized she could hear the now-familiar sounds of a smithy. Hildr continued, pointing to the left and then ahead, "The barracks for the single men are over there, with quarters for smaller families farther in. In the main building is the great hall, where fighters sometimes spar and where we have our great feasts every night. It also contains the Master's quarters, a set of rooms reserved for Freyja when she visits, and quarters for those humans whom the Master promotes to officer status. You, being the only single female on the grounds, as well as the most honored wife of Tyr, will be in one of those rooms."

They entered the grand hall at the opposite end of the courtyard. Crystal stopped for a moment to allow her eyes to adjust to the dim inside light, glad that the cacophony of battle had vanished with the closing of the thick wooden door. In front of her were many rough wooden tables, arranged haphazardly through a hall that was nearly as large as Matt's dining hall, though apparently based on the arrangement of tables meant for far fewer inhabitants. "Does everyone eat dinner in here at the same time?"

"The warriors do, yes. Their spouses eat as well, but in the kitchens. It's one of those hallmarks of Valhalla."

"Oh. I wonder if, as a woman, I'll be expected to eat in the kitchens. I should ask Thor, shouldn't I?"

"No. Don't ask," Hildr said, turning to face Crystal. "It is a sign of weakness to ask permission. You should walk in this evening and assume your position at Thor's table as a head warrior in training. If he feels strongly about it, he'll tell you so."

Hildr spun around again and led Crystal through a side door into a hall; she opened a door halfway down and walked in. "Your chambers are here. The privy is at the end of the hall on the left. It's the only one, but you're the only human housed in this wing so you needn't worry about privacy." Hildr bowed and said, "And now I leave you to your peace."

Crystal sat on the single bed in the small room. As she had expected, the furnishings were sparse; a bed, a wardrobe, and a small desk and chair. She held up her blue glass shard, and then on impulse put it down and reached out for elemental essence with her mind. Pushing her thoughts across the distance, she focused on Matthew and, pretty quickly, found a consciousness that she sensed was his. "Matthew?" she projected.

"Crystal? Are you calling for me without the glass shard?"

Now that the connection was made, Crystal found it much easier to maintain. She smiled and thought back at her husband, "Yep! I looked at the flows in the glass shard and figured I could duplicate them. Pretty good, yes?"

"It is, but…. Remember the first time you latched onto the essence of magic? How it wiped you out for a day and a half? You shouldn't spend your energy like this. I'm sure that Thor won't go easy on you just because you're tired."

Crystal felt a pang of chagrin at Matt's words and said so, following it with "But aren't you proud that I figured it out?"

"Of course I am, but use the shard next time. Anyway, are you in your room? Send me a mental image of your room, especially the spot where I can send your trunk."

She did, and a trunk appeared on the floor where she had imagined it. "Thank you, Matt. I bet I can figure out how to teleport things if I watch you do it a couple of times."

"I bet you can figure it out without watching me, but don't. Keep in mind that you're there to learn physical combat, and keep the magic out of it. All right?"

Crystal chuckled. "Sure, Matt. I should probably get ready for my first lesson now. Talk tonight?"

"Sure. Enjoy!"

Crystal closed the connection, not sure if she was likely at all to enjoy what was coming. Still, she had begged for it, and she had managed to meet every challenge so far. No sense, she thought, giving ground to her fears now. She opened the chest and quickly repacked the clothing inside in the wardrobe, moving the empty chest out of the way to stand against the wall during her stay. Deciding not to leave her weapons out, she took them off of her belt and stowed them inside the chest, weaving a magical flow of earth and air to create a simple lock. It wouldn't keep Thor out, she knew, but it would make the chest seem sealed to most humans or thra—er, Valkyrie, she corrected herself. She took off her weapons belt, but remained in the rest of her clothing. The light silk tunic let her torso move well, as did the linen pants, and she didn't understand what Thor's objection could have been. It looked, she thought, like the same type of outfit that Aphrodite had worn when she had attacked and nearly killed Crystal.

"You're gonna fight in a silk shirt?" Thor asked as she walked back into the main hall. "Suit yourself, I guess. You'll need to do more than dress like Aphrodite to beat her, you know."

Crystal smiled and moved toward the god, unwilling to show the slightest doubt. "It fits well and lets me move around. I have plenty of shirts if this one is ruined."

"It's not just a comfort thing, or a wardrobe thing either, Crystal. Silk has the wrong energy to fight in. It saps the power from your body instead of holding it close to you. Today you should be fine, but in the future find a good stout linen or wool tunic."

"Yes, Sir. I'd never heard that about silk before, so I didn't know it was bad."

"How much have you fought hand-to-hand or with melee weapons?"

"None."

"NONE?" Thor roared, rising from his chair. "You've never been in combat in your life?"

Crystal held onto her resolve to avoid the intimidation Thor was pressing her way, but only barely. She breathed in once and replied, "I didn't realize there was a prerequisite."

Thor settled back on his heels and crossed his arms over his chest. "Hmmph. You realize this is going to take a while, right?"

"I was counting on it," Crystal said, surprising herself with the steel she was able to place in her voice.

"I guess I can say that at least you don't have any bad habits. So how are you with pain?"

"Giving or taking?" Crystal smiled.

"Well, miss smart aleck, if you've never been in a fight before, it's a pretty good assumption that you have no clue about giving it."

"Yes, Sir. But in the same vein, since I've given birth to twins, it's a pretty good assumption that I know something about taking it."

"We'll see. Now, see that pile of weapons over there? I want you to grab one of the sticks and a practice shield and bring them over here."

Crystal did as she was told, feeling silly holding the pieces of wood that felt more like toys than battle implements. "Thor, I need to learn to fight with a short sword and a war hammer, not with a stick and a shield," she said.

"You have to start somewhere, and this is it. When you fight with two weapons, one of the standard techniques is to have one of them functioning as a sort of shield most of the time. In fact, the shield weapon method is about the only way to fight with a sword and a hammer. Learning with an actual shield will help you get used to that. The stick, meanwhile, is lighter and requires less finesse than the hammer at first. Now, are you going to question everything I do, or can I get on with training you?"

"I'm sorry," Crystal said, letting her voice go soft. Having been a teacher herself, she knew how annoying constant questioning could be. "I won't..."

The attack came without warning. Crystal barely had time to get her shield up as Thor's wooden hammer came smashing down on it. Even with the blow successfully blocked, its force propelled Crystal back several steps. She managed to regain her balance, barely, and then straightened back up into a defensive posture in the hopes of successfully deflecting the second attack that she knew was coming. She growled, brought her pretend sword up, and looked Thor in the eyes—and then realized that he was watching her intently rather than preparing another attack.

"Nice job," the god said, sincerity evident in his voice. "You weren't ready for the attack, which is something we can work on, but you managed to block it anyway, and you recovered nicely. Most people—most women, especially—would've covered their heads and screamed. It takes a warrior spirit to slip right into a defensive posture and ready yourself for another blow. We've definitely got our work cut out for us, but at least I have something to work with."

Crystal bristled over the sexism inherent in Thor's compliment, but he hadn't sounded like he was trying to be insulting. Letting it slide, she asked, "So how do I make that blow not push me back and off-balance as much as it did?"

"You ask good questions, too, when you're not being a smart aleck," Thor said. "Battle with heavy weapons, like a mace or a hammer or a broadsword, is all about energy. If you're the one swinging it, you want to put every ounce of energy you can into the contact that the weapon makes with your opponent. If you're the opponent, meanwhile, you want to shunt all that energy to one side or another. Think of the energy as a line following the swing of a weapon. You can move it to the side, but you can't stop it. The trick is in figuring out which side to deflect, or shunt, to. That'll be an especially important lesson for you to learn when you switch from your shield, which can take some beating, to the sword, which cannot. Then again, I don't think Aphrodite will fight with a heavy weapon. It's not her preference. Regardless, you need to learn the basics."

"So what of battle with light weapons?"

"Light weapons, like rapiers and short swords, are a matter of speed and accuracy. You can win a battle with one with the lightest of attacks, if it's well placed. That's where you're going to have the hardest time, dear. You're going to have limited protection, and a heavy weapon, and so you'll need to work hard on building an agile defense with your off hand."

"Why are some swords considered heavy weapons?" Crystal figured that as long as she was asking questions and learning, she was giving her throbbing shield arm a chance to recover from the blow Thor had landed.

"Big swords are for bashing and cleaving, the former more often than the latter, actually, while small swords are for thrusting and stabbing. Slicing, too, sometimes, but that's rare."

Thor's words brought back a memory. "So what kind of weapon will Aphrodite use? In her battle against Matthew, she used two swords."

"You remember that battle, eh? That was epic. Anyway, you asked about Stacy. She's always liked dual-wielding matching blades that fit more into the light category than the heavy one. She can be just as deadly with a quarterstaff, though, or a short sword and dagger combo or a whip and dagger combo. Don't expect to see her heft a shield, regardless."

"You're looking forward to the battle, aren't you?" Crystal had caught a hint of excitement in Thor's voice, a kind of reverent intensity.

"Yes, and no, Crystal. Viewing it as the battle-master that I am, I say this will be a very interesting matchup. You and Stacy will, by the time we're done here, if, of course, you survive my training, be very closely matched, both physically and in skill level. You're very similar to her, you know, in body type, and now that you've filled out a bit I can say that the two of you could almost be twins. You're like night and day, though, in your personalities, which correlates directly with your battle styles. When I attacked her like I did you, she actually came right back at me, stick flying and all. You're pretending to be confident—and yes, I can see through your act. She was confident, though, to the point of belligerence. It nearly killed her more than once during our training. When the two of you finally meet in the arena, it'll be an epic battle of two women, both of whom I taught to fight, and both of whom Apollo taught to wield the flows of magic, who are opposite yet equal in personality and styles. Yes, it's going to be grand to watch. The only bad part is that one of you won't make it out."

"She's tried to kill me, so I don't feel too bad about the prospect of doing the same to her."

"Yes, Crystal, but you're mortal. No, I don't mean that as an insult," Thor interjected, seeing the flash of annoyance in Crystal's eyes. "Humans are born, they grow up, and they die. If you live a long, healthy, happy life, how long would you say that is for a human? A hundred years? Maybe a few more or a few less? That's nothing in the life of a god or a goddess. It's a sad thing indeed to consider the loss of an immortal life, no matter how well you get along with her."

"So why require a fight to the death? Why not, oh, I don't know, play checkers? Or more seriously, have a magic contest to see if the upcoming goddess is strong enough in the flows? Why does it have to be a physical battle?" Crystal asked.

"Well, if you think a battle to the death with Stacy will just be a physical battle, then you're already beaten. She'll be using every flow she can against you, and you'll need to be as agile in your counter-spelling as you are with your blocking sword to survive."

"Okay, granted, but that wasn't what I was really asking. Why does it have to be a battle to the death?"

Thor shrugged. "Why, when you fall, is it down and not up? The world is as the world is, dear, and it's useless to question it."

"One would think the gods would have more power over the way the world is."

"Yeah, yeah, yeah—you gonna sulk about it all day, or can we get back to training?" Thor said as a grin widened across his face. As she readied herself for another attack, he continued, "Anyway, don't try to understand what the gods can and cannot do. If you win the battle you're settled in to fight, you'll become one of us, and then it'll be another few millennia before you really come to grips with why the world is as it is. I will tell you this now: rules are as important to us as they are to you, and the fact that we can change things doesn't mean that we should, or that we will. Got it?"

She nodded, and barely got her shield into the path of his hammer blow. This time, though, she was expecting it, and his talk of deflection of energy was still fresh in her mind, so she angled the shield to her left and the hammer bounced to the side. She raised her stick over her head, grinning triumphantly.

Thor glared at her, his practice hammer raised again to strike. "You gonna celebrate or fight, dearie?" he asked.

"Sorry," she said. "I was just overjoyed at handling the energy of the blow, and...."

This time the attack came unseen. She was holding her shield up to be able to block the next hammer blow, and as a result she didn't see his leg swinging around until too late. Both of her legs left the ground, and she fell hard on the arm that was holding the stick. She heard a bone snap just before she felt intense pain in her forearm. She picked herself up gingerly, holding the shield in front of her while willing her right arm to function. It refused.

Thor crossed his arms over his chest, right hand still holding the hammer's shaft. He glared at Crystal. "Well, what are you going to do?" he asked with steel in his voice. "Are you waiting for me to call the medic? Do I need to tell Apollo how little you learned there?"

Crystal suddenly saw through the shock that she was feeling. Yes, her arm was broken. But Apollo had taught her how to fix fractures. It was easy, in fact—just, not when it was her own arm that was fractured. She closed her eyes against the pain and looked for the violet energy using her mind rather than her eyes. She gathered enough of the flow for a simple binding and wrapped it around the bone in her upper arm, watching and feeling the bone shift back together with a sense of detachment. She opened her eyes and flexed her arm tentatively; it was as strong as it had ever been.

Meeting Thor's gaze, she said, "I did learn healing energy, but never when I had to apply it to myself. Thank you for teaching me that."

Thor grunted. "You need to be quicker on the uptake next time, dear. Were I a real opponent, you would have died while you had your eyes closed healing your arm."

"I understand," Crystal said. "I'll keep a purple flow open while I fight."

"Good," Thor said. "Many a battle has been lost while a combatant worried over a minor nick on his arm or slipped on a trace of his own blood. And while you're at it, keep your shield down so you can see the battle." With no warning again, Thor spun his leg around, but Crystal leaped over his spin and brought her stick around and down in a powerful blow.

Thor's platter-sized hand stopped her stick in mid-air. "Yeah," he said, "Nice leap, but your swing leaves some to be desired. Then again, that's why you're here, right?"

They spent a long time sparring, Thor teaching Crystal both theory and practical movements. He explained to her the concept of defensive zones formed by both her shield and her stick, and showed her how to watch the same zones of her opponent's defense. He coached her in properly swinging the stick itself, forcing her to use her shoulder and upper arm to increase her power while avoiding wrist and forearm fatigue in a longer battle. "Light weapons, you can zip around with your cute little wrist flicks all day long, but you only get one or two of those in with a heavy war hammer before your stamina gives out, and then you're tired. And, usually, tired means dead."

They took a late lunch break, and Crystal welcomed the breather. A thrakkon—no, a Valkyr, she reminded herself again—brought her a tray of meat and cheese and a mug of beer. "Beer for lunch?" she asked Thor as she self-consciously accepted the service of the Valkyr.

Thor noticed her hesitation. "Eat, Crystal," he growled. "The Valkyr live to serve the warriors in this hall. You spar with me, so no matter how new you are or what gender you may be, you mark yourself a warrior. And yes, we have beer for lunch in Valhalla. Unless you'd prefer something with some twinkle for your toes?"

Crystal took a big gulp to swallow the piece of sausage she had been chewing on and shook her head. "No, your beer is wonderful for lunch, Thor," she said, mimicking his manly voice.

Thor snorted and rose. "Yell for me when you're ready to get back to your lessons, Miss Deep Voice." He walked out the front door of the hall into the courtyard.

Crystal finished quickly, having no one to talk to. The Valkyr appeared from somewhere across the hall, hurrying to remove Crystal's table setting as she rose. Crystal watched the Valkyr's speed and gracefulness, impressed, and also in a vain attempt to assess her prowess as a competitor on the field. Finally she turned toward the door, wondering if Thor had meant his command literally. "Thor!" she yelled loudly, deciding it was best to assume so, and then go to the door and yell if he didn't appear. But he did appear, teleporting in immediately after her yell to stand before her.

"Well, you eat fast like a warrior too. That's good. Back to training?" Thor picked up his wooden practice hammer for his right hand, and this time pulled a stick for his left. Crystal equipped her shield and stick again and faced off against the thunder god.

Thor feinted with his hammer and then sent the stick arcing down a vertical path toward Crystal's left shoulder, the blow intended to cleave her left side from her body had it been a sword. Crystal was too fast for it, though, stepping back with her left foot and letting the sword pass harmlessly by what was now her front. In doing so she didn't see Thor's hammer, which had finished its first course to fly around and in a sideways arc, connecting powerfully with her now-unguarded pelvis. She felt her core muscles contract around bones that were no longer whole, the force of the blow snapping her spine and splitting her hip bones apart as she flew backward through the air, coming to land in a heap against a table.

Dazed, she looked up at the giant. She was sure the blow must have hurt, but she couldn't feel anything. Once again, she summoned the purple energy flows, tenderly knitting back together her spine and the nerve column it carried, her hips, and all the organs in between. It was the first time she had healed an injury this severe, so she took extra time to make sure she was putting everything back together correctly. Finally satisfied, she rose again, feeling an annoying tingling in her legs as though they had gone to sleep. Otherwise, she was back to healthy and able.

As she took up a defensive stance again, Thor nodded. "Nice healing. But don't do that again. Do you even know what you did wrong?"

"Wasn't fast enough," Crystal said quietly, still unsure of her voice after such a crushing blow to her midsection.

"Very true, but I mean something more fundamental. Show me your zones of defense." She waved her stick in the two roundish areas to the left and right of her front. "Now show me where those go when you spin sideways to your opponent." She did as he commanded and flushed as she saw that her defense had completely gone away when she had twisted her body sideways. Thor confirmed it by saying, "Don't spin sideways against an opponent. The loss of your defense will get you killed, as you now know."

The two spent the rest of the afternoon sparring. Though Thor was only moving at partial speed, he was still swinging hard enough to hurt. Finally he called, "Enough. I need to get down to the field to see how the other newbies are doing. Tomorrow you will spar against one of my warriors. But dinner will be served soon, and I need to look in on everyone before then. Go to your room and rest a while; you've had a long first day of it. Listen for the horn."

Crystal was pleased that he hadn't gotten any more crushing blows in on her, but she knew she would later feel the multitude of little welts he left up and down her body. She put the shield and stick back in the rack where they belonged and walked to her room. Her arms, despite all the toning she had gotten while at the forge of Hephaestus, felt like rubber. She was glad, now, for Gaia's frank words and advice; to have come here and survived before her time in the forge would have been impossible.

Gingerly, she felt the bone in her upper right arm. It was tough to tell, with the corded muscle sheaths in the way, but her bone felt completely knitted together. Tentatively she put both hands on her abdomen and pressed in, surveying the damage. It felt like nothing was out of the ordinary there, either. She quietly rejoiced at Apollo's thoroughness in teaching her the art of healing magic.

Taking movements from memories of a routine she had learned in a class many years ago, Crystal began stretching out. She had never been athletic, but she had gone through a phase where she wanted to do aerobics. The class she had taken at the college had spent what seemed an inordinately large amount of time on warm-up and cool-down stretches. Now, she understood why, to the very core of her body. The work at the forge had mostly provided its own stretching, but combat training was all about keeping everything tight and compacted into a set of defined poses and defensive zones, and she had never completely extended her arms or legs for fear of a lesson from Thor's practice hammer. Now, she was happy for the chance to stretch her limbs out, forcing knotted muscles to move again and shaking out the strain of the sparring.

Before she was quite done, a deep and vibrant note pealed through the keep. She finished her stretches quickly, realizing as she did how hungry she was, and headed back out into the hall to heed the call of the dinner horn.

She walked into barely-ordered chaos. Warriors were moving tables and chairs around, filling in the area where Crystal and Thor had sparred. Thor stood at the head table, looked over to Crystal, and motioned to the chair on his right. She joined him, and he grinned.

More warriors entered the hall, filling in the side and rear tables. Finally the door to the courtyard closed, and Crystal saw that nearly every spot was taken. Thor sat, and all the warriors followed the cue to sit also.

Thor stood again and bellowed, "ALLRIGHTLISTENUP!" The warriors quieted down instantly and looked to their master. Thor said, "Most of you men won't know what to do with a woman who can battle, but for tonight and the next several weeks you'll get to find out. We have a special guest." He pointed to Crystal, though the gesture was unneeded as every eye in the hall, male but for Crystal's, was on her. "Crystal here is the wife of my good friend Tyr. She is already a warrior in her own right, and is here to learn the Thor way of battle. You will welcome and respect her, or I'll let her kick your ass."

The hall resounded with the noise of cups banging on the table; Crystal assumed it was their version of applause. As she beamed at the attention, a Valkyr reached over her shoulder, filling her mug with beer. At the same time, another Valkyr reached over Thor's shoulder and filled his mug. Other Valkyr, about a dozen, moved around the room dispensing beer from large pitchers. Crystal looked at Thor, assuming she should wait for him to drink first, but he nodded for her to enjoy. She drank a small mouthful and decided that she liked it. The beer was lighter-colored than the ale she had been served in the volcano, but it tasted stronger and a little more bitter.

She put the heavy mug down. As raucous conversation filled the hall, she turned to Thor and said, "Your ale is good, Thor."

"Not a beer drinker, are you, Crystal?" Thor said.

Crystal shook her head. "Not really. How did you know?"

"That's a lager you're drinking. It's all we make here."

"Oh," she said, confused. "At the camp of Hephaestus, they said that the weak American beers I drank were lagers. This has a lot more flavor, so I thought it was...."

"...a better lager," Thor interrupted, winking. "Besides, what the blazes do the Scots know of beer?"

Crystal shrugged, conceding the point. "Who brews it?"

"The Valkyr. They're quite handy, as you can see," Thor said, ending with a nod toward the Vaklyr who was bringing a huge tray to the head table. On the tray was a whole roasted pig surrounded by roasted potatoes and vegetables. She laid the tray in front of Thor, dipped the quickest curtsy Crystal had ever seen, and darted back toward the kitchen.

"I'm honored," Crystal said, nodding toward the platter in front of them.

Thor looked Crystal in the eyes, humor invading his expression. "Well, yes. Tonight's feast of roast pork is laid out just for you. Tomorrow night, it will still be in honor of your presence. After you've been here a few weeks, if you find us still honoring you at dinner, then that is just a measure of how wonderful it is to have you here." The thunder god hefted his mug and, without raising his voice, said, "To Crystal!"

Crystal felt her face turn red. "Oh, I saw the magnitude of the feast and assumed it was a celebration. Do you actually eat this well every night?"

"Look around you, my dear. The men work long days preparing for battle. They need a feast at night that will keep them happy and well fueled. Besides, this is the mythic pull of Valhalla: battle all day, dine every night on roast pig served by the beautiful Valkyr. Who am I to go against custom, eh?"

"I can tell you hate it, yourself, and would change the custom if you could, oh mighty Thor."

Thor burst into loud peals of laughter. Raising his glass and his voice this time, he yelled, "A toast! To Crystal Silvertongue!" All the warriors yelled and then drained their mugs, slamming them down on the table as though the drinking were a race. Watching closer, Crystal realized it actually was a race, the first at each table to slam his stein down celebrating the fact heartily while everyone refilled from the pitchers set out. She heard Thor's quietened voice rumble, "The men don't really give a crap what I say when I toast something. They love having a reason to down their beers." Crystal smirked at the god, noticing that he had drained his tankard also only to have it refilled immediately by a Valkyr.

The rest of the evening flew by. Valhalla was a noisy place over dinner, Crystal found, but the food was good and the beer kept flowing. After everyone had eaten their fill, wrestling matches began, men seeming to pick opponents at random. Crystal watched from behind her mug, glad that none of the warriors beckoned to her.

One of the smaller, wirier men rose and walked to the center of the hall after a particularly violent match. He pointed to an older man of about the same size, and held up his chin. The hall quietened. When all were silent, the man in the middle of the hall said:

"The elder Albert,
He tried to avert,
Any suffering to his frame,
Was known to sit clear,
And whisper 'O Dear,'
Whene'er was time to game."

The dining hall erupted in cheers, and Thor leaned toward Crystal, laughing and applauding as he said, "You've probably never seen flyting before. Mattias's purpose is to insult Albert in rhyme. If the insults are good enough, it will draw Albert into more flyting, or even physical battle, though weapon-based combat is forbidden in my hall over dinner."

Crystal saw that Albert was on his feet, walking toward Mattias at a measured pace. She hadn't thought the rhyming all that great, but it apparently passed in this hall. Taking a spot in the center of the floor facing the first flyter, Albert crossed his arms and said:

"The youngster in truth
Has far too much youth,
To challenge a real man to fight.
He's strong in his head,
But he's late to his bed,
We should all bid him now a good night."

A roaring applause greeting Albert's verse. Crystal thought he had won the verse match, and the assembled warriors seemed to agree. Suddenly Mattias flung himself at Albert, and the two connected in a wrestling match even more intense than the previous ones had been. It lasted for many minutes, Albert finally coming out on top. Thor, laughing and clapping, stood and thanked both men for a great bout.

The warriors in the hall seemed to take Thor's speech as a suggestion to leave. They rose and staggered out through the door of the hall, leaving Crystal and Thor by themselves except for the Valkyr who were busy cleaning the tables and righting the chairs that had fallen over when their inhabitants stood up out of them on unsteady legs.

"That was interesting," Crystal said, horrified that she was slurring her own words a bit. She had no idea how much she had drunk, since the Valkyr had filled her tankard at every opportunity. "I wouldn't have expected a rhyming battle."

Thor smiled and nodded. "It's a traditional Norse form. Physical battle, as in 'I attack you now,' happens all the time and is kind of commonplace. It's far more interesting when the two combatants hurl insults at each other first, isn't it?"

Crystal agreed, and said so in a slurred voice. Realizing it was well past time for her to be in bed, she rose and staggered to the door. She heard Thor's chuckles and a soft, "Good night, Crystal, wife of Tyr," as she carefully picked her way down the hall and into the room, collapsing fully clothed into the mattress and losing consciousness.

Pain, Pain, and More Pain

The lovemaking with Matt over, Crystal laid at his side, his arm around her shoulders. She was spent, barely able to stroke his chest. Why was he shaking her shoulder? No, it was Sorscha shaking her shoulder, saying her name over and over....

Matt's body dissolved into a spare pillow as Crystal came awake. She twisted her neck around in a painful attempt to figure out who was grasping her shoulder and saw Hildr, a grin on the Valkyr's face. Crystal jerked up. "What time is it?"

"Good morning, wife of Tyr. The warriors have already eaten and are in the field." The Valkyr was, in fact, laughing at her, Crystal realized.

Crystal pushed herself from the bed and, once her swaying was gone, called on healing magic to calm the throbs in her head. The rest of her body hurt too, but she left the bruises from battle to be trophies. She walked unsteadily to the wardrobe and opened it, reaching inside for a fresh change of clothing that— wasn't there. The wardrobe was empty. She looked over at the corner, and realized her chest containing the war hammer and the blade was gone also. As panic set in, she rounded on Hildr.

"Where is my stuff?" Crystal asked, panic seizing her being.

"In your room, wife of Tyr," the Valkyr said, her smirk not wavering.

Crystal glared at the Valkyr, angry for the game she was playing, and then she realized what Hildr was implying. Looking out into the hallway, she counted doors, and then swiveled her head back inside to meet the gleefully bright eyes of Hildr.

Crystal shrugged.

"I had a bit too much to drink last night, I guess," she said, trying to keep her voice upbeat and defiant despite the queasiness in her stomach, and then drew herself up and strode down the hall to her own room. Hildr followed her in, still carrying the tray of fruit and cheese that Crystal had failed to notice earlier.

Crystal's eyes warred with her stomach as Hildr thrust the tray into her hands. "You must eat," the Valkyr said over Crystal's objections. "Today you are to spar with some of Thor's warriors, and you need strength to do so."

Crystal put the tray on the bed and picked a slice of apple up from it. She bit into it and chewed. And chewed. It was strange, she thought, how chewing food with a hangover seemed to take more effort than chewing any other time. It actually seemed to tire her out, so she lowered her cheek into her left hand for support as her jaws kept working. Ow! Crystal tenderly examined her cheek with her fingertips; it hurt. Still chewing, she walked to the privy and looked in the mirror and then gasped. Both eyes were blackened and her left cheek had a purple bruise starting to show itself. Curious, she walked back to her room and stripped, examining each bruise as it was revealed.

"I look like I lost a fight with a tornado," Crystal said to Hildr after she finally managed to swallow the bite of apple.

"You didn't expect to win any matches against the Master, did you?"

"No, but—I don't remember him getting in this many good hits."

"Maybe the floor and the furniture helped him a little."

Crystal spared a moment from her self-examination to glare at Hildr. She was in enough pain without sarcasm from the Valkyr. "Yeah, they must have. I'll have to teach them a lesson next time." As Hildr's expression changed from a subtle smirk to a broad grin, Crystal decided to leave her bruises unhealed as reminders. All except the face, anyway; she gathered healing energy and smoothed away the bruises on her cheek and around her eyes as well as the one she couldn't see yet on her forehead. It wouldn't do to go down to spar looking more like a beaten wife than a woman warrior.

Well—might as well get started, she thought. Crystal walked by Hildr, grabbing a large chunk of cheese from the tray against the Valkyr's protest and eating it on the way down to the field where she had met Thor.

"Good morning, sunshine!" the god said as she approached. "Did you get enough beauty sleep? The Valkyr who went by your room to wake you this morning said the snores from the room next door to yours were loud enough to scare even her away." Crystal stood, silently accepting the approbation, as Thor turned and looked at her. His eyes lingered on the bruises she had left on her body. "Can't you heal those?"

"I can," Crystal said with a dismissive shrug. "They help me remember the lessons you taught me yesterday."

Thor's grunt carried the smallest touch of approval. "David!" he yelled. "Give Crystal a chance to show you what she learned yesterday."

Crystal sparred with several of Thor's warriors throughout the day, creating many new bruises as the day progressed. They helped her by giving suggestions on how to hold her shield or club better for different types of attacks. The warriors, Crystal noticed, tended to be as interested in sharing their knowledge and skills as the blacksmiths of Hephaestus had been. She supposed it had to do with some sort of sense of brotherhood, though that was easier for her to reconcile when Angus had been showing her how to smelt iron than now, with a never-ending line of warriors seeking to apply bruises to her body.

As they tromped back toward the dining hall that evening, Crystal thought that she could still feel every old bruise and every new one as well. Her resolve had only wavered once during the day, as a long line of men had used sticks and hammers to pound lesson after lesson into her body. Thor had sensed her doubt; the god had suddenly been there, helping her to her feet. He whispered in her ear, "Embrace the pain, Crystal. Use it as fuel. Stacy will, and she will use it against you if she can. The more pain you feel and work through now, the stronger you will be in the coming battle."

Crystal groaned and ground her teeth in frustration. She knew Thor was right, and the lesson was still with her as she moved toward a well-earned dinner, but it was painfully obvious how far she still had to go. She was being crushed by mortal men, many of whom were only swinging at half or three-quarter speed despite Thor's exhortations to really test her. How could she hope to defeat a goddess?

Dinner was a replay of the night before, though this time Crystal carefully monitored how much she drank. She found the beer served as a kind of inner salve, just like that at the forge had; her bruises didn't hurt any less, but the immediacy of the pain went away. Crystal enjoyed watching the wrestling matches and even the flyting contest, though she thought the rhyming a little weak again tonight. Thor seemed to read her mind, leaning over and saying, "You can join in, you know. The men would love it, in fact. I bet you could toss out insults like nobody else in the hall could."

Crystal shook her head. "Certainly not tonight. My entire body is sore after the lessons your men taught me today."

Her talk that night with Matt and the girls was short; all she could really think of was the throbbing pain in every inch of her body. She mentioned it once to Matt, and resolved to say nothing of it again after barely resisting his urging to heal herself. As the connection closed, she lowered her head onto the pillow and re-laxed, closing her eyes and drifting immediately to sleep.

Crystal woke gently with fingers caressing her hair. She murmured her pleasure and stretched like a cat, feeling her bruised muscles protest and then give in. Suddenly she recalled where she was, and her eyes snapped open as her head swiveled around, bringing her face to face with Aphrodite.

Matt's ex-wife said, "Wakey wakey, lovey," a mocking expression on her face, as she rose. An evil laugh reminded Crystal of the battle at her estate as Crystal reached out with flows of elemental air, unlocking the trunk and calling her weapons to her hands as she sprang from the bed. "Oooh, such pretty pretty weapons. Too bad you don't know how to use them," the goddess taunted her, a pair of swords appearing in her hands.

Crystal felt her anger rising. She tensed and threw the hammer at Aphrodite as hard as she could. It bounced off a shield the goddess raised, and Aphrodite laughed again. *Damn you! I'm not ready!* Crystal thought, and then gripped the returned hammer tightly as she moved in for close combat. As she closed the distance, Crystal gripped all the elemental flows and threw a mélange of energy bolts at Aphrodite, hoping against hope that she could distract the goddess enough to get in a good strike with her sword. Aphrodite's shield deflected every flow, though, as the goddess arrogantly waved Crystal forward.

Knowing she would only get one strike, Crystal gathered the essence of magic and threw it, missing on purpose, sending it around Aphrodite's shield to behind her and setting off an explosion. She sprang in at the same time, wondering where Thor was, hoping that Aphrodite would be distracted, willing her god-killing sword to find its mark. She was horrified, though, to see her sword slide harmlessly off of Aphrodite's shield, the goddess's face a picture of gleeful radiance as her sword struck Crystal's chest, diving in and finding her heart.

With a gasp, Crystal woke. Wide-eyed she stared around the room, seeing only darkness and—a shape in the door. Out of reflex Crystal unleashed a flicker of elemental flow to light the room, and saw Hildr's face clearly enough to recognize the Valkyr. "What....?" Crystal said, still breathing too heavily to finish the question.

"I heard what sounded like struggle, so I came to see if you were alright. Are you okay?"

"Yes, it was—I guess I had a bad dream. Weird, I've never been prone to having bad dreams. Not until recently, anyway."

"A dream of battle? Against a goddess?" Thor's voice imposed itself upon the room as he pushed around Hildr. When Crystal nodded, he smiled. "Valhalla has a way of calling dreams of glorious battle to its inhabitants."

"But why her, then? Why not the battles I've been fighting?"

"Why are you here, Crystal? Is it to fight against me, or any of my warriors? No, you are preparing yourself to fight to the death against a goddess. Right? Does it not make sense that your subconscious would tell you that it's worried about the outcome?"

"My subconscious was pretty clear on the outcome, actually. I died."

"You almost died, you mean. You can't see yourself die in a dream—at least, not one that you wake up from."

"Well, okay. Fine, then. She ran me through with that magical sword of hers, and I almost died. How do I guard against that in the future?"

"By training more. You'll get there, but not in two days."

"So what do I do if she comes after me before I get there?" Crystal said, wincing at the whining tone she heard in her own voice.

"She won't. First, she knows I would never permit it. Here, in my hall, you are under my protection, and my Valkyr make a better response team than your husband's thrakkon do. Yes, I remember your earlier battle at Tyr's estate. I was there, remember?   But she won't want to, in any event. Gaia has initiated you as challenger, and so Stacy does herself dishonor if she harms you anywhere other than the arena in Olympus. So relax, wife of Tyr, go back to sleep, and join me in the morning in the great hall for more lessons."

Crystal did join Thor in the great hall the next morning, where he continued the training regimen he had established. That day he spent tutoring Crystal privately, and the next he had her join his warriors on the field to work with the men in turn. On the following day, when she joined Thor in the great hall he handed her a wooden replica of her hammer. "You've done well with the club learning your basic offense and defense," he said, "but now it's time to continue learning with your main weapon."

Exhausted by dinner time, Crystal sat at the table awaiting the arrival of the pork platter. She had to admit that she agreed with Thor about the skill level of the hammer. It was similar to the club but required more finesse, since it didn't matter where on the club the strike was made, yet the hammer's attitude on impact made all the difference in the world. She enjoyed it, though, because it was her weapon. Hephaestus had made her a hammer, rather than any other type of weapon, because he knew it would be the right choice for her. She had felt at the time—and she knew now—that he was correct. She loved the combination of strength, knowledge of physics, and finesse that it required, and she cherished the way the hammer felt like part of her body when she swung it. As Thor had pointed out early in the day, a hammer wielder couldn't afford to overbalance on a swing, and so combat with the hammer felt like a dance. Crystal loved to dance.

****

"Nice," Thor said, a surprised look on his face.

Crystal had a hard time staying in her defensive stance when what she wanted to do was jump up and down and scream her excitement, so she just nodded, a wide smile on her face the only hint of celebration she allowed herself. Still, she was proud. It had taken nearly three weeks of training, a day of lessons from Thor followed by a day of practice in the field followed by repetition of the simple cycle, but she had finally landed a solid hit on the thunder god: a rib-crushing blow to his side.

She had earned the hit, also, damn it. Thor had taught her there were two ways of getting inside an opponent's guard to land a solid and perhaps decisive blow. The first was to watch for mistakes, a method she had been frequently using with the warriors in the practice field, to the point where she won nearly as many bouts as she lost. Thor didn't make mistakes, though. Ever, she assumed. It made sense that anyone who had been fighting for millions of years would be supremely well-practiced at it, but that hadn't lessened the frustration she had felt at never, ever, ever, getting a hit in on him while he still, though definitely less frequently, continued getting powerful and occasionally bone-crushing blows in on her.

Thor sat down in a nearby chair. "Go ahead. Dance. I see that you want to. You've earned it."

Well, if he ordered it, she could only oblige, so Crystal held both arms up and whooped. He was right that she had earned it, because Thor still hadn't made a mistake. No, she had landed a blow the second way Thor had taught her: a perfectly-executed combination. Thor taught combinations to her; they were essential to success in a melee but they were difficult to carry out in the heat of battle. Each combination was intended to move the opponent's defense to one side or the other, which required not only accurate placement of threat but also the ability to fool the opponent through phony weight shifts and eye movements. When executed well, if the opponent made a mistake, the combination resulted in a good hit. When executed perfectly, it didn't matter whether the opponent made a mistake or not.

Crystal had been perfect. For that, she celebrated.

Thor rose and picked his weapons up after allowing Crystal a couple of minutes for celebration. "Party time's over, wife of Tyr. Getting a good blow in is a sign of improvement, but it will take more than that to defeat Stacy. Let's go," he said, and Crystal obediently settled back into a battle posture.

When they set their weapons down that evening, Thor congratulated her again. "Nicely done today, Crystal. Very nicely done. Let's meet back here tomorrow morning." Crystal nodded, curious why Thor was breaking the rhythm, but unwilling to ask.

The next morning, Thor walked in to the hall to find Crystal there already equipped with her shield and hammer. He chuckled and asked, "Are you that eager for a beating, young lady? This is the first time you've gotten here before me."

Crystal smiled over her shield and said, "You've changed the cycle of training, Master. I'm most curious as to why."

Thor guffawed. "Well, I confess that it's partly in consideration for your training, but surely you don't think I've gone and made you the focus of my camp, do you? The Valkyr tell me the men at the training field slack off a little when I'm not there, and they've been getting used to the day on, day off schedule. It's good to switch it up; they'll spend all of today working hard in the belief that I'll show up, and tomorrow they'll work hard because I'll actually be there. But as for your training, it's time to switch that shield out in favor of a sword. You've gotten—well, quite acceptable, I'd say—at single-weapon fighting. It's time to add dual-weapon fighting to your training."

Crystal set her shield down and replaced it in her left hand with a stick. "I have to admit that I'm a little scared of this. You said, a long time ago, that standing behind a defensive shield while using an offensive weapon was difficult enough, and you've since taught me that you were right. Using two weapons seems like it'll be an entire level of difficulty above what I've already done."

"Oh, it is," Thor said. "As a single-weapon fighter, you have to read your opponent and be able to block his attack while pushing your own attack into his vulnerable area. As a two-weapon fighter, you have to do all of that, but your second weapon must serve as both defense and offense at the same time. It's especially true in your case, since you're preparing for a battle in which your secondary weapon is the one that must deliver the killing blow. You've really presented me a tough nut to crack, you know that, right?"

"That's probably why you took on the challenge, isn't it, Thor?"

"Indeed. Now, put the hammer down. We're going to work on your left hand sword ability today."

Thor directed Crystal to keep her right hand at her side as much as possible, while he selected a stick to hold in her left hand that was about the same length as the god-killing sword Gaia had given her. "For styles that are truly dual-wielding, typically with matched bladed weapons, you want both weapons acting as a single pair, hands moving together most of the time but striking separately when needed. That's how Aphrodite will come at you, so it's important that you understand the stance. Dancing with two weapons is a relentless style. Your opponent will press you, press you, and press you, till you slip up and die. At least, that's what she hopes. The only way to survive in dual-weapon combat against a shielded foe, she will know, is to be as aggressive as possible."

Thor summoned two swords that looked like what Aphrodite had used and demonstrated the aggressive combat he had described, attacking the air in front of him. His twin swords carved parallel serpentine paths in front of him and then split to separately strike at his imaginary opponent. "See?" he asked.

"Now, your style will be significantly different. Trust me, she'll know this and she'll adapt. She was trained by the best, you know. But then again, by the time you're in the combat, you'll be able to boast of the same trainer." The twin long swords flickered out of his hands, replaced by a short sword in his left and a hammer in his right. "This," he said, waving the short sword, "is your shield, mainly. What you must have, or develop, is the ambidexterity to use your left hand as artfully as your dominant one." He demonstrated by waving the short sword in front of him, appearing to block blows and then strike a blow of his own. "Your dominant hand will be using the hammer. Its purpose is to inflict crushing blows on Aphrodite when an opening exists, and to distract her when an opening doesn't exist. Keep in mind that your hammer really can't hurt her, though. Its main purpose is to get her off-balance enough to allow you to strike a mortal blow with your sword. Got it?"

Crystal said, "I think so, but matching physical action with what I understand is difficult. Can we practice a bit?"

Thor nodded. "That's why we're going one-handed at first. You need to practice with just the sword in your left hand. Keep in mind as you do it that blocking with a sword is actually your worst choice, since it requires as much energy to stop a blow as your opponent put into starting the blow. Here, swing at me so I can show you."

Crystal swung the stick in her left hand at Thor as hard as possible, and he demonstrated blocking using a summoned sword in his own right hand. Seeing the action-reaction pair made Thor's warning clear to Crystal.

"Blocks, then," Thor said, "are inefficient. It's far better, when using two weapons, to redirect or avoid strikes. That way, instead of using your strength to stop your opponent's momentum, you can use her momentum against her strength."

Crystal spent the rest of the morning with her right hand hanging at her side, training her left hand to move the stick it was holding in sinuous patterns, fending off Thor's attacks. She surprised herself by being mostly successful; Thor landed a few strikes, but most were shunted off to the sides.

For the afternoon, Thor had her equip the hammer in her right hand. He started attacking and defending half-speed, to get her used to working both weapons at once, but the god rapidly progressed the training to full-speed dual-wielding. Crystal found the concentration on both hands to be both exhausting and exhilarating at the same time. Thor landed blow after blow on Crystal's body as her left hand refused to adjust to his attacks quickly enough, but Crystal's bruises had long since stopped being an issue for her training. She healed the fractures she suffered, while all other blows just created painful memories that served as lessons.

The next day Crystal faced off against Thor's warriors. One after another they beat her down, several suggesting bluntly that she had perhaps chosen the wrong fighting style. She continued getting back up, though, no matter how soundly she was knocked to the ground. At dinner that night the raucous environment that was Valhalla failed to penetrate her brooding silence. Thor stopped her with a hand when she rose from the table early to seek her room. "You did as well as could be expected today," he said, his stare holding her eyes with its intensity. "It's a hard style to learn, but you'll do it if you just keep getting up."

Crystal nodded and left, nursing both her injured body and her injured pride in the privacy of her room for the rest of the evening.

****

"Good morning, sunshine," Thor greeted Crystal. "Ready for the next phase in your lessons?" Crystal nodded, made wary by his uncharacteristically bright greeting. The past several weeks had brought much more bruising, but the time had also proven the truth of Thor's words about success through resilience. On each day working with Thor, Crystal had been taught a specific method to use in her chosen style, and she had spent most of the day practicing it over and over against the master. The other days she had spent in the field squaring off against the warriors, whose attacks slowly became less effective against her and whose admiration she seemed to be winning. Her bruises, though always present, had bothered her less and less as the days wore on. She even was invited to join in the wrestling at dinner, a contest she had proven herself competent in from the start.

"What is the next phase, Master?" she asked.

"General training, Crystal. I've taught you every technique there is to know in fighting with a hammer and a sword. You've learned astonishingly quickly, and so you're pretty good at the individual techniques. It's time to start putting them together, though. With magic, by the way, and your pretty hammer too. You need to start practicing like you'll actually be fighting."

"Oh," Crystal said, unable to put words around her feelings that mixed excitement with terror. She had been looking forward to a more broad approach to sparring as the next step in the training without really knowing if she could handle it. There were a lot of techniques, and while she had executed them all flawlessly on their own, actual combat flow meant taking them all out of their individual compartments in her mind and using them together without a script. She thought back to the days early in her marriage when she and Matt had taken ballroom dance classes, in part for the opportunity to get out one evening a week, and in part because the tango had sounded so sexy to learn. The pair had stepped expertly through each move, but putting them together into something resembling a dance had been rough—at least, it had till she had learned to let Matt lead. This exercise, though, was the opposite; if she let her opponent lead she would die.

"Crystal?" Thor said, breaking her out of her memories. "Are you ready?"

"Sure. Sorry, Master," Crystal said, making a snap decision to share her fear with Thor to get his advice. "At least, I think I am. You've taught me lots of techniques, but I'm a little nervous that I'll try, say, the sword sweep to the left when I should be sweeping to the right." She wished he had given her catchy names for the techniques like she had seen in the cheesy kung fu movies. It would be so much cooler to refer to the moves as, say, Lily Catching the Light or Downward Facing Dog—wait, was that a yoga stance?—she couldn't remember—than to have no labels at all. "I'm worried that I'll use the wrong one at the wrong time."

"Oh, don't worry. I can tell you with certainty that you have no reason to worry about that." Thor said.

"How can you be so certain?"

"I've been training warriors for a long time, Crystal. You don't need to worry because you will, for sure, use the wrong technique at the wrong time. Everybody does. And when you do, most students get up and do the same thing again, and then on the fourth or eighth time they get off the ground they learn not to do that. You've proven yourself smarter than that, though, so I bet you'll learn quicker. Say, the third or the fourth time you pick yourself up off the floor."

Crystal sighed. Thor's words hadn't improved her mood. "So, do you have any words of wisdom on how to determine which move to use when?"

"Well, yes, of course I do. Don't do it." Thor laughed at Crystal's incredulous look, and said, "No, I haven't lost my mind, girl.

Hand to hand combat is just like every other contest in this regard, only there are much higher stakes. Do you play chess?"

"Not well," she said.

"Fine; this isn't a chess game. But when you've played chess, do you worry about how you're going to move the pawn, or stress yourself over the correct execution of a castling move? Of course not, because the actual moves are trivial. Your hands play chess in the current round, but your brain plays chess many rounds ahead. If you're to be any good at it, anyway. Combat is the same, only faster. You don't have time to consider your strategy, to evaluate it a number of moves into the future. You also don't have time to think about whether to sweep your sword to the left or to the right. A warrior has to resign that level of thinking to her subconscious, thus allowing her main thought to focus on observing the opponent and evaluating the flow of the fight. But to do that, you must learn to trust your subconscious, and there's only one way to get there. Know what that is?"

"Sparring?"

"It's not standing here gabbing about sparring, that's for certain. Get your hammer—leave that damn sword where it is—and let's go."

Crystal turned and started toward the door, but Thor stopped her. "Wait. Are you seriously going to take time out of our training to go back to your room to get the magic hammer that is enchanted to return to your hand?"

"No, of course not," Crystal said, an impish smile playing across her face. "I was just trying to find the right spot in the light here where I can dramatically call my hammer to me. Oh, here it is, a great spot." Crystal waved her arms in a grand flourish and thought of her hammer, and was rewarded with the sudden feel of the hammer's weight in her right hand.

Thor snorted, unimpressed, and used a flow of air to toss a sword from the stand against the wall to Crystal. She squeaked in surprise and ducked the flying sword, and Thor's deep peals of laughter rattled the beams.

Thor pulled two matching swords to himself and brandished them.

"Why are you letting me use my magic hammer, but you're using unenchanted swords?" Crystal asked.

"A few reasons, Crystal. For one thing, you need practice with the weapons you'll be using in a combat that's already set into destiny. I don't. Second, your opponent in that combat will be using unenchanted swords. Third, Mjolnir would cause more damage to your flesh than magic can heal. I'm trying to teach you, not break you."

Thor attacked suddenly, both swords coming at Crystal on her right side. She jumped back, one of the sword tips grazing her chest, and fell to the floor. Blood streamed from her new wound.

"Those are sharp," Crystal said, adding an ironic twist to her voice as she knitted the skin on her chest back together.

"Indeed. Unfortunately your reaction wasn't. Diving backwards to sit on your butt isn't one of the techniques I worked so hard to teach you."

Crystal stood and then leaped back into battle. Through the day she healed herself frequently, each time making an effort to remember how she had been beaten. By evening, she thought she was holding her own.

"Tomorrow, it's back to wooden weapons," Thor said. "My warriors don't have magical weapons, and it's best for now that you don't use one against them. Later, we might test them against you, but you're not ready for that yet. Go put that hammer away now. I'm hungry."

Two days later, Crystal was surprised to see Hildr in the hall with Thor. "I want to see you matched against a Valkyr today, Crystal," Thor said. "Hildr is close in size, speed, and strength, to what you'll face in your battle with Stacy." Hildr proved a tough opponent; she wielded twin blades with unbelievable speed and accuracy and added several cuts to Crystal's body in the first few flurries. Frustrated, Crystal moved in closer and tried to use her strength against Hildr, but the Valkyr reminded Crystal of the thrakkoni strength by throwing her across the room with a negligent one-handed flick. Thor, watching Crystal pick herself up, said, "Stacy will probably enhance her strength magically so she can do the same. You should, too, but your better bet is to stay out of reach and use the skills you've gained in weaponry. Regardless, you shouldn't try the crowding trick again. It's a losing gambit against an accomplished swords-woman."

Crystal growled in frustration as Hildr's blinding speed beat her again and again. The Valkyr threw her sword down after slicing through Crystal's guard and her chest. "Stop fighting me with your head!" Hildr said, frustration peaking in her own voice. "I strike, and you think about what I'm doing and what you can do to counter it, and by the time you figure it out, I've already dealt you what would probably be a mortal blow in real combat. You don't have time for all that thinking!" Hildr stormed out of the room.

Thor walked over to Crystal and took the weapons out of her hands. "Okay, let's try something," the thunder god said. "Look in my eyes. Don't think about anything. Just be—just stand there. When I strike, you block, but don't think about it."

Crystal relaxed and stood an arm's length from Thor, eyes locked on his, waiting on his strike. She saw his eyes tense, and saw them shift to her right, which she knew meant he was striking that direction. She blocked to her right, and felt his palm connect with her left side.

"You were thinking, weren't you? Stop it. Clear your thoughts. Your mind isn't fast enough to block me, but your subconscious is. Picture yourself back in the repetition of beating on metal in Hephaestus's forge, and let your peripheral vision warn you of the attack and your subconscious defend against it. Now—again."

She did as he said, imagining herself back in the forge, and was both shocked and pleased when her hand, acting of its own volition, caught Thor's attack. They tried the exercise again, and Crystal blocked again. A third success brought a smile to Thor's face.

"Hildr!" Thor bellowed. The Valkyr appeared, arms crossed. "I think Crystal is ready for more lessons."

Crystal settled back into the forge work in her mind's eye, and was surprised at how easily she was able to block Hildr. She got in a solid hit with her hammer, knocking the Valkyr to the ground to rub her shoulder. Her giggle earned her a glare from Hildr.

"Sorry," she said. "I was just—well, amazed at how well this works, for one thing. But I also used to make fun of the various movies and shows where the main actor or actress was told to 'beeeee the blaaaaade' or 'beee the baaaat' or whatever. I had no idea at the time how well that could work."

After lunch, Hildr switched from twin swords to a polearm, Thor explaining that Aphrodite was nearly as good with that class of weapon and might switch up in the hopes that Crystal hadn't practiced against it. The blocking action, Crystal found, was completely different, but she had no problems adapting.

Dinner that night was a repeat of the many dinners before. Crystal wondered how many pigs Valhalla must keep in order to serve pork every night, but experience now told her it made for a hearty meal. She understood, now, for the first time, how it was that tales of Valhalla could sound so enticing to the northern warrior clans.

Celebration

"Glad to hear everything is okay and your training is going well, Crystal. Before you go, though—is there any chance you can take tomorrow off to come home for a bit?" Matt's voice was comforting as always, but the question put Crystal on edge.

"Home? Why? What's wrong, Matt?" Crystal asked.

"Wrong? Nothing, really. But—you don't know what day it is today, do you?"

"Thursday? Thor says it's always Thursday here."

"I wonder why," Matt said, his voice making it clear that he didn't wonder at all. Crystal had been fairly sure he would know that Thursday was named after Thor, but the joke seemed funny anyway. "Do you know which Thursday, though?"

"Noooo..." Crystal said. "How about a hint?"

"Just a hint. All right, I'll try a hint. Here's one, my love. At right about this time, fourteen years ago today, we were rushing you to the hospital."

Crystal gasped. "No, it can't be. There's no way it's November."

"Okay, love, but good luck convincing the girls of that. They've been following one of those new inventions that they call a calendar."

"But I got here..."

"...in July."

"Okay, fine, but there's no way I've been here for..."

"...almost five months. Yeah, that's about right."

"I just expected it to get cold, or maybe snow."

"Tell Thor that. I bet he can make it snow at Valhalla when he wants it to. Or not."

"I guess it never snowed on the kids' birthday when we lived at home."

"It never snowed much at all in the Bay area. If you waited for snow to celebrate their birthday, they'd still be playing with dolls."

"They still play with dolls."

Matt chuckled. "Okay, you win. But it is true that tomorrow is their birthday. I think they're counting on their big buff warrior princess mommy to make an appearance."

"I'm sticking my tongue out at you."

"Not very much if you can talk around it that well."

Crystal blew a raspberry across the link, and Matt chuckled. The couple said their farewells for the evening and closed their magical connection.

"Thor?" Crystal called out, hoping the god of thunder would hear her.

The door opened. "Yes, Crystal?" Thor's massive bearded head poked in.

"Can I take a day off?"

"A what?"

"A day off. Tomorrow is my girls' birthday, and I'd like to surprise them by being home on their special day."

Thor laughed. "Ah, yes, the beauty that is a woman. No matter how much battle rage she shows on the battlefield, she still remembers her children's birthdays and asks for a day off from the rage. I bet Tyr forgot the birthday, didn't he?" Crystal smiled in response, unwilling to correct Thor's mistake. "Well," Thor said, "Your time here is drawing to a close, anyway, so maybe it's best that we call an end to your training."

"No!" Crystal panicked. "I'm not ready, Master."

"Crystal, you're as ready as you'll ever be. You've taken every lesson I have to give. You've started consistently beating my warriors, sometimes two or three at a time. You've proven more than a match for the Vaklyr with that enchant you do." Crystal smiled, proud of her discovery of the resonance that allowed her to increase her strength and speed with a spell that didn't require holding on to. "You even fight me to a draw as many times as not. What else do you seek to gain?"

"I've only been training for a couple of months. Aphrodite has a lot of time on me."

"It's been quite a few months, actually, and you could train for the next several decades and not come close to Stacy's millions of years of experience. Besides, the shorter your stay, the more likely she will underestimate you. I think your time to leave has come."

Crystal agreed, but couldn't prevent her sadness at leaving Valhalla from showing in her face.

"Oh, you can come back anytime you'd like, wife of Tyr. How about tomorrow night, we throw the girls a birthday dinner here? It will be quite a bit different from the cake and ice cream they usually get, but it will give the Valkyr and the men a chance to say their goodbyes. You can even bring that husband of yours if he'll lower himself to eating in my hall. What say you?"

Crystal nodded. "That sounds wonderful, Thor. If it's all right, then, I will teleport back tonight to sleep in my own bed, and we'll make plans to return as a family tomorrow night."

Thor nodded and turned to leave.

"Wait," Crystal said. "Aren't you going to teleport me back? ...Master?"

Thor stopped and turned, a confused look on his face. "I'm sorry, I must have misheard you. Didn't you say you would teleport back? As in you, yourself?"

"I can't teleport myself."

"And why not?"

"Well, I don't know how."

"Ah! Well, can't and don't know how are two different things, aren't they?"

"Indeed. Mind helping me figure it out?"

Thor chuckled. "Of course not. Watch me teleport myself." Thor gathered magic around him, and suddenly his body blinked out of one spot and into a space a few feet in front of where he had been. "It's a fairly easy twist, but the key is to focus on the spot you wish to go to while you un-focus on everything else. You have to be able to see the spot, at least in your memories, or have a strong emotional connection with it in some other way. That's why the gods all have a gold spot for teleporting to; it makes targeting easier when we visit each other. The only trick for us is in being very clear on whose gold spot we're popping out onto."

Crystal, who had been watching closely, nodded. "I think I have it now," she said. She gathered the essence around herself and tweaked it just as she had seen Thor do it, and suddenly she felt the familiar shifting of the world. She looked around and was pleased; she had moved to the exact spot she had been targeting. "Is there any significant difference when teleporting a long way?" she asked.

"None at all," Thor said. "It's precisely the same weave. Your subconscious guides your mind on the actual location, so you have to be specific when you're focusing on the target. For example, if you just think of teleporting onto a gold circle, you might end up visiting Stacy instead. You can also use the kind of coordinates that the old earth science systems used, but that's a little dangerous since you never really know what you'll be teleporting into. Teleporting into the middle of a tree doesn't feel good, trust me."

"I'll keep that in mind," Crystal said. Then, on impulse, Crystal lunged at Thor, catching the giant god of thunder in a hug. Thor seemed startled for a moment, and then returned the hug with gusto. "Thank you, mighty god of thunder," Crystal murmured into his beard. "Your faith in me, and your teachings, mean the world to me."

"Tyr's an old friend—older than you probably realize, Crystal. I hated to see him in with Stacy, but I'm pleased as I can be to see you with him. Go now, wife of Tyr, and come back tomorrow night for a grand party."

"Will do," she said, and stepped back. She picked up her two magical weapons, smiled at Thor, and then un-focused enough to grab hold of the white swirling essence around her. Soundly in control, then, she focused on a spot at the foot of her own bed. She twisted the essence just so, and felt the world shift. Opening her eyes, she found herself staring through darkness at her empty bed.

"You really should either warn me that you're coming, or teleport to the gold spot next time," Matt's voice sounded behind her. She jumped in surprise and whirled around. Matt was rising from one of the chairs, putting down the book in one hand and the drink in the other. As he walked toward her, he said, "I love having you back, but your hasty teleport set off every alarm in the estate. Once I realized it was you I had to let all the thrakkoni know to stand down. They...."

Crystal didn't really care about the alarms, so long as no one had gotten hurt, and so she silenced Matt in the only way she knew. Summoning the white essence again, she teleported to him and kissed him deeply.

When she finally released him, she sagged. He caught her easily and carried her over to the bed. "Love," he said, gently undressing her and laying her down, "I'm overjoyed to see this new-found power in you, but please take it easy. There's a reason we usually walk around the room instead of teleporting. Two teleports in a row is exhausting."

"Three," Crystal said, smiling from her pillow. She really was exhausted; she couldn't move her head off the pillow.

"Of course. You teleported once at Thor's to make sure you could, didn't you?"

She gave a tiny nod, and Matt smirked. "Well, regardless, I'm very glad to see you. I've missed you, Crystal. Are you home for the night, or for a while?"

"I'm home for good, sort of," Crystal said, having trouble keeping her eyes open now. "Thor said I was done, and ready to face Stacy." She shook her head, trying to keep from slurring her words too much. "He wants to have a—a—a birthday party—for the—um, for the girls. Tomorrow."

Matt smiled tenderly. "That sounds grand. You need sleep now, though. Close your eyes, and let me just take this god-killing sword to somewhere safer."

Crystal closed her eyes, and knew nothing more till the morning.

****

The sunlight blinded Crystal as it blazed in through the freshly-opened window. She growled as she sat up; she had grown used to being woken up more gently, without the sun's forcefulness. She was exhausted, too; it felt like she could use another couple of hours of sleep.

"Did you enjoy your visit with Thor and his Valkyrie, Crystal?" Sorscha's voice chimed over Crystal's growl.

"I did, yes. None of them ever opened a window and prismed it directly into my eyes."

Sorscha chortled her low-pitch huff-huff sound, and Crystal realized how much she had missed the thrakkon. She said, "Then again, you've never stuck a sword or a pole arm in me, so I think you're still my favorite."

"They are rather fond of fighting, aren't they?" Sorscha said. Crystal didn't see a point in answering, so she rose and let Sorscha begin dressing her. "I do hope they were sticking swords and pole arms into you to fulfill a training purpose, yes? They didn't treat you badly, did they?"

"We had some glorious practice battles, is all. Do you know a Valkyr named Hildr?"

"I do. Hildr is, I believe, the Valkyrie who attends to visitors, as she serves the Master when he is there also. Was Hildr your attendant, or one of the ones teaching you?"

"Both. She's an amazing fighter."

"They all are. The Father God gave each of them a third shape long ago, and they've always trained the hardest and been the best warriors of all of our kind."

"I don't see the connection."

"Neither do I, Crystal. But to them, being a Valkyrie is a very special thing. Oh, sorry."

Crystal had reacted to Sorscha's accidental pressure on her rib cage as she was putting on her shirt by jumping away. It hurt. Crystal looked at the spot, wondering why it hurt with no bruise over it. Then she realized that the lack of a bruise was unusual, and she looked over the rest of her body. Her bruises were gone. The spot on her ribs still hurt, but it was an internal injury that Crystal hadn't cared about enough to heal. "Where's Matt?"

"Right here," Matt said, rising from the chair that was turned toward the window and the white fields outside. Crystal gasped—white?

"Did you cause it to snow just for me?" Crystal asked.

"You, and the girls," Matt said. "They've never had snow on their birthday, so I figured it would be nice."

She gazed out the window at the snow-covered landscape that looked more like a portrait than a real scene. "It's beautiful, Matt," she said, and then remembered why she had asked about him. "Hey, did you heal my bruises?"

"Guilty. I couldn't bear to see those things all over your body last night. I hope you weren't collecting them for some sort of bragging festival, were you?"

"No, actually, I just left them unhealed so they would remind me of the lessons learned. Now that I'm a graduate, I guess it's okay if I throw away the texts."

"The texts, sure, but you still have a final exam, if you still wish to go through with it."

"I do. Why wouldn't I, after coming this far?"

"Well, I can't think of a single reason you wouldn't, but I still wish you would."

Crystal closed the distance between them quickly and embraced her husband. "My love, I'll be alright," she said into his ear. "I've had the best trainers available."

"So has Stacy," Matt said. "Now, don't get upset. I have every confidence in you and your abilities. But I also don't wish to see you hurt, so forgive me if I seem a bit over-protective of the love of my life."

Crystal kissed him on the cheek. "I forgive you."

"Oh, good. And if you're dressed sufficiently, I'm sure you'd like some breakfast to go with that forgiveness. And so would your daughters, I bet, who still don't know you're home."

Crystal gasped. "I don't have a birthday present for them."

Matt shrugged. "Taken care of. While you were gone, you asked me to get our beloved daughters a pair of glass orchids, each in its recipient's favorite color. They're wrapped and in the closet now."

"Oh, that was very wise of me," she said, knowing that she had made no such request. She kissed him again. "You're such an awesome father."

"I know," Matt said, winking and pulling away. He strode to the door. "Girls!" he said, his magically-enhanced voice echoing in the room. "Are you ready for breakfast?" Heidi and Linda exited their room at the same time Crystal walked out of hers, and the girls squealed and ran to their mother.

Breakfast was an excited affair, with the girls spending more time asking their mother questions about her long stay away than they spent eating. Birch and his wife also joined them and listened intently to Crystal's stories. Birch was saddened that Crystal had been there for months without seeing Mjolnir, but his sadness was lessened by Crystal's description of the great hall and its attendant Valkyr and replaced by joy when Matt informed him that he and his wife and some of the other mages had been invited to attend the birthday party at Valhalla.

The rest of the day went quickly. The boys, Steve and Corey, joined them for lunch, and were told to be prepared to travel for dinner but not to where. Heidi asked her mother repeatedly what the plans were, but Crystal kept quiet and smiled at Matt.

Finally dinnertime came. Matt led the family along with Birch and Frita, Ben, Natalia, and the boys, Phoenix, Krista, and RJ, up the stairs into his throne room and all crowded onto the gold circle. "Girls, you remember the times you've teleported on the backs of the thrakkoni?" Matt asked, voice raised so everyone could hear. When they nodded their heads, he said, "This is very similar. We're going to teleport someplace special, but the sensation in your guts will be the same."

"Where are we going, Dad?" Linda asked. Heidi continued, "It would be nice to know what to be prepared for."

Matt looked at Crystal, who nodded, and so Matt said, "Girls, we're going to where your mother has been for several months. You've heard of Thor, right?" Both girls had, so Matt continued, "He's invited all of us to Valhalla for tonight to celebrate your birthdays. The Norse would've probably considered this sacrilege, to celebrate girls' birthdays at the great hall of Odin, but we're gods, right? The women there are like the thrakkoni here, only they're called Valkyrie and are warriors in their own right.

The men are all humans training to be some of the greatest warriors of the coming years. Now, are you prepared for transport?" Both girls nodded, and Crystal watched Matt envelop the family and friends in white strands of magic as they blinked to Valhalla.

Crystal looked around; they had decorated the hall grandly for the occasion. The wooden beams of the ceiling and those supporting it were wrapped in colored ribbons, and multi-colored lights shone all around. The Valkyrie all wore fine silk instead of their warrior tunics. The assembled warriors, for once strangely quiet, were the only ones who didn't seemed to have changed; they were all still dressed in fighting leathers.

Thor's voice bellowed down the hall, saying, "Tyr! Crystal! Magi! Welcome to Valhalla! And who are the lovely young ladies you bring with you?" The giant, dressed in an outfit that was much furrier than anything she had ever seen him in, waved them up to the main table. Matt walked boldly down the hall, suddenly seeming nearly as tall as Thor. Crystal saw her husband wave his left hand, and noticed that his right hand was missing. She pushed the girls along behind, waving at all of the men who, just days prior, had stood against her on the field of battle. Chaos erupted as over one hundred large, hairy, and loud men cheered. The mages and family followed, Birch staring wide-eyed around at the grand hall.

The family took their seats at the main table, and Thor motioned it to be quiet. He said, "My comrades, today we celebrate two grand events. The first celebration is the anniversary of birth of these two young ladies, twin daughters of my ancient friend Tyr. Tonight, we celebrate their birthday, and I, being lord of the hall, get the first kiss!" Thor turned and, lifting each girl up in turn, kissed her on the cheek. He allowed the cheers to die down before continuing, "The second is bittersweet. Many of you have come to respect the hammer and sword of Crystal, wife of

Tyr, as she has stayed with us and learned our ways. Tonight marks her return home. She is always welcome in our hall, of course, and I am sure she will return, so tonight is but a temporary farewell. Still, a sad farewell it is."

Crystal was amazed as all around the hall the men and Valkyr alike rose and applauded her. Moments later, both Thor and Matt joined them. She started to rise also, but a cushion of air on her shoulders forced her to remain in her seat, and Matt's voice sounded in her mind. *Sit, my love. They do you honor by standing for you, and you should accept it by remaining in your seat and looking pleased.*

"Tonight, then, a grand feast!" Thor called, and the Valkyr quickly brought a platter of roast pig and vegetables out to the main table. Crystal reached in and grabbed some meat for her board, and then realized that her daughters were watching her, horrified. She shrugged, and said, "It's a warriors' hall, girls. Eating like this is expected. Hey, it's fun, too. Try it."

They did, and soon they forgot their insistence on manners enough to enjoy the meal. Matt obviously enjoyed it as well, one-handed though he was. Midway through, the men began bringing gifts to the girls. Crystal was amazed at the workmanship; most of the gifts were hand-carved pieces of wood or stone, some more ornate than anything she had seen before. One, a towering man named Seth who Crystal remembered could pack a wallop with his hammer, brought the girls matching nested wooden egg sets, each egg set comprised of one intricately carved egg inside another, inside another. The generosity of the normally-ferocious warriors brought a tear to Crystal's eyes.

The tear was short-lived. Immediately after the gift-giving ceremony, the warriors settled in once again for their normal dinnertime amusement. Birch clapped and yelled while the girls looked at their mother in horror as grapplers faced off in the cleared area in the middle of the room.

"It's normal, girls. At least, it's normal for Valhalla," she said quietly, smiling to them. "It's actually kinda fun."

"You did that?" Phoenix asked from several seats down, destroying Crystal's idea that her explanation had been quiet.

"Well, sure," Crystal said, shrugging her shoulders as though participating in after-dinner wrestling on the floor of the grand hall of Valhalla were something she'd always done.

Phoenix snorted; Birch looked at Crystal with wide eyes.

Crystal, watching the matches, wasn't surprised when Seth stood again and sauntered toward the head table, saying:

"The Master's guest is all done,

Going home to bask in the sun,

To her very last breath,

From the war maul of Seth,

She's learned that it's better to run."

Phoenix leaned over as she switched her gaze from Seth to Crystal. "A limerick? In Valhalla? *Really?*"

Crystal's smile widened as she stood and walked around the table to face Seth on the floor. "Yes, really," she murmured as she passed Phoenix's chair. "He's an Irish Viking."

Feet planted wide and fists on hips, Crystal faced Seth with her smile still glowing. Loudly, she answered:

"The challenger dear

has nothing to fear

from this tired and beaten-down lass.

But he'll need a friend

to see to the end

this contest, for I'll kick his ass."

As most of the crowd cheered, Crystal could hear Matt behind her quickly explaining to the girls what and why flyting was. She chuckled softly to herself as she imagined the shocked looks they must be giving him.

Another man, Olrud, rose and joined Seth on the floor. Crystal had wrestled the pair of them before, and she'd also fought them as a pair several times with various weapon combinations. The two men made a good team, but neither was an overly-competent wrestler, especially against someone whose weight was as well-balanced as Crystal's.

"By Seth I shall stand,

to give him a hand,

though likely he needeth me not,

to challenge this lass

who has lots of class,

but wrestling skill? Probably not."

Crystal barely had time to register the sigh behind her that was Phoenix commenting on the poor quality of the rhyming that evening before the two men moved into an approach and the match was on. Seth, the larger man, came at her first. She took his right arm in her hands, flipping his hand sideways and bringing the elbow up and over her shoulder, controlling his weight as she rapidly shifted her hips under his body and used them as a fulcrum to flip him over. Wham! The big man's body made a loud sound as it hit the ground and Crystal turned to face Olrud's onrush.

Olrud had apparently learned from their previous wrestling match, as he approached cautiously and carefully in balance. No matter; Crystal matched the older man in strength and was more agile than he, so she slipped into a hold where each of them wrapped arms around their opponent's head and shoulders. She knew Seth would be up soon and so she didn't have much time, so she ducked under Olrud's arm and used her hips as a fulcrum again to flip him over onto his back with her own back landing across his chest, knocking his wind out.

She saw that Seth was back on his feet, so she flipped up quickly and went after him. She repeated the cycle several times, alternatively flipping one then the other onto the hard wood floor. They began getting up more and more slowly, till finally each remained on the floor for long enough that Thor declared her winner. Everyone in the hall leapt to their feet and cheered; the noise of beer mugs hitting tables was deafening. Matt and her daughters were beaming in pleasure at the head table.

Dinner finally ended and the Valkyr brought large boxes for the girls' gifts. While they were boxing the gifts, Matt teleported the mages back while Crystal led her family down to the room she had called her own during her stay. The girls were shocked at the room's simplicity, but Crystal assured them it was grand compared to her first room at the estate of Apollo. They helped her pack her clothing into her chest, and Matt returned the chest to their room with a wave of his hand.

"An Irish Viking?" Thor asked Crystal, arms crossed over his chest and a playful scowl stretched across his face.

Crystal shrugged, eyes twinkling.

"I am not good with goodbyes, Crystal," Thor's voice said from the door, "so I expect you to return with or without your husband, who seems to hang out at his own estate far too much. For now, anyway, I'll bid you good night. The gifts for your daughters are in these boxes, and so all is ready for your return."

Both girls hugged the massive thunder god, whose face quirked with tender happiness. "You're a lucky man, Tyr," he said, and then he left to return to his own room.

Matt teleported the family back to their estate to find that Sorscha was already working on unpacking the trunk of Crystal's clothes. Crystal kissed the girls and wished them a happy birthday again and sent them to bed talking excitedly about how awesome their mom the wrestler had been, and then pushed Matt toward the bed also. "You're a lucky man, Tyr," she said, mimicking Thor's voice.

"I know I am, wife of Tyr," Matt said, smirking, and pulled Crystal to him. Crystal saw Sorscha leave out of the corner of her eye, and then she started to work on showing Matt how lucky a man he was.

To Kill a Goddess

"So, lovely wife of mine, when do you plan on challenging Aphrodite to a battle?" Matt asked the next morning as they dressed.

"The sooner the better, I suppose," Crystal said. "I doubt there's much advantage to waiting."

Matt exhaled a long, slow sigh. "No, I guess you're right. I can summon the gods as early as tonight."

Crystal stopped dressing and went over to Matt, running her hand down his cheek. "If I fail, will you mourn me?"

Matt stopped what he was doing and went over to the windows, staring out at the forest for several entire minutes before replying without turning back to her, "Yes. I've mourned every wife I've lost, Crystal, but I would mourn you more than any. You're the closest I've ever found to an equal on this plane of existence." He turned and said, "I love you, Crystal, and will rejoice with you when you win. I respect the choice you have made, and stand behind you win or lose. But know this—I will be destroyed, too, should you lose the battle."

Crystal's eyes met Matt's but couldn't hold there; she sank into a chair and looked at the floor. Finally she breathed in, and then out, and said, "Call the gods tonight, then. I must finish what I've started, and tonight I will be your true goddess mate." Crystal felt strange doing nothing to lighten the mood, but her response felt—right.

"Matt?"

"Yes, Crystal?"

"Should I fall, you know how to take care of the girls, right?"

"Feed them and clothe them every day and marry them off at the first opportunity?"

"Wasn't what I meant," Crystal said, glad for the touch of levity.

"You won't fall. But be assured that if you do, the girls will be taken care of."

"Thank you."

The day passed quietly. Crystal spent most of the day in the war room gloomily practicing moves with her weapons. She originally had intended to awaken the figurines and fight them, but she found she only had a taste for fighting one being, and that goddess wasn't available yet. So she paced, and paced, and paced.

In mid-afternoon, a knock sounded on the door. She opened it, and was greeted by Sorscha carrying a package. The thrakkon opened her bundle and took out a set of leather armor. Crystal began to object, but Sorscha shushed her. "The Master asked me to bring this to you," she said. "He commissioned it for someone else, who left him before it was done. It would please him greatly if you would wear it into battle against her. It's not very encumbering, as you can see," Sorscha made her point by holding up the top piece that really was just a chest plate with shoulder pauldrons, "but it has some magical protection against modest injury. It won't make or break a battle such as the one you face, but it might allow you to maintain your concentration at just the right time. May I help you put it on?"

Crystal nodded, and Sorscha began fitting the hardened leather pieces to her body. It fit very well, forming itself to her body and allowing her an entirely free range of movement. The arm guards were separate pieces, tying below the pauldrons, and the leg pieces were separate as well. She allowed Sorscha to finish adjusting the buckles and straps, and then moved to the mirror in the corner. It really did look good on her, she allowed herself to admit. "Thank you, Sorscha," she said.

A low whistle sounded from the door. Matt came in and said, "My goodness. That armor looks absolutely stunning on you. How about you and I run away to some deserted island somewhere for a few months while I let you know how sexy you look?"

Crystal stuck her tongue out at him, forcing some levity in the hopes of it making her feel better. It did work. A little, anyway. "Once the battle tonight is over, dear Mars, you can take me wherever you'd like."

"I'll take you up on that. By the way, keep in mind that though everyone will know you're my wife, I must maintain an air of indifference during the battle. I also can't celebrate in the arena when you win. If Gaia shows up, which is doubtful, she'll be senior, but if not then the seniority cloak falls on my shoulders." He walked over and embraced Crystal. "Are you ready?"

Crystal, who had spoken with the girls at length that morning, was ready, and said so. Matt nodded, and Crystal felt the lurch of the teleport taking her away. She had forgotten how jarring the teleporting to Olympus could be, though, and she staggered slightly in Matt's arms. After regaining her balance, she looked around. She was in the bar, which was now empty except for her, Matt, and the barkeep, who winked at her and then went back to studiously ignoring her.

"When you're ready, walk through the curtain. I must take my place," Matt said, and after a prolonged gaze into her eyes, winked out of the room.

"Good luck, lass, and Godspeed," Crystal heard the barkeep say, barely loud enough to carry to her ears.

The time had come. She had trained for months. She didn't feel it was enough, but four gods had assured her it was. She didn't feel ready, but there wasn't any additional time to get ready. She set up the oscillation magic to improve her strength and speed, breathed deeply, exhaled, and walked through the curtain.

****

What had been a soft murmur of talking ceased as Crystal walked through the curtain. She looked around; she was on a marble arena floor. The walls were white. The ceiling was white. The columns holding up the ceiling were white. All around the arena, faces stared at Crystal from above the wall. She looked around and saw Thor, and closer to the middle of the wider part she saw the cold, disinterested expression of Apollo. Right in the middle she saw Matt, sitting in apparent judgment.

Across the arena floor lurked Aphrodite.

Aphrodite, she saw, wore no armor. Then again, she was a goddess, so she likely didn't feel the need. Instead of leather, Aphrodite wore flowing silk, which was comfortable to the touch and made movement easy, but gave no room for error in dodging.

Aphrodite's eyes focused on Crystal, and then on the hammer, and then on the sword. "I see you come well armed," she said, a sneer on her face. "I'll be glad to claim that hammer as my own when I defeat you."

Crystal smiled. She had watched, and then participated in, the flyting at Valhalla, and there was no way Aphrodite was going to approach the offensiveness of the men in Thor's hall. She replied, "And I will be glad to claim your seat here as my own when I defeat you."

Aphrodite laughed, and Crystal saw power flow at the goddess's bidding as two swords appeared in her hands. *Good, then, she's using the weapons I trained against the most*, she thought. The goddess took the initiative, sending a bolt of white energy at Crystal. Crystal, though, had her shield ready and easily deflected the bolt.

"The mighty Aphrodite missed her target oh so widely," Crystal said with a snide grin, trying to pull Aphrodite out of her cool pose and into an angry battle—the angrier on Aphrodite's part, the greater Crystal's chances to win.

"Can't you do better than kindergarten rhymes?" Aphrodite asked as she released a barrage of elemental magic that Crystal also deflected. Crystal noted that the onlookers seemed protected by some sort of shield, but she wasn't willing to turn her attention away from Aphrodite long enough to study it.

"What's wrong, Stacy? Scared? Is that why you stand way over there and throw your magic at me?"

Aphrodite aimed a white ball of the essence of magic at Crystal's face in response to the comment, but Crystal deflected it just as easily. This time Crystal was ready; as soon as the magic ball was diverted she threw the hammer at Aphrodite and brought the god-killing sword back to guard position quickly. That her move worked shocked Crystal. Aphrodite apparently knew that the hammer would return, and took the opportunity of it being in the air to duck around it and, at an impossibly fast speed, charge Crystal swinging both swords. She was brought up short, though, by Crystal's effective defense with the blade, and Crystal sent Aphrodite a few steps back with a well-aimed blow to her shoulder.

"The great Aphrodite is mighty tough, but it seems that she's just not fast enough," Crystal taunted, grinning over the grey sword that was the only weapon in existence which could steal the life from the goddess.

Aphrodite regained her composure and attacked, a smooth flow of both weapons simultaneously to one direction and then to another. Crystal easily countered, letting the goddess control the flow for the moment in order to gauge her abilities better. Aphrodite wasn't, it seemed, anywhere near as good as Thor was. The two traded blows for several minutes while Crystal digested this fact, measuring the goddess's reach and speed and strength. To Crystal, the battle felt exactly like watching a chess match from above, her subconscious taking care of the mechanics involved in parrying and dodging Aphrodite's blows and returning a few of her own while her conscious mind examined, evaluated, and recorded the goddess's strengths and weaknesses.

Crystal went on the offense. The god-killing sword danced around perfectly in the zone of defense, blocking any attempt Aphrodite made while forcing the goddess to maintain a defensive stance herself. Meanwhile, the hammer swished in a wicked S-shaped arc, catching Aphrodite on the tail of the S and kicking her body around and back. The goddess lifted herself off the floor with a burst of air energy, quickly regaining defensive posture as Crystal pressed the attack.

Finding themselves to be almost perfectly evenly matched, the pair went through a series of moves that Thor had taught Crystal meant suicide in bladed battle, Aphrodite's blades dancing back and forth down Crystal's defenses and Crystal's blade moving in closer and closer to Aphrodite's body. The speed and strength of both combatants was all that saved them; with inhuman agility each spun out of the combination before they impaled each other, but neither escaped injury. Crystal felt blood pouring from her stomach. Apparently Aphrodite had sliced her across her middle as Crystal had used the god-killer across Aphrodite's chest. Crystal cast the spell that would close her own wound as she watched Aphrodite's wound close also.

Huh? This is supposed to be a god-killing sword, she thought briefly before smothering her confusion. It wouldn't do to take a chance that Aphrodite would see her confused, even for a moment.

Suddenly it occurred to Crystal to do something new. She had established oscillations in other types of magic. Apollo had mentioned oscillations in healing; why not set one up for permanent healing?

Quickly she set up a healing oscillation of purple energies through her body as she stalked Aphrodite from across the arena, a victorious feeling taking over as the cut across her stomach stitched itself back together. Why hadn't she thought of it earlier? It proved challenging to set the oscillations to precisely the right tempo, especially in battle, but when they settled in successfully, Crystal felt like crowing.

The expression on Aphrodite's face was priceless. As the healing oscillation set in to Crystal's body, Aphrodite looked on in horror and then resignation.

Suddenly the goddess threw herself into the attack, surprising even Crystal with her ferocity. Crystal was beaten back to the wall at first, but then the exercises at Valhalla took over and she began shunting Aphrodite's attacks to either side.

Crystal saw Aphrodite's mistake after a few minutes. The goddess was telegraphing her intent. She was clearly taking every swing at Crystal's neck, apparently doing her best to behead the mortal woman. With a start, Crystal realized that her oscillation hadn't included her head, and modified it the slightest amount so that it would. Aphrodite's dual attack remained constant, but her groan told Crystal that she had seen the modification.

Wait.... Crystal realized she had missed a main point. *If I can set up a healing oscillation, then I am....* Crystal allowed one of Aphrodite's swings through her guard to verify her suspicion. Sure enough, the cut that opened in her chest quickly closed itself.

I'm—immortal.

As Crystal's wound closed, Aphrodite seemed to lose steam for the fight. Crystal beat her back, attacking with both the hammer and the god-killing sword. She pressed Aphrodite into the center of the arena for the kill.

But if I'm already immortal, what's the point? Crystal's study of defense against two blades was now soundly controlling Aphrodite's forms. *And I've already seen her heal from a cut with this 'god-killing' blade, so....*

With a flick of her sword, Crystal succeeded in disarming Aphrodite's right hand. The battle, she knew, was nearly over, and would be hers to win if she maintained her cool. A massive bash with her hammer later, Crystal removed the weapon from Aphrodite's other hand and drove the goddess to her knees. She was one strike away from winning the battle, killing the goddess, and finishing the contest....

No.

This had never been, she realized with a shock, about killing Aphrodite. The secret was within herself. Crystal now saw clearly what the key was to becoming a goddess, and it didn't involve the beheading of another deity.

Crystal changed direction of the blow she had been about to make. It wouldn't have made a difference, anyway, she was certain. Instead, she went low and swiped Aphrodite across the tush with it, and then threw the 'god-killing' blade to the side onto the floor. Hefting her hammer, she strode across the arena and looked up at Matt, a challenge in her eyes.

"I claim my place among you," she said, using magic to project her voice. She was struck by a moment of doubt; if she was wrong, she was leaving her back open to Aphrodite's swords. She forged ahead anyway, saying, "I have learned magic from the master of the arcane after passing his test. I have learned combat from master of battle. I have bested one of your own in the arena of combat using both skills. I have even done my time in the forge of Hephaestus, working and proving my mettle. I would sit amongst you now, a fellow immortal, an equal in the eyes of all."

Crystal had been making it up as she went, doing what felt right, but she was pleased that she hadn't felt either of Aphrodite's swords cleaving her body. Something, then, was going well. She watched Matt's eyebrow quirk up in a questioning expression as he looked around the room, locking eyes with each god and goddess present. Finally, his eyes having made their rounds through the onlookers, Matt looked past Crystal at where she had left Aphrodite. Crystal desperately wanted to know what Aphrodite did or said in response, but she refused herself the pleasure of turning around. She held Matt's eyes until they returned to hers, solemnity radiating from his face.

Matt rose. "Crystal," his amplified voice rang out, "the assembled deities have watched your test and find you worthy. Ascend now, and take your place."

A cheer erupted from the viewing area, and Crystal finally let out her breath and allowed herself to look around. Thor was literally bouncing up and down, clapping with all his might. Apollo was more serious, yet his smirk told her that he was pleased as well. Hephaestus bore a huge grin on his face and gave Crystal two enthusiastic thumbs up when their eyes met.

Finally Crystal turned to meet her former foe, now her equal. Aphrodite was standing, arms crossed, glowering across the arena at the newest goddess. She inclined her head slightly, admitting defeat, and Crystal allowed her a tight smile in return.

Crystal turned and, using a cushion of air, ascended into the stands next to where Matt waited. "You done good," he said quietly into her ear. "Now, how about some nectar and ambrosia to celebrate the newest goddess?"

The pair floated down together and walked through the curtain hand in hand, husband and wife, god and goddess.

Tea and Cookies

"Tea and cookies it is, then," Gaia said, and a table holding an exquisite porcelain tea set and a plate of cookies shimmered into existence in the middle of Gaia's forest glade. Matt held Crystal's chair for her as she sat, and then seated himself elegantly as the earth mother joined them.

"I'm glad you decided to stop by," the Mother said.

Crystal, pouring a cup of tea for the other two deities before filling her own cup, smiled and said, "We had to, Mother. I've wanted to take you up on your invitation to tea and cookies and get to know you for quite some time. Matthew has always spoken reverently of you. Besides, it seemed appropriate that my quest bring me back here after beginning in your glade so long ago."

"That, and she's been teleporting everywhere she can, Mother, ever since she mastered that spell. She even teleports into her closet from the bed when she gets up. The idea of teleporting to your glade got her so excited she was shaking," Matt said.

Gaia's laugh seemed to be echoed by the trees around them. She said, "That's quite normal, Matthew, for a newly-ascended goddess. Speaking of that, Crystal, how are you enjoying your newfound status?"

"It isn't all that different," Crystal said with a shrug. "Sorscha tried to call me ma'am again once, but I convinced her that I was still Crystal. You do know Sorscha, don't you, Mother?"

"Oh, I certainly do, child. She's one of my favorite thrakkoni, in fact. If she ever leaves Matt's service, I might actually consider allowing a dragon to live here in order to have her around. Now, I assume, I'd have to compete with you for that honor."

"I'd fight you for her, that's for sure, but somehow I can't imagine her ever leaving Matt. But back to being a goddess—the kids still treat me the same, and pretty much everybody else at the estate does too. They had their big adjustment when Matt went from guy to god, so my change isn't a shock to anybody."

"Well, you and Matthew make such a cute couple that I'm sure you'll both enjoy it for millennia to come."

"We will, and thank you." Crystal hesitated slightly, and then plunged into the next topic. "Mother, I've been really curious about one thing. May I ask what might be an indelicate question?"

"Of course you may, daughter. You're one of us now."

"Right. About that. All I really had to do to become a goddess was set up a healing oscillation for immortality, right? I can understand the long hours under Apollo's tutelage, but what about the rest? Couldn't I have been useless at fighting, but able to self-heal, and do just fine in the arena? And why was the arena even needed at all?"

"Have you forgotten what happened at the end of the test?"

"No, of course not. I was found worthy by the assembled pantheon. But why was that necessary?"

"Daughter, over the eons, many humans have and will continue to become powerful mages. Some will discover the healing oscillations. Some of those will even be able to wield ka. They will all, being infected with the arrogance that plagues the human species, declare themselves gods or goddesses just like us. They might even possess the discipline that you proved when you mastered Apollo's special test—oh, come on, you don't think his average adept has to learn differential equations and classical mechanics, do you?" Gaia asked in response to the surprised expression on Crystal's face.

When Crystal sat back again, finally understanding the rigor of Apollo's test, Gaia said, "The human mages may be physically strong, but they won't have demonstrated the quiet resolve you did in splitting tons of firewood just to engulf it to make charcoal. They won't understand the connection to the world that comes from smelting iron by hand instead of by magic. They won't have earned the respect of Valhalla's residents by being beaten down again and again only to continue rising and learning. Most importantly, they won't have held what they believed to be the life of an immortal they hated in their hands, and chosen not to strike. The mortal children, no matter how powerful they become, will have none of the wisdom of the gods they pretend to be, and unfortunately for them, allowing them to go about their business isn't usually an option for us.

"It wasn't just a test that you passed, Crystal. It was a whole series of trials, and had you failed any yet still declared yourself goddess anyway, we would have had to beat you down from it. I wasn't lying when I said it was a life or death battle for you, daughter. You merely assumed wrongly about where the death might have come from."

Epilogue

"Why not?" Crystal asked, sitting up in the lounge chair in the secluded cottage back at Matt's estate. Her questioning gaze bore down on Matt, who was actually lounging in his lounge chair near hers. The couple had rejoiced, along with their daughters and all of their friends, for two days after Crystal ascended, and now they rested in their quiet retreat to recover from too much partying.

"Love, recall your first test as a potential goddess was to learn magic," Matt said. "Those who can't touch magic, can't learn it. Those who can't learn magic, can't be goddesses."

"Why can't they touch magic, though? You and I can both do it."

"I don't know. Nobody really knows why that ability is prevalent in some but not in others."

Crystal was angry. She had come to grips with her status as a new goddess, but now it only stood to reason to her that her daughters should become goddesses too. "Well, what made the difference in me was setting up the oscillation for healing. Why can't I just do that for the girls?"

"Come on, now, you already know the answer. Oscillations can be set up in ourselves, if and only if we know ourselves well, or in inanimate objects, but never, ever, in other people. You can't set up an oscillation in the girls because you can't feel their innermost body rhythms to match them."

"So the girls will end up growing old and dying and we can't do anything about it."

"Well, yeah. On the other hand, that is the nature of humanity, right?"

Crystal glared at Matt in frustration. "No! Well, yes! I don't know. I just wish I could help."

"Help? Love, the girls have a god and a goddess as parents. Every need they'll ever have will be taken care of. Their peers will consider them the luckiest humans on the planet. One of the toughest lessons we deities have to learn is to accept our limitations, and this is one of them."

Crystal sighed. "Okay, fine. I just want to know why the ability to touch the elemental flows isn't inherited."

"It is, sort of," Matt said. "At least, it usually runs in families. But sometimes it skips generations, like your red hair or other recessive genes."

"So you're saying that, since Natalia is a strong mage but her boys aren't, and you and I are strong magic users but our girls aren't, that if they...."

"That's exactly what I'm saying. If they breed...."

"That's such an ugly word."

"Fine. If they fall in love and have wonderfully fulfilling lives together and bear us beautiful grandchildren—how's that? But yes, your conjecture is correct. If one of the girls and one of the boys happens to have a child, we may have an extremely powerful magician on our hands."

"Wouldn't that be wonderful?"

"Maybe. Depends on what he or she does with that power," Matt said drily.

"Well, we'll have to wait and see, I guess."

"Yes, we will, love. And you and I have plenty of time to do just that."

ABOUT THE AUTHOR

Dean by day and writer by night, Stephen H. King grew up being asked whether he was "that Stephen King." "Not the author," he'd say until his writing addiction took hold and made that into a lie. Now he writes and reads and blogs as The Other Stephen King—you know, the one who writes fantasy and science fiction. When he's not writing, he enjoys thinking about writing while going on hikes or long road trips. When he's not thinking about writing, it's usually because he's fishing.

Find other Stephen H. King works at:

http://TheOtherStephenKing.com

Read his ongoing thoughts about writing, authorpreneurship, and other key parts of life at his blog:

http://TheOtherStephenKingOnWriting.blogspot.com

www.ingramcontent.com/pod-product-compliance
Lightning Source LLC
Chambersburg PA
CBHW060955120726
47910CB00002B/649